DISTORTED VISION

DISTORTED VISION

SUSAN LEWALLEN

KONSTELLATION PRESS

Published by Konstellation Press, San Diego

www.konstellationpress.com

Cover photograph: Ellen Crystal

Cover design: Scarlet Willette

ISBN: 978-1-7346421-6-2

To the many dedicated African health professionals I've worked with over the years

CONTENTS

1

MARCH, 2017

My brother Jared disappeared when I was thirty-five.

I'd looked up to him as far back as I remembered. The fact that he got more charming and successful every year drew me in deeper. Our parents were well-known human rights workers and their careers moved us around different countries in eastern Africa every few years. From tawny plains to deep green forests, hustling cities to sleepy villages, it was an education in geographic and cultural variation. We were classic "third culture kids," uncertain how to respond when asked a simple "Where are you from?" We had American passports but little real experience in the US — and a different view of the world than most American kids. We mostly hung around kids who grew up like we did. At home, our tight little family formed a safe, cozy nest. I coped with frequent moves and new schools because other kids were also coming and going and, besides, Jared was always there as a ready-made best friend on day one. We might bicker at home but, out in public, we had each other's backs.

We spent a bit of time in the US most years, with family friends or in summer camps. Our parents didn't want us to end up ignorant about the country that issued our passports. They went along with us at first, but Jared and I traveled together on international flights, as unaccompanied minors, from a young age. It was a surprisingly loose system, where supervision was sloppier than our parents imagined. We took advantage of it, and a couple of times plotted ways to sneak away from our hapless airline chaperones. I used to fantasize that we were co-conspirators in a spy plot. Safe with my big brother, it was the two of us against the world.

He wasn't perfect. He was sometimes pushy and at times unreliable — although he usually had a good excuse. In fact, he missed the grant award ceremony on my big day, months before his disappearance.

He texted me a few minutes before it started. *Sorry Ana. Can't make it. Trauma case. Swamped in surgery.*

My spirits sagged. Jared had encouraged me while I worked with a colleague to write the proposal for this grant. We got the award, but now he'd miss seeing me — or, at least, my university department — accept it.

That morning, with support from the Azar Foundation, we launched the Global Health Initiative at Honnelly University. I gave a speech for the occasion. Of course, so did my colleague, Brad Hicks. The head of department, Dr. Andrew McCaskey, gave a keynote address, and Mr. Azar himself had more than a few words to say. So several of us were sharing the glory.

I'd had to remind myself not to fiddle with my earring, which Jared said was a dead giveaway of anxiety. In truth, my boss, Andrew, had eroded my confidence a bit with his introduction. "Ana is the daughter of the late Robert and Alicia Lotner. Their names will be familiar to many of you for their outstanding work in international human rights on the Arusha Tribunal. And among those rights is the right to health."

A ripple of dismay washed over me. I was proud of my parents, but I'd worked hard to make this initiative happen. This was my best, if not my last, chance to try to have it all. The career in global health I envisioned would give me the opportunity to combine development work with research and life in different places. I'd open the possibility to live for stretches in African countries that felt like home to me. If all fell into place, I'd recreate a family life like the one my parents had given Jared and me.

I pulled myself back from my mini-reverie to hear Andrew introducing Brad, my faculty colleague on the grant, as a former Peace Corps Volunteer who'd worked to bring a reliable water supply into the lives of women in a little village in Mali. He didn't mention Brad's parents.

I SCANNED the reception room after the ceremony. I'd have to mingle and talk to several individuals but just for a moment I amused myself by watching people. Jared had taught me how to identify the richest man in the room, a skill that served him well as he developed his non-profit organization. "It'll be the guy who's most nonchalant. He won't need to impress anyone." It was clear that Mr. Azar, CEO of the Azar Foundation, was that man here. He leaned on a post near the edge of the room, one foot crossed over the other, while he held a small plate of hors d'oeuvres and gazed around the room with a half smile. I'd need to navigate over that way to speak to him soon.

I wished Mark were here but he hadn't been able to

come to the celebration. He'd dashed into the back of the auditorium just before the speeches started, then caught me afterward as everyone migrated toward the reception. "Sorry, Ana. Just broke away from my meeting to hear you speak. You were terrific! Gotta get back." He delivered a quick kiss, then raised a suggestive eyebrow. "We'll do better after dinner tonight. I'll text you."

"Yes, please," I said, feeling a grin broaden my face.

"And that outfit looks great." Then he was gone.

Nice that he noticed. I'd gone all-out dressing for this occasion — at least by my standards. I was proud of the fact that I didn't spend much on clothes. Most of mine came from thrift stores, consistent with my anti-consumerism. Plus, mistakes — and I made them — didn't set me back much. I was in an ongoing internal sparring match over my wardrobe. In one corner was just enough vanity to want to look good, but in the other — usually victorious — was a robust unwillingness to be uncomfortable. Now, vanity was on the ropes. I slipped my finger inside my waistband to ease the pressure of form-fitting black trousers. They did look classy since I'd dropped ten pounds, but I loathed anything tight. Lycra — ugh! — the embrace of a python. I wished the sack dress would come back into style. Meanwhile, the balls of my feet were protesting at bearing my weight in unaccustomed high heels. Ballet slippers would have been a better idea.

I put sartorial thoughts aside and, studiously ignoring waiters carrying silver trays of tiny sandwiches, samosas, and bacon-wrapped meatballs, I moved in the direction of Mr. Azar.

"Dr. Lotner," said the CEO, straightening up and running his eyes over me. "Let me congratulate you. Honnelly's going to have a great global health program.

Absolutely critical nowadays. Thanks to advances in transportation and a globalized economy, health issues are crossing international boundaries. Pandemics don't respect borders."

Recognition disconcerted me for a moment. His final two sentences were right out of a section of the proposal I'd crafted. He probably didn't realize he'd swiped my words, and I didn't comment. Embarrassing him wouldn't be a good idea. I smiled, nodded my agreement, and we small-talked for a few minutes.

A fiftyish man with a half-empty champagne glass approached us. "Ana," said Mr. Azar, "this is Kevin Klant, CEO of Mountain Medical Devices." He turned to take us both in with his magnanimous gaze. "Ana needs no introduction."

"Of course not," said Kevin, stretching out his hand to shake. "Congratulations on the new program." He pulled his arm back to flag a passing waiter with a tray of something savory wrapped in bacon. "I saw a short piece on public television last week about your brother, Jared. He described the eye surgery he does in poor countries. Too bad we don't have more like him." He popped the tasty-looking tidbit into his mouth and chewed as he eyed me.

A spontaneous smile spread across my face along with a sense of largess toward Mr. Klant. "Yeah. Jared's in a class by himself."

Kevin swallowed. "I guess it runs in the family." He wiped his fingers on a little napkin, and fished a business card from his jacket pocket. "Tell your brother to contact me. We'll arrange some donations for his organization." He turned to speak to someone else.

Mr. Azar nodded politely at me and signaled to someone

lurking behind me, waiting their turn with the big man. "Congratulations once more, Doctor. Excuse me."

Alone again, I looked around the room. I'd rooted through a bathroom drawer that morning to unearth a wand of mascara. A sticky chunk of the stuff hung ready to dislodge itself into my eye, bobbing across my visual field every time I blinked. If I took a swipe at it, it would smear. I wriggled my shoulders to adjust a scratching tag in my sweater and tried to relax into the glow of a successful kick-off for the initiative.

I wished my father were around to see this. And I wished again that Jared, who so often stood in for Dad, had made it today.

Brad approached, crunching into a samosa. He held up a hand to indicate his full mouth, chewed for a few seconds, and swallowed while I debated whether one little pastry-wrapped sausage would really do that much harm. "Sorry about that," he said with a grin. "Nice comments you made earlier. We'll need to map out next steps soon. It's a good award, but it'll only stretch so far."

One thing I disliked about academics was the hyper-competitiveness among those scrambling their way up — like hyenas fighting over a carcass. At thirty-five, I was a bit late finding my feet on the career ladder and I didn't have more time to waste. After my undergraduate years in the US, I imagined I wanted to work in human rights law. I went to the UK for training, then spent a few years working in London before I was captivated by public health. That lateral move meant another six years of graduate work, all of which I did in London. When I was ready for a real job in my new field, I made the big move back to the US. I loved specialized study but I was keenly aware of my lack of field experience. When Andrew selected me for this new program I was delighted, but I had to remember that he'd selected Brad too. I hoped the competition wouldn't be gladiatorial.

Brad continued his complaints. "We'll have to crank out lots of papers for academic journals." He looked back over his shoulder and lowered his voice. "I'm afraid that's Andrew's priority, but I hope it's not all we do. I want to create opportunities for research to intersect with service programs."

I nodded. This was exactly what I envisioned for the GHI. "I'm sure we'll be able to form good collaborations. I've got contacts in eastern Africa. And my brother's been involved for years in medical service projects. He runs his own non-profit. We can count on him for advice and ideas."

Brad raised one eyebrow and hesitated before producing an unconvincing smile. "Yeah. Maybe. Fly-in-fly-out projects aren't what I was thinking of. We want to focus on development, not disaster relief." He sighed. "Africa's a hard place to work. It's easy to feel like those at the top are always on the make — and some of them are. It's usually complicated."

"Sure, I know. I spent eighteen years there," I said, wanting to kick myself for sounding defensive. To be honest, Brad's Peace Corps background intimidated me. He'd lived for two years in a thatched hut without electricity, where the nearest water meant a serious hike to a stream. Years at international schools in eastern Africa didn't equate to life in a village. And my PhD was theoretical stuff focused on public policy.

Brad continued, as though he was reading my mind. "Sometimes I feel like I learned more about development from life in an undeveloped village than I did from my academic degrees." He turned the corners of his mouth up just a smidge — maybe it was a smile — and excused himself to talk to someone else.

I studied him as he walked away. Was he a colleague or the competition? Funding limitations over time could mean that one of us would be pushed from this career ladder. I didn't want to be the one tumbling off. It would probably come down to which of us could develop the best collaborations overseas. That's what would bring money from funders into the department. I didn't want to fail at this.

EARLY APRIL

"We oughtta have a party with your friends to celebrate the new program," Jared said, rummaging through the fridge in my little condo one evening shortly after the award formalities. He'd arrived after work, shrugging off his cashmere topcoat and dropping his suit jacket on a chair as he loosened his tie. "Sorry again I couldn't make it to the ceremony. That case couldn't wait." He opened the fridge and pushed containers and bottles around on the shelves. "Don't you have any good cold white wine?"

I wondered if his exasperation was due to the surgery schedule or the lack of good wine.

For the past year-and-a-half, for the first time in a long time, Jared and I had lived in the same city. I'd had a choice of several universities where I could take the young researchers' award. Finished with my PhD, and fleeing a failed relationship, a move to the American Midwest, where Jared had his practice, felt like the right thing to do.

I reached for a bottle from the shelf where I stored my

limited liquor inventory. "Here. Put this in the freezer and we can have it after a bit."

He made a this'll-do face at the label and shoved the wine into a narrow space he excavated between two heavily frosted lumps of something. "Wow, wasn't this here last summer?" he said, poking at a third, weirdly shaped block — maybe meat.

I threw a grubby oven mitt at him. He whirled and snatched a dishtowel, snapping it out like a cobra's head.

"Tell you what. I'll foot the catering bill for a celebration here and throw in a Molly Maid cleaning before and after."

I laughed, turning back to the potato I was slicing.

"I'd do it at my place but Beth's been prickly lately." He slammed the freezer door and slumped on a kitchen chair. "After my last trip overseas, it took her a solid week to warm up."

I abandoned the potato and sat down across from him, folding my hands on the table and nodding slowly. "Yeah, I thought she seemed frosty when I took you home from the airport. Is everything okay?"

He let a few silent seconds elapse while he got up to get a glass of water, a pained expression on his face. "We're going through a rough time. We'll work it out."

I hoped so. The family we'd grown up in hadn't always been good at resolving conflict, or even admitting we felt wronged — ironic in view of our parents' careers in international justice. My mother was the chief offender. Maybe she gave all she had at work and just wanted peace in the house. "Least said, soonest mended," she'd say briskly as she turned away from my yearning for acknowledgment of hurt feelings. Sleeping dogs were left to lie, and we learned to step right over them until they died. I looked to my father for warmth and sympathy.

I understood Beth's grievances — or I thought I did. Jared worked long hours in his private ophthalmology practice, and then his volunteer surgical excursions took him away for days or even a couple of weeks at a time. Beth admired the trips when they were first dating and he was flying around, but her enthusiasm faded when they had a child. It was nonexistent now that Sean was nine and Jared's non-profit organization was growing.

I waited for him to say more, but he took a long drink of water and changed the subject. "How about that party?"

"I guess I could have it here." I glanced around the small space. "We can squeeze in twenty-five if we stick to drinks and hors d'oeuvres."

"Only twenty-five?" He rubbed his forefinger over the fashionable stubble on his upper lip. "Let's make sure a few of them are well-heeled. Maybe some foundation-board types?"

I raised my eyebrows.

He chuckled and punched his right fist into the opposite palm. "Just kidding, Ana." He snapped his fingers and sat up straighter. "Hey, didn't you have a contact for me? Some guy you met at the university's grant award party?" He widened his eyes. "Support for my non-profit?"

"Oh, yeah." I rose and grabbed my backpack from the doorknob. "I'm glad you reminded me." I rummaged through the mess, found Kevin's card, and handed it to Jared.

I turned back to the potato slicing. "Check the wine, will you?"

Jared's relentless search for opportunities to benefit his work was one reason why he was successful. I could probably learn something from it. He was always pushing, and his charm was hard to resist.

"Open the oven for me, will you?" I shoved the roasting pan into the hot stove. "Sure. Let's do a party here. And thanks for the offer to pay."

"Will it be two glasses or three?" he asked, brandishing the wine bottle.

"Just two for dinner. Mark'll be over later. He's helping a couple of Ugandan friends with a project. Sustainable energy stuff. He's eating with a potential business investor."

"Hmm. Sorry I'll miss him," he said with a smile that didn't reach his eyes.

I wished, not for the first time, that Jared appreciated Mark more. We'd been together for almost six months. "What've you got against him, anyway?" I asked, striving for an off-hand tone as I turned toward salad making.

"Not a thing," Jared protested, making an aggrieved face. He hit the table with the flat of his hand and smiled. "Just want the best for my favorite sister."

"Hey, Ana." Jared rushed into my office two weeks later, a day before the party, with an enormous grin and a glint in his eye. His clothes said he'd just come from the gym — high-end workout stuff.

He shrugged off an athletic jacket. "Got a great idea!"

I was wading through a student's draft manuscript on a study. English wasn't the guy's first language and it was slow going, but I was determined to help him get this published. "Whoa. Hold on a sec, Jare." I deleted two paragraphs, replaced them with a single sentence and a good reference to previous work, and hit "save." Turning away from the screen, I leaned back in my chair. "Okay. What's the idea?"

Jared had plunked down in the armchair across from my desk, the built-up soles of his Nikes resting on the little coffee table.

"Tanzania. For one of your first projects. You need to make a trip to suss out ideas for your program. Tanzania's perfect. You know the place. We've both got contacts there. I can line you up with a couple of good sites for collaboration."

I sensed a steamroller heading my way and I eyed him warily. "I've thought about it as a place to begin. But I'm considering other countries too."

He leaned forward. "You've gotta start somewhere. Why not Tanzania? Think about it. We could go together." He winked at me. "Traveling like the good old days." He waggled his brows.

I sighed and rolled my eyes, overcome by a familiar sense of defeat in the face of his exuberance. "Why are you suggesting Tanzania? I loved my four years there but it wasn't *your* favorite place."

He took in a deep breath, closed his eyes, and blew out through loose lips. "Come on, Ana! I was a kid. I was hauled out of high school in a place I liked and hustled off to finish my last year-and-a-half in Moshi. So, I didn't love it then. But I enjoyed it when I was back there a couple of years ago to do surgery in Dar."

He studied me for a moment and pulled out his ace. "How about if we take Sean? As you've been saying, he's a great age for the game parks, right?"

I didn't recall saying that at all, but someone might as well have yelled Bingo! Jared knew my soft spots.

Sean. That little imp looked so much like our father. The sandy hair and green eyes were part of it, but he also made faces and moved his hands in ways when he talked that had to be genetic, since he'd never met his grandfather. Sometimes I got weepy seeing it. The resemblance got stronger every year.

I still hadn't replied, but Jared knew a toe-hold when he had one. "We'll talk about this again soon," he said, grinning, standing, and pulling on his jacket. He rapped his knuckles on my desk in a done-deal way. "See you tomorrow night!" He was out the door before I blinked.

I turned back to the computer screen and moved chunks of text from the "methods" section into the "results," then dragged other chunks the opposite way. I smiled, imagining my student's pleasure when this paper was published.

It wasn't until later that evening that I realized Jared hadn't said anything about Beth going to Tanzania.

"I LOVE THESE PHOTOS," said Kate, scrutinizing the family pictures on my living room wall. "Look at your parents. They're always hanging together, side by side."

I paused from pushing an antique trunk into the bedroom. "You're right. I guess that's how I always think of them." I bit my lip. "I'd like to be half of something like that someday."

Kate had become a good friend since my move to the Midwest. I met her through my sister-in-law, Beth, with whom she worked. She was fun and the two of us hit it off. She'd come early to help rearrange furniture before the party.

"Look at this one!" she said with a laugh.

The picture was my favorite, taken for a holiday letter

that year. Jared and I, ages twelve and nine, stood in front of Mom and Dad. We'd trooped outside for the snapshot at the end of a sudden short downpour, and the smell of rain on dry earth filled the air. I'd been fidgeting in a scratchy blue blouse my mother insisted I wear. Jared and I had exchanged taunts, which escalated into slugs, over some perceived injustice. Mom dug her fingers into my shoulder to turn me toward the camera as Dad bent forward to elbow Jared into place. When the shutter opened we were leaning every which way like dry maize stalks after the harvest. But we were a family, laughing and full of life against a rain-washed sky. Water beaded on the leaves of the avocado tree and trickled from the creamy frangipani flowers behind us. Best picture we ever took. Many times I'd longed to turn back the clock to those days we were together.

Kate studied the picture, swung her head to me, then back to the photo. She frowned faintly. "Yeah, it's you. Jared looks a lot different though." Her frown deepened. "Where is he anyway?"

"Dunno," I answered, grimacing. Snow was piled on the outside windowsill of my condo and stacked eight inches on the cars parked in the street. It was coming down so thickly it was hard to see the apartment building on the other side. "He said he'd be here by six forty-five to help." I glanced at my watch. Seven thirty. People would start arriving any time, and twenty-five guests milling around my place would be a crowd. We needed to move a few more pieces of furniture.

I cast a critical eye around my little condo, satisfied with the place. I liked my minimalist theme, free of knickknacks and suited to a small space. I had comfortable basic furnishings, but a group this size would have to perch on a variety of stools and chairs if they wanted to sit. The lucky ones would grab something near a horizontal surface and the others would have to balance plates however they could.

A few errant items caught my attention. I shoved a book under the couch and swept a half-finished research paper into a half-opened drawer, bumping it closed with my hip. A clean hand towel in the guest bathroom and a swipe at the sink completed my efforts to make the place ready.

At 7:50 it looked like twenty-five people had arrived — and still no Jared. As I expected, the place was chock-a-block. I turned the music down a notch.

"Great job on the award! Way to go, Ana!"

I basked in congratulations from friends, which dampened my annoyance with Jared's tardiness. I wouldn't even be having this party if it weren't for him.

The front door creaked, and I looked up as he entered.

Jared was a knockout. Sometimes people couldn't believe he was my brother, which I didn't especially appreciate. I was average height, and no matter what people thought, had to work at staying slim. Jared was tall, a natural athlete with solid musculature that he labored to improve by regular workouts. We both had dark thick eyebrows, but his golden hair contrasted with my dark too-curly frizz. While my hazel eyes looked muddy, his changed through from sea green to aquamarine or emerald depending on what he was wearing. Thanks to orthodontia, we had straight, even teeth, but his actually sparkled. A grin from Jared went a long way to convince the doubtful.

"Nice of you to show up, Jare." I gave him the fish eye. Then I looked again. Stomping and shaking snow into my vestibule, chatting and beaming, seven more people crowded in behind him.

"This is Sam Hearny," Jared said, with a big smile and a

slap on the guy's back. "He runs a great optical instruments company." He turned to introduce me to other unfamiliar faces, a woman from a local pharmaceutical firm and someone else who might have been a grateful patient — likely a wealthy one. Partners accompanied all three, so this made six extras at the party. In addition, a sheepish-looking young man whom Jared introduced as Thomas, a resident in ophthalmology at Honnelly, tagged along at the back. I welcomed them, but, really? Seven additional people in my little place? Jared was going to have to gear up and do some hosting duties. I rubbed at the spot on my neck where a seam in my collar scratched.

I needn't have worried about hosting. Jared turned up the volume on the music, served drinks to the new arrivals, and started glad-handing his way around the room, moving smoothly from one group to another. I caught sight of him several times, rocking back on his heels and chortling, with his hands in his jeans pockets and thumbs hanging on his belt. Anyone else standing like that would look like a country bumpkin. Over the next hour, something shifted in the room.

"Hey, Ana, your brother's amazing! Sounds like his non-profit's gonna rid Africa of cataract blindness."

"Hey, hear you're going to Tanzania. Is that right? Sure hope you and Jared can take his son with you. Be great for the kid!"

"Where is she?" I heard Jared say somewhat later as he moved to turn down the music. "Hey, hey." He raised his glass and waited for the room to come to attention. "How about some toasts? Here's to the new Global Health Initiative at Honnelly and its someday director. My sister, Dr. Ana Lotner!"

Jared and I exchanged a look, and he flashed a grin at

me. All we'd been through together tumbled through my mind and warmed me.

Later, I went into my small kitchen for a break. I perched on the top of a little stepstool, the only seating left in the place. As I leaned back against the fridge, Kate came around the corner.

"Jared's in good form," she said, propping herself against a counter.

I looked at her closely, sensing some implied criticism. But I dismissed it. It's one thing to criticize your own brother but quite another when someone else does it, and most people realize that. Besides, he *was* in good form.

"Yeah, he's great. I'm lucky to have him — although bringing seven extra guests into this place is a bit maddening."

She chuckled. "I guess he can use the strokes though. I'm sorry about Beth."

"Huh?" I sat up straighter and turned to face her. "What're you talking about?"

She blanched and her eyes widened. "I don't mean to be telling tales." She set her glass on the counter and wrapped her arms around her waist. "I figured you knew about it. It's not a secret at the office." She looked down at the floor.

I stared at her, open-mouthed with bafflement.

"We don't have to talk about it," she said, turning and letting her gaze slide off into a corner.

"Yeah, Kate, I'm afraid we do now."

She looked back at me, swallowed, and chewed her lower lip.

"I understand Beth moved out a couple of weeks ago. I'm sorry, Ana. I assumed you knew."

I inhaled sharply. Beth and I hadn't seen each other for a

while. I knew things were tense but hadn't seen this coming. At least Kate didn't try to talk more about it.

I dragged myself off the stool. "I've gotta go back to the guests."

But I didn't enjoy the rest of the party. Why hadn't Jared told me?

3

LATE APRIL

I called my brother from my office the day after the party. "Jared, I heard about Beth. I'm so sorry. When did she leave?"

The pause was long. "A month ago. But she'll come around. Change her mind. I'm working on it. That's why I hadn't mentioned it to you."

"Are you going to tell me more about what happened?"

"Not now. Like I said, we've been going through a rough spot."

"How's Sean taking it? I guess he's with Beth?"

He spoke slowly. "Yeah, they're in a new apartment she's rented. He's doing okay according to Beth, but I'm sure he misses me. I see him a couple times a week." The silence was heavy for several seconds. "I'll convince her to see things my way."

"Sure, Jared. You have to try." But, really? Beth's work colleagues knew about it and Jared still figured she'd change her mind? My mood darkened. "You won't care if I call her, will you?"

He wavered so I pushed on. "I want to see Sean."

"I dunno. Well...okay. I told her about us taking Sean to Tanzania. Maybe you can help convince her it's a good idea."

I sat down hard in the armchair. "You told her we're going to Tanzania?" I bit back annoyance. "But Jared, we hadn't agreed to that yet. It's a possibility, but there's a lot to work out first. I haven't decided if Tanzania's the best place to start."

He said nothing.

"If this trip's part of the program, I need to develop a budget, to contact projects we might partner with."

The steamroller lumbered toward me but Jared still didn't say anything. Not for the first time, I wondered if he understood what I did with my doctorate in public health. Some medical doctors didn't have a clue.

"What exactly are your plans in Tanzania, anyway?"

"I'm an eye surgeon, Ana. They need surgeons desperately to deal with all the cataracts." Impatience tightened his voice. "I'll go to a small mission hospital in the south of the country, near Mtwara, to operate. Thomas, the resident you met at the party, will meet me there. Great experience for him."

"And Sean? What do you imagine he'll be doing?"

"I want him to see what I do when I travel. I figured you and I and Sean would enjoy some holiday — game parks, or maybe Zanzibar. I need to take him, to show him how much he means to me. And he needs to see what I do."

"Holiday sounds good. But Sean's nine, Jare. He'll be bored at the hospital." Jared had a big blind spot about his work. He loved it and assumed everyone else would too.

"Well, he could hang out with you for part of the time. We'd trade off. You're always saying you want more time with him. There're lots of possibilities."

I sighed. He had a point, as usual. I did want more time with Sean and having him to myself was an irresistible treat.

"Okay. But I'm not agreeing yet. I need to think it over and talk to Andrew. And I want to talk to Beth. I'll get back to you after that."

I hung up and slumped against the chair back, flattened in the wake of Jared's persuasion. After a few seconds, I took a long sighing breath and sat up straighter. I did need to move along on planning and maybe the nudge wasn't a bad thing.

I wanted to go back to Tanzania. For most people, East Africa means exotic animals, and Tanzania has the best of those striking creatures. The world's celebrities — along with tons of tourists — tend to go to Kenya, where the highest-end safaris draw them. But I preferred Tanzania, where our family had often viewed the game off-season and avoided crowds. I loved the variety of landscapes in Tanzania, the tropical beaches, mountain forests, and vast plains. Who wouldn't be impressed by the sight of snowcapped Mount Kilimanjaro, nineteen thousand feet rising directly out of the dry plain below?

I opened my file on Tanzania and started reading. Several projects caught my interest. By the end of the day, when it looked like a visit might be realistic, I called Beth.

A WEEK PASSED before Beth and I met. Another freak spring snowstorm raged as I drove through crowded streets to reach the penthouse apartment where she and Sean were living. It was luxurious, though not as large as the house she'd had with Jared. Beth had inherited money and, in addition, she made an excellent salary as an investment banker. Right now I was glad of that. I didn't want Sean to suffer any more than necessary, although a nice apartment wouldn't go far in salving the pain of a broken family.

Beth had a parking space across the road for guests in addition to her own underground spot. I stomped snow off my boots and rang her residence. Buzzed inside the warm lobby, I took the elevator to her floor. She opened the door to her apartment as I emerged.

I hadn't warmed immediately to Beth when I'd first met her a decade before. I don't think I was intimidated by gorgeous women, but I viewed them suspiciously. I didn't want to spend my time in the painting, plucking, and fussing I figured went into making Beth look like Beth. Her job in investment banking required that she dress up. Mine didn't, and I saw no reason to torture myself in uncomfortable clothes or dangerous shoes.

After we got to know each other, she gently laughed off my grievances. "Ana, it's not that much work. You'd get used to high heels if you wanted to." It took time for me to see there was a great brain under the hair. I'd come to appreciate her more when she and Jared saw me through a traumatic breakup with a guy I was living with in London during the years I did my doctoral work. I figured we were heading for marriage but he was only focused on his own path forward.

"Look, Ana," Beth had counseled long distance, through my sobs, "those successful marriages with two careers that look so amazing? Well, they may be, but you can bet there's been compromise. One person can't always have what they want. You've got to find balance."

Jared had agreed. "It wasn't gonna work with him. He wasn't right for you."

Maybe that was true, but the rejection hurt like hell and

I was determined to be careful in future. Still, my clock was ticking louder all the time. When Beth introduced me to Mark, a guy who worked in her office building, I was interested — cautious, but interested.

"Ana." Beth threw her arms around me and pulled me inside, brushing snow from my shoulders. "Take off those wet things. Isn't this foul? I hate spring snowstorms. Just when we think we're through winter."

Sean barreled into the entryway. "Ana," he shouted, wrapping his thin arms around my waist. "Can you stay for dinner, Ana? Can she, Mom?" He turned back to me. "And stay to hear about my book when I go to bed?"

I'd managed to spend a lot of time with Sean, in the US or the UK, and I'd read to him since he was old enough to sit up. As he outgrew this, we worked out a cozy pact where he summarized his latest book for me. He loved the audience, and it might have helped me develop patience, which I needed. It was getting more interesting as he matured into more complicated books and, even though he could be a chatterbox, I'd miss it when he grew past our ritual.

I bent over to hug him hard, biting my lower lip and fighting back an onslaught of sadness. I looked up at Beth.

"Of course we'd love to have her," she said, looking straight at me so I knew she meant it, "but we'll have to see if she has time." She raised her eyebrows at me in a silent question.

I tightened my arms around Sean, hoping my voice wouldn't crack. "What's for dinner? And what are you reading?"

B<small>ETH</small> and I wouldn't have a chance to speak privately as long as Sean was around. He stuck to my side as I moved to the kitchen to pitch in with dinner.

"If you guys can clear that counter I'll use it," Beth said. The corners of Sean's mouth turned down. He was no more eager than most nine-year-old boys to help with meals.

"No problem," I said, before he balked. Behind Beth's back, I dried a wet knife on my jeans, stuck it in the butcher block holder, and winked at him. He grinned.

Sean babbled about his teacher and friends over the meal, and I was glad to see him acting normal, even if I knew these good times couldn't happen every night. Beth interrupted the flood once to inject her congratulations on the grant award.

"You mean you have a new job, Ana?" Sean asked, a shadow of worry on his face.

"No." I laughed. "Just new money to do interesting things in my old job."

Only once did he mention his dad. "He was on TV, Ana! I heard him talking about how he helps people in Africa." He'd seen the PBS interview. Beth looked away, and abruptly got up for a glass of water. Sean raced off on other topics.

"Doesn't your tongue get tired?" I asked, not entirely as a joke.

"'Course not. Do I really have to clear the table tonight?" he asked Beth, giving his best puppy dog look.

"Yep. You know how it works, kiddo. Dessert when it's all finished."

SEAN PROVIDED me a reasonable summary of an Alex Rider story while Beth cleaned up the kitchen. I tucked a fat down duvet around him and turned off his lamp, wondering if I were doing the boy a favor, encouraging him to engage with page-turners before bedtime.

Too often I'd gone to bed with a good book and been horrified to realize the light coming in my window wasn't a truck's headlight at midnight — it was dawn. I'd be miserable with exhaustion the next day, unable to drum up the faintest memory of the energy I'd enjoyed in the wee hours. Jared's diagnosis was mania. He wasn't serious, but, in the middle of one sleepless night, I read the brilliant descriptions of the condition in Kay Jamison's *An Unquiet Mind,* and I had to admit I recognized something of myself.

In the living room, Beth poured us each a glass of Merlot. I collapsed into what had always been my favorite chair. I was surprised she'd brought it from her previous home. Looking around, it appeared she'd moved much of the furniture and spent time and energy making things look like the former house. I guessed this was for Sean, but what had Jared been left with? I recognized a number of paintings and photographs. Even the wall colors and soft furnishing were similar. She watched me looking around.

"I didn't take as much from the house as it may appear," she said, gesturing around the beautiful living room. "The art, of course, was mine, but I had the photos copied and purchased new furniture like what we had in the house." She arched her perfect eyebrows. "Maybe it was crazy, but when I bought this place I wanted Sean to feel it was home."

"Wait. I thought you were leasing. That's what Jared said."

She put her wine down and turned to face me full on.

"No. I bought it. The marriage is over, Ana, and that's final — at least in my mind. In fact, I'm seeing someone else."

My spirits sank as she spoke, not just because of the words, but because she said them with such calm confidence. I wasn't sure how much she was willing to say, nor what I wanted to know, besides the fact that this was final.

"I know how much you love Sean," she said, picking up her wine again. "He loves you, too, and I will never do anything to hurt your relationship with him. You're always welcome here, Ana. But I cannot live with Jared any longer."

I wasn't as good at holding back my tears as Beth was. Or maybe she'd cried all she needed to; but I hadn't. She handed me a tissue and sat quietly for several minutes while I made no effort to stop weeping. She didn't offer more details, and I didn't ask. Maybe I'd never know. I couldn't imagine how she could throw away a marriage with Jared.

I finally quit sniffling and pulled myself up. I wanted to hear her feelings about the trip. "I know Jared spoke to you about taking Sean to Tanzania. Can we talk about that?"

"He mentioned it. The discussion got sidetracked and we didn't finish."

I smiled weakly. "The idea was a trip with the three of us — or four, if Mark comes. I need to investigate projects for our new program at Honnelly. I can take vacation time and arrange my schedule so we can trade off with Sean if needed."

We sipped wine for several moments while the gas logs in the fireplace made realistic crackling sounds. Beth was never impulsive. She took a while before she spoke.

"How long would you be there?"

"I figure about three weeks. I'm considering an itinerary that would let both Jared and me do what we need to do, and also make sure Sean has a good time. I'm really hoping Mark can come."

Beth cocked her head. "Jared's okay with Mark going along?"

"I'm sure he would be. I haven't talked to Mark about it yet. Why not?"

Beth waved the question aside. "What about Sean's school?"

"If we go in mid-August, Sean won't have to miss much, at least not more than a week. Plus," I added, as though I were making a package irresistible, "we'll miss the rainy season."

Beth smiled with half her mouth at my ploy. But it was a unique opportunity for Sean. She'd only been in Africa as a tourist, or short-term with Jared. She'd been enchanted by the game parks, and I hoped this would sway her decision.

I leaned over to refill my wine glass, then, picturing the roads outside, I went to the kitchen for water instead. Beth didn't appear to have moved when I came back.

"Let me think about it, Ana. Will you send the itinerary, with all the details?"

"Of course." I reached over to give her arm a squeeze, and moved to leave. We shared a hug, and I girded myself to face the nasty night. I hoped Sean could go, but with or without him, I was looking forward to the sun in Tanzania.

"ANA?" Beth caught me at home by phone two days later. "I've decided it's okay for Sean to go. I'll be honest and tell you I'm a little worried about it. Still, it's a great opportunity for him and knowing you're there makes a difference."

"Good. I'll talk to Mark. In fact, he'll be here soon with the fixings for dinner."

Mark arrived an hour later with the grin that made joy bubble in my heart. "Got a little surprise for you."

"What? Tell me."

He raised one eyebrow. "Go look at your Kindle."

I searched for a second before I spied it on the living room couch. It opened onto the last page of the book I'd finished the night before. I hit the "home" icon, and there was Mark's surprise — a new book.

"*Last Bus to Wisdom*, by Ivan Doig. Hmm. Never heard of it."

He gave a satisfied smile. "You'll love it. It's a coming-of-age story about a boy a couple of years older than Sean."

Who doesn't adore an unexpected gift? I reveled in fiction — for entertainment, new ideas, to laugh, to cry, and sometimes just for distraction and escape. Mark loved it too, and that was not so common in men I'd known. There's no denying the intimacy in shared love for certain stories. We didn't always like the same books, but that made for good discussions. What we did agree on was the magic — living briefly in someone else's life and discovering all that humanity had in common.

I hugged him and brought up the Tanzania trip.

"Sounds like a dream right now," he said, grimacing at the window, where sleet pelted the street. "I'd love to go, and I'd do it in a flash if you could delay it by a week or two." He finished slicing the onion for a chicken tagine he was experimenting with and turned to face me, knife in hand.

I rubbed my forehead, accidentally flinging a piece of preserved lemon onto the floor. The scent wafted up. Nice. I picked up the slippery rind, then rinsed it and threw it in the skillet — I wasn't going to waste this stuff. Mark smiled because he'd have done the same.

I'd looked at the scheduling conflict from every angle. Jared wasn't enthusiastic about alternative travel dates, arguing I had more flexibility than he did because of his obligations to patients. Even if he'd been willing, there was Sean's school to consider. Sean was a big part of the discussion.

"Ana, we gotta make this trip work for him," Jared had argued. "I'm afraid he thinks he's responsible for my separation from Beth."

"So have you talked to him about that?"

"Yeah, of course," Jared had said, folding his arms across his chest. "But I want to give him a treat."

No arguing with that.

"And I want him to see what I do."

Now I skimmed off a spoonful of the tagine to offer Mark a taste. "I really want us to go together. I just can't figure out how to make this work."

"Yeah, I guess. Too bad about the timing. It's rotten. But it's critical for me to be at this energy conference. It's the first time it's being held in the US. Several African colleagues are coming to present innovations for decreasing emissions in Kampala and Kinshasa. It's good stuff."

I knew about his meeting. My shoulders sagged. "This is the only time Jared and Sean can go. And I told Beth I'd do it."

His face fell and he laid down his knife. "What if you didn't try to go with Jared and Sean? You and I could go together almost any time after my conference."

"Jared can't take Sean unless I'm along to help."

His disappointment filled the space. He shrugged. "You have to do what's right for you."

I couldn't look him in the eye. I set down my knife and put my arms around him, feeling the tension in his back muscles. "I want Sean to have this chance."

He didn't reply.

I hugged harder. Mark was the best thing that had come into my life in a long time. Sometimes I got dizzy imagining where it might go. But he just had to see that I couldn't let Jared and Sean down. I let go of him and returned to dicing the slippery pungent peel.

The tagine was delicious. Mark was a good cook. The wine was great, the vinaigrette perfect on the crisped greens, and the candlelight provided just the atmosphere I'd hoped for. We ate slowly and savored each bite. We laughed ourselves weak sharing stories of past travel mishaps. So more than a ripple of dismay washed through me when he said he had to leave soon after dinner.

SNOW HAD TURNED to dirty slush and ice chunks ten days later when Brad, Andrew, and I met after work at a popular bar near the university to discuss our next steps. I broke through a thin crust and soaked a foot in an icy pothole between my car and the front door. Brad and Andrew were waiting in a booth, munching chips and pretzels when I entered. I hurried over, pulling off my overcoat and scarf as I squelched across the floor.

Andrew was expansive. "The Azar grant is a great start. We can take it in a number of directions. But it's seed money. In the long run, success with the GHI depends on our ability to develop collaborative projects in developing countries." His smile, over the top of a beer mug, took in both of us.

"That's where you two come in. We need to agree on criteria for appropriate projects."

This made sense; everything in the grant had been couched in the most general words possible. It was time to get more specific and Andrew got to it.

"One major requirement is to find projects we can scale up. The big donors — USAID, Gates, NIH — aren't going to be interested in small schemes."

Brad set his jaw and I figured he was thinking about his Peace Corps experiences, which were small schemes.

Andrew flicked his eyes back and forth between us and I felt uneasy, a bit like trapped prey, as he continued. "We've got to bring in money for your salaries, as well as project expenses. And we have to include significant overheads for the university. We'll need the big grants."

That was a down-to-earth reminder of the realities of academia in the twenty-first century.

Andrew wasn't finished. "And we need to create opportunities to involve Honnelly students. A strong global health department will attract the best students to our university."

"I'll be checking out a school eye screening project involving medical students," I said. "It's something I learned about from my brother."

Andrew rubbed his chin. "I didn't realize he was involved in public health."

"What about training programs?" asked Brad. "Building local capacity ought to be part of anything we do."

"Good point," said Andrew. "Ana, I want you to check out a nurse training program in Moshi. It's a great example of manpower development – ought to be right up your alley with your human resource policy background."

I reviewed my upcoming trip to Tanzania. I'd take half of the three weeks there for holiday. We agreed we'd work with governments or with local and international NGOs, and we'd consider community development schemes like water and sanitation.

"And another thing," Andrew added, taking the last pretzel. "Projects should lead to academic publications."

Brad caught my eye and nudged my squishy foot, just a fraction, under the table.

My enthusiasm was high, but my stomach was growling when Andrew looked at his watch. "Got another meeting," he said, grabbing the bill. We broke up, retrieving our coats and hats. I was satisfied that Brad and I had emerged as equals in the planning.

I was determined to wring out my sock, although the water saturating it had come up to body temperature and I wondered if it were worth the effort. As I neared the ladies' room, I was startled by the sight of Beth, sitting at a corner table. She was smartly dressed as always, but that evening, it wasn't just her sophisticated jacket and scarf — she sparkled and exuded energy. She was laughing and deep in conversation with a man I didn't know. He wore jeans and a sweater and didn't look like he came from her work world, but the electricity between them was unmistakable.

My instinct was to sneak out and hope she didn't see me, but we caught each other's gaze before I managed that. She smiled and gestured me over to the table. I pasted a smile over my apprehension and ambled over. The man she was with was clearly an intimate partner — not a work colleague, but a romantic interest — and she made no effort to hide it. They were holding hands and he stroked her manicured fingers with his thumb. She introduced me to Paul Rosenstein as Jared's sister, and her good friend.

"Oh," said Paul, smiling. "This is the famous Ana, who Sean dotes on. Join us, please."

"I'd love to," I lied, "but I'm late to meet someone for dinner."

Beth was at ease, not hiding anything from me or this man. I hadn't seen her so relaxed in a long time. They laughed as we exchanged a few pleasantries, before I repeated my excuse and fled, not taking time to wring out the sock. I wanted to get out of there. How much did Jared know about Paul?

4

FRIDAY & SATURDAY, AUGUST 18 & 19

Sean hopped up and down, running around looking at every display in the Detroit airport as we waited to board our plane to Schiphol. We had a direct overnight flight to Amsterdam, four hours to recover, and ten more to Dar es Salaam. Jared and I knew this route to eastern Africa's big cities well; it was as painless a way as possible for the long trip.

Hours after we left Detroit, Jared rubbed his creased face as we rolled our carry-on bags up the jetway at Schiphol. "Let's grab a shower before the next leg."

Courteous security agents checked our boarding passes onward without wasting a second, and we were in the lounge, signed up for showers within twenty minutes. Sean, who'd stayed up all night watching movies, stumbled to a couch and curled up there, conked out after thirty seconds.

"He doesn't care about a shower anyway," said Jared with a yawn. "You take the one that's about to open, and I'll wait here. I asked them to put a space or two between us in the sign-up list so one of us can stay with him — although he's going nowhere from the look of it." He tousled Sean's hair.

The hot water in the sparkling clean white cubicle, followed by a rubdown with a thick white towel, revived me. I'd be good for a few more hours before jet lag brought me crashing down.

Jared was slumped over next to Sean when I came out of my refreshing cleanup. My handsome brother looked the worse for wear, thanks to the night flight. His forehead was shiny with grease and his jaw hung half open. I couldn't resist. "Jare, you're drooling," I said, right into his ear as I shook his shoulder. He came to with a start, and punched me lightly on the arm before he disappeared for his shower.

I roused Sean. "Come on, sweetie. It'll be easier if you stay awake for a bit." He rubbed his eyes, looking like he wanted to cry. "Let's see what they have to eat. I bet there're packets of hot chocolate mix over there. When your dad comes out we can go look at some of the cool exhibits downstairs." I more or less dragged him over to the counter for a mug of rich chocolate, comforting in the air-conditioned room. His eyes flashed some life at the sight of trays loaded with buttery Dutch waffle cookies.

"How many can I take?" he asked.

I laughed. "Whatever you can fit on your saucer — use the tongs. You can come back for more when you've finished those." This was no time to worry about good nutrition. We just needed to stay awake.

Jared came out of the shower looking considerably better than he had going in. The three of us left the lounge and walked down a couple of long corridors.

We stopped in front of a small display titled "Heroes of the Dutch Resistance."

"Hey, Sean, check this out," said Jared.

Sean sounded out the word: re-sis-tance. "Yeah. Sometimes Mom tells me not to put up any resistance. But what's the Dutch Resistance?"

"Let's find out," I said, noticing an arrow pointing toward a larger exhibit. We needed to kill an hour and this would do it.

Sean liked the stories of small-scale sabotage at the beginning of the war. The short video and displays were well done, realistic about the difficulties of choosing to adapt or even to collaborate during an occupation, rather than taking the considerable risks involved in resistance. His eyes widened as he learned about the resisters and the systematic extermination of Jews. "But Paul's Jewish," he protested. "He'd have fought against those guys!"

Jared scowled. "Look, Sean," he said, pointing at a picture and pasting on a wide mechanical smile. "This guy, Gerrit Kastein, a major hero, was a doctor — like me." They read some of the details of his life and activities while I underwent a small jet-lag-induced sinking spell. "It says he died trying to escape after he was taken prisoner."

I came out of my fog to hear Sean. "I'd try to escape if I was a prisoner. You would too, wouldn't you, Dad?"

"Of course," Jared insisted.

By the time we got to our boarding gate for Dar es Salaam, the temporary stimulation of my shower was long gone. I staggered to my seat and let my head fall back on the headrest, closing my eyes. I must have dozed because the next thing I knew we were gaining altitude. I lowered my seatback and readjusted my body in the cramped space. Unfortunately, it was 10:00 a.m. and most passengers were full of life. It was fun time for Europeans heading for holidays in

East Africa. Window shades were up and lights were on all over the cabin. Groaning, I pulled a blanket over my head.

A few minutes later I felt a nudge. "Ana, how does this remote work? Dad's asleep and I wanna watch a movie."

Surely the kid knew more about electronics than I did, but I took the little black box, fumbled with it, and handed it back. "Sean, I'm going to sleep." To forestall future interruptions, before I dropped off, I raised my groggy head. "You can eat or drink anything you want. No need to ask."

5

SATURDAY, AUGUST 19

I didn't wake up until we started the descent to Julius Nyerere International Airport in Dar. It was dark outside and Sean's screen had gone off. He was sprawled across his seat and spilling into mine — essentially comatose. I hoped he'd get a second wind. We'd all need one to make it off the plane and through the immigration process ahead.

The airport had been renamed several times after it was built in the 1970s, but the arrival hall hadn't changed much since I'd been using it. We queued up to old wooden counters where officials lounged behind the glass, seemingly indifferent to the time required to process the crowd. We collected forms to complete, with tiny spaces into which we were expected to squeeze information no one would ever check, then queued again to pay visa fees. A big rubber stamp hit the wooden desk when it marked my passport, startling me out of my wits as I dozed on my feet.

We still needed to retrieve our bags. We jostled our way into the crowd at one of the three old worn revolving baggage carousels, doing battle with carts teetering under enormous boxes and suitcases. Metal screeched as tractors pulling trailers of luggage lumbered along outside on the tarmac. Travelers rolled their shoulders, craning their necks to catch a glimpse of the next bag emerging through the slapping, swinging rubber flaps that covered the openings from outdoors. Jared heaved a sigh of relief when his large box of surgical supplies appeared on the belt.

I scanned the room and made for the one free trolley, flashing Jared a thumbs-up as I grabbed it. But, no wonder it'd been abandoned. One wheel was stuck at an angle and the only direction it rolled was backward. There was nothing else, so we piled our baggage on to tow toward customs. Jared pulled the ailing contraption behind him and swore when it bit into his Achilles tendon.

It was better not to be among the first going through. The officials were only human and, as the crowds fatigued them, they were inclined to wave people through with minimal checking. Or maybe they'd satisfied their curiosity about what was in the luggage of strangers.

"What's in that box?" asked an official in a peaked cap so large he disappeared under it.

"Surgical supplies," Jared said with a respectful smile. "I'm an eye surgeon, and I'm taking them to Mtwara."

"Open it. We need to inspect."

Peaked Cap gazed off in the distance. Jared peeled back tape, pulled the box flaps out, then stood back and crossed his arms over his chest and watched. Peaked Cap rummaged through the contents, scowling as he picked up a cellophane-wrapped box of fine sutures and examined the writing on the side. An official I presumed to be a superior came out from a nearby office; he and Peaked Cap exchanged brisk Swahili.

The supervisor studied Jared for a moment before speaking. "Do you have the inventory list for these goods?"

Jared stepped forward and pulled an envelope out of the side of the box.

The man squinted at the list for several minutes, glancing between it and the contents of the carton and moving his lips. "The declared value of these items is two-thousand-five-hundred US dollars, correct?" Jared nodded, without a glance at the sheet.

Exhausted tension replaced my sleepiness and I ground my teeth.

"You'll have to pay duty on these items," said the supervisor, "unless you have a letter from the hospital where you plan to use them."

"But, sir, these medical supplies were donated. My hospital at home gave them to treat people who need them in Tanzania."

"That may be, but we have laws about importing goods, as I'm sure you have in your country. Do you have a letter from the hospital where they will be used?"

A muscle in Jared's jaw twitched. He was holding himself carefully. "No, I don't have a letter. I didn't realize I'd need one. I've never needed one in the past. Can I pay a fine to you now?"

The supervisor's nostrils flared on his otherwise stony face.

Jared, I pleaded silently, don't try to bribe this guy. Let's finish this as simply as possible and not break any laws.

I spoke up. "Thank you, sir. I think what we're wondering is if we can leave the supplies here and pick them up with a letter in a day or two? I'm sure we can get the document you require."

He glowered at Jared for a few seconds before he turned

his gaze on me. "Yes, we can keep them. We have a process for that, but we'll charge storage for every day you leave the box with us." He turned back to Jared. "Come with me."

This was promising, but it also meant we'd be here longer. Sean and I found a couple of peeling plastic chairs and sank onto them while Jared and the official disappeared into an office.

Sean leaned his head on my shoulder where it lay heavily, slipping off every few minutes as his neck gave way. I tried to lean my own head on the wall behind us, but it was about three inches too far back. My neck snapped painfully and I let my head fall forward instead. Anxiety gnawed into my tired brain. What had Jared been thinking, offering to "pay a fine"? Relief flooded me when he came back out of the office.

"Is it sorted out?"

"Yeah," he grumbled. "Paying duty was an option — but it's fifty percent of the value. No way! I'll ask for a letter from the nuns in Mtwara."

"Did the guy hint for you to pay under the table?"

"No. Gotta admit, they're organized and the procedures were straightforward. I've got an official receipt for the supplies."

"How come you didn't have a letter? Doesn't customs usually want one?"

"I've got through without it before."

We roused Sean, changed some money, and hauled ourselves outside into the open-air terrace in the front of the Dar airport. The air weighed on my chest like a thick layer of wet cotton wool. Several little shops around the periphery were open in spite of the late hour, selling carved animals, cloth, pharmaceuticals from who-knew-where, or simply changing money.

Jared and I half dragged Sean. Taxi drivers assaulted us, eager to hook a customer. Ours was the last flight arriving for the night. We didn't want to go far. Traffic between the airport and town was grueling, even late at night, so we were headed to a place close by. There was no point in driving somewhere special since we'd leave the next day for Zanzibar.

Jared made eye contact with one of the drivers and they exchanged a few words. "This guy'll take us," he said, and we followed him to a tiny battered taxi. We crammed our luggage in the boot, already partly full with a spare tire, blackened tools, and greasy rags. Jared got into the front. Sean and I piled into the back, where weak springs caused the seat to sag so badly on my side that he tumbled into my lap. The decrepit vehicle lurched out of the parking area. The driver stopped to pay the lot fee and made a sharp turn off the main road into a rutted narrow alley.

"I've stayed here before," said Jared, turning to face us in the back. He grinned, watching me try to shove Sean into a better position to relieve my pinned leg. "This route may not look promising, but we'll end up at a decent guesthouse. Not much, but the price is right and it's close."

We rocked our way through potholes, as Sean's head bounced off my shoulder in the back seat of the car. There were no lights on the road, but the full moon and an occasional long fluorescent bulb fixed to a building or hanging in a tree allowed a ghostly view. The land on either side of us was divided more or less into rectangular plots. We passed a variety of small buildings, some crumbling cement, others mud bricks, many patched together with odds and ends of corrugated tin sheets. Some kind of barrier surrounded most of the plots — whether it was a concrete

wall, pieces of pressed board, chain link, or upright sticks
held in place by wire.

We stopped outside a tall metal gate, part of a solid
heavy enclosure. A single light illuminated it and I made
out that this was the "Wellcome Guesthouse." The driver
blew the horn and someone peeked out through a small
window cut in the solid sheet metal gate. Once the driver
got out of the car and exchanged a few words with the gate-
keeper, the heavy door swung open. We drove into a
compound with what looked like a large house. The lights
inside silhouetted a man in a light blue skull cap and
jellabiya standing in a wide doorway.

"Welcome, welcome! Good trip? You are Mr. Jared, I
think? Party of three?"

I sighed with the pleasure of being expected at the end
of a long journey.

Jared was out of the taxi and shaking hands, launching
into the obligatory greetings with the owner.

"*Karibu.* Come in," said the man. "You speak Swahili."

"*Kidogo,*" said Jared, with a modest smile.

I suppressed an eye roll. Sure, Jared and I both spoke a
little. He'd just used most of his entire vocabulary. I was
tired and grumpy again and working hard to appear
pleasant.

We entered an old stone building and what must have
once been the sizable main living room for a large family.
Four tall stools stood in front of a rustic heavy timber
counter, which occupied one entire side of the room. A shelf
crowded with bottles hung above it. The seating arrangement on the other end of the chamber consisted of two
wooden couches, facing each other, with a low table in
between. Heavy wooden chairs, sized for a yeti, stood at
right angles to the couches. A variety of pamphlets, adver-

tising safaris and tourist adventures in Tanzania, lay scattered over the low table. The covers of a few glossy magazines showed off pictures of Zanzibar beaches and high-end holiday spots on those islands.

"You would like tea? Water? Shall I open the bar?" the proprietor asked. "Hassan!" Then louder, "Hassan, we have guests!"

A tousled boy shuffled in from a side room, rubbing his eyes as his straw slippers made a swooshing noise on the clean-swept tile floor. He made a move to take our bags.

"Thank you, we're very tired. May we go straight to our rooms?" I said, to forestall any ideas Jared might have about socializing. I was afraid his body clock was telling him it was early morning — he'd be getting a second wind.

I propelled Sean forward with a grip on his upper arm and dipped my head at the boy to lead the way, which he did, with Jared's bag on one shoulder and a pack in the other hand. We went out a door in the back of the big living room and entered a narrow stone passage, dimly lit.

"Pick up your feet, Sean. It's uneven." I tried not to snap. Last thing I wanted was for him to stumble on the rough concrete floor, nor did I want to go down myself with a twisted ankle or stubbed toe.

The corridor opened into an open hallway, and the night sky glowed overhead. A faint smell of sewage wafted from a drain in the corner. Frogs croaked and I heard a splash. We faced a narrow, wrought-iron spiral staircase, where I humped and thumped my roller bag around to the first landing and on to the second. These damned things were so hard to maneuver on.

"I'll do it, Madam, just leave it," said the young boy, waving toward my luggage. But I didn't want to wait for him — I wanted to stretch out in a bed. There were times I didn't have the patience for the graciousness of African hospitality.

The stairs opened onto a tiny balcony where a small fridge was plugged into a mass of junction boxes that swung from a tangle of electrical cables coming out of a ragged hole in the concrete wall. The balcony opened into a large family room with three beds, a baby crib, a couch, and several tables. The floral smell was stronger here, and I saw a cylindrical can of air freshener in one corner.

I dumped my bag, then pushed Sean toward the single bed. "Take that one. Your dad'll be up later." Sean shrugged off his backpack and was stretched out before I could tell him he needn't bother to brush his teeth — as if he planned to. I untied the mosquito net over Sean's bed and draped it over him.

Hassan dropped the bags he carried and flipped on the air conditioner. While it wheezed to life he opened the fridge to show me bottles of cold water. I wished he'd hurry. I wanted to push him out the door.

"Thank you, we're fine," I said, as a rush of cool air blasted from the wall unit. I closed the door behind him, stripped down to a t-shirt, and was horizontal and dead to the world a minute later.

6

SUNDAY-TUESDAY, AUGUST 20-22

The call to prayer woke me as the sun poked a finger of light through the gap in the curtains. I was groggy and stuffy from the refrigerated air, but lying flat on a bed instead of cramped in an airline seat had been delicious. I stretched under the sheet and a cotton blanket. Sean was still sleeping. I levered myself up and peered around the room, through the faint white haze of the mosquito net. Jared lay across the largest bed under his own net, a lumpy log beneath a rough, rumpled bedsheet. Sean still had on his travel clothes and looked like he hadn't moved from the position he'd fallen in last night.

A small rip in Sean's bed net, overlooked the night before, caught my eye. Not ideal. I hoped the net had been properly soaked in insecticide. I contemplated the place of mosquitoes in the web of life. There were other pollinators, and surely the geckos I loved watching could eat something else — likewise the fish. As vectors of malaria, yellow fever, and dengue, mosquitoes caused plenty of trouble for tropical countries. I was glad Beth wasn't here to see the hole.

I imagined Jared and Sean would be asleep for another

hour or so. Insomnia had plagued me all my life. I rarely slept in the daylight and, half the time, not at night either — didn't matter how tired I was. "Strong circadian rhythms," was the best that therapists, hypnotists, and doctors had come up with over the years. Not very helpful. Jetlag was a killer for me. Over the years I'd learned to manage the insomnia, waiting a reasonable time in the dark for sleep, and, if it refused to come, taking out a book. I read a lot of books.

The problem with reading in bed, and especially in the middle of the night, was how to keep enough light on the page but not in my eyes, or someone else's. I'd MacGyvered several partial solutions over the years. I slept best lying on my left side so I dreaded the even numbered pages, difficult to position in the light. I developed an inflammatory lump on my wrist from the contortions. I tried different gadgets made for night reading, but none worked well.

Jared kept telling me to try an e-reader, and I ignored him. He finally gave me a Kindle. I thanked him and left it in the box for months. I was sure only a real book could satisfy me, holding it and feeling its weight, turning pages and flipping back and forth to find specific sentences. When he asked me for the third time how I liked it, I reluctantly gave it a try. I loved it and never looked back. With the device in my backpack I had a dozen books along wherever I went, and my lighting problem was over. I sheepishly admitted the favor he'd done me.

I reached under the mosquito net for the little backpack I used instead of a more conventional purse, and pulled out the Kindle. Bunching the pillow under my head and neck, while the air conditioner chugged and Jared snored lightly, I got through several chapters of an Ann Patchett book I'd missed when it'd come out years before.

I was immersed in the story when Jared sat up, rubbed his eyes, and yawned hugely. A smile of satisfaction spread across his face. "Hey, Ana. It's great to be back here. Can't wait for Sean to wake up. May have to drag him from bed."

I took the first shower. The instant hot water nozzle zinged me with an electrical shock when I tried to adjust the spray, so I made do with the few misdirected streams and drips of tepid water dribbling from it. Not great, but it was still good, and I savored it. The minute I stepped outside in the sticky air of Dar, it would be a dim memory.

Back out in the living room, when I emerged, Sean was awake and dressed in clean clothes, bouncing with energy and not a bit interested in washing up. I glanced at him and turned to Jared with a shrug. "I'll take him down to break-fast while you grab a quick shower."

Sean flung open the door to a gust of warm wet air. He raced down the circular stairs and I followed, startling and stumbling when a rooster's crow split the air. Sean stopped at the bottom, uncertain which way to go. I didn't remember either. The narrow stone hallway, open to the sky, didn't look anything like it had in the dim light of the previous night. In one direction, two women were bent over washtubs at what might have been the end of the corridor, so Sean and I went the other way. A sharp right turn led us to the big entrance room with the bar where we'd come in the previous night.

A faintly sweet floral smell permeated the air. The big double doors at the front were open this morning to a sunlight-filled courtyard. Beyond that hung the creaking metal gates we'd driven through in our taxi. Lush tropical plants, some with leaves a foot wide, grew out of ceramic and plastic pots of every imaginable size and color. Small-leaved trailing vines crawled out of tin cans and climbed the walls of the compound, twining with branches that drooped from brilliant magenta bougainvillea.

I turned from the plants in the courtyard to the interior of the room. Rustic hardwood dining tables and chairs, painted with many coats of shiny gloss, were scattered around. I took note of the chairs' sharp-edged rungs, made without benefit of a lathe. They were positioned at ankle height, perfect to wound an Achilles tendon when an unwary diner tried to scoot the chair forward with her butt on the seat. That had happened to me; I resolved not to be a victim again.

A smiling man in clean white shirt and trousers, arms folded across his chest, entered from a side room to greet us. "Ah, *habari za asubuji*, Madam. How are you this morning?"

"*Nzuri sana. Habari yako.*" I turned and grinned at Sean. "You remember the greetings?"

He smiled uncertainly. "*Habari za...asubuji?*"

"*Nzuri sana,*" said the older man, solemn-faced, looking at Sean. "*Habari yako?*"

"*Nzuri,*" Sean said with more confidence as the man's face split into a wide grin.

Greetings were critical here, as in most African countries. I'd come to appreciate the air of civility they lent to almost every interaction, although it took some time to understand that the answer to "how are you" always had to be "fine." Someone on her deathbed might admit things were only "a little fine."

"What would you like for breakfast? Tea? Coffee?"

"Do you have Cheerios?" Sean asked.

The man frowned, his face uncertain. "We have juice, eggs, toast, paw paw, pineapple. How do you like eggs?"

I jumped in. "One more person will join us. We'll all have scrambled." I glanced at Sean. "Okay?" Looking back at the man, I added, "Tea for me, and my brother will have coffee when he comes down. We'll also have toast, paw paw — with lime, please — and juice."

The man disappeared and Sean and I settled at a table.

"Maybe they'd have a different cereal," said Sean with a pout, more curious than sulky. "Maybe Frosted Flakes?"

I laughed. "Sean, these guesthouses don't serve American cold cereals. They're available in the big shops, but expensive. You know they're rubbish. You'd be hungry again in two hours."

Jared bounded in, clean shaven, comb marks in his wet hair, interrupting my lamentation about junky American breakfast food. He tousled Sean's bedhead. "Gotta wash this tonight, Buddy." He picked up a glass of juice and swigged it down. "Guess it's the usual selection for breakfast?"

"Yep, some things don't change." We shared a smile. The luscious fruit varied by season, but the only choice in most small guesthouses was how the eggs were cooked. "I went with scrambled, and tomorrow it can be a 'Spanish,' and then we can do boiled, and then there'll be fried." We snickered. It was good to be back in Tanzania with my brother.

WE NEEDED ferry tickets to Zanzibar, but the first priority had to be the document from the nuns in Mtwara. That took over an hour, with a complicated phone call. Their email arrived with an attachment, a problem to access. We finally got it downloaded but had to take it to a nearby shop to print. "The ink is finished, sir," said the owner, when we tried to use the guesthouse printer. Once Jared had the letter, he took a taxi to the airport.

I arranged for a messenger from our lodging to make

reservations for us on the ferry to Zanzibar. "Make it for the last crossing. Not sure when my brother will be back from customs. And buy one-way tickets. I don't want to be stuck if we change the time of the return." No matter what was printed on the ticket, getting a refund or exchange was impossible unless money passed under the table. Ill-informed foreign crusaders for justice could end up paying several bribes instead of the one originally demanded. The joke was that entry into a police station cost nothing — you only paid when you wanted out.

Jared returned from the airport with his box and many complaints about customs.

I resisted the urge to ask him if he'd learned a lesson. The guesthouse proprietor was happy to store the supplies for him until he went to Mtwara. Jared's schmoozing often paid off.

WE TOOK the last ferry for the two-and-a-half-hour crossing from Dar to Zanzibar. We'd opted for business class rather than the pricier VIP section. It made little difference, since we spent the entire journey on the deck hoping the fresher air would quell the nausea induced by the rocking boat on a rough sea. We did get a snack and drink out of the deal, but the faint smell of diesel, impossible to avoid, even outside, robbed me of any appetite. I gave the sweet biscuits to Sean. The crowd on deck was thick. Scantily clad tourists mingled with Zanzibari women in coverings ranging from simple *hijabs* to full *burkas*. We stood at the rail, pointing and yelling, spotting jumping fish. Screams of gulls pierced the dull chugging of the engine from time to time.

We got stuck at arrivals behind a tourist who had no

passport; he hadn't realized that Zanzibar considered itself independent of Tanzania for purposes of immigration. By the time we dealt with entry formalities, the sky was turning a deep blue. The noise and jostling outside the terminal were ferocious. We let ourselves be hustled into a taxi to our hotel.

"See you on the terrace for dinner. Eight o'clock okay?" asked Jared, steering Sean toward their room as uniformed bellhops took our bags.

I smiled at the thought of a quiet hour alone.

"ANYTHING YOU WANT, Sean. Check out the seafood on this menu!" Jared waggled his eyebrows and grinned. "Guarantee you'll love the prawns."

"Go for it, boys. I've been dreaming of grilled red snapper, myself." It was an old argument between Jared and me, which seafood was better.

"Tell you what," said Jared. "These portions are huge, let's order one of each and let Sean taste both and decide which he likes best."

Chefs in white double-breasted jackets and tall white toques barbecued fish and other sea creatures over coals behind an outdoor counter, their laughter and chatter muted by the crashing waves below.

The indigo sky had gone black, but it was cloudless, and we tried to identify constellations in the southern skies. Waiters in black trousers with bold, colorful, geometrically printed shirts brought our meals, and we had far more than we needed.

"So which is better, Sean?"

He wrinkled his forehead and chose the snapper. Then,

with a glance at Jared's face, he changed his mind. "No, the prawns!"

"That's my boy," shouted Jared. They high-fived and he sprinkled vinegar and hot sauce on the communal plate of chips. He didn't ask if everyone wanted the fiery red stuff, and he put on far too much for my taste.

THE NEXT DAY, we walked around Stone Town for a couple of hours. I loved the old stone buildings, with their huge medieval-looking, heavy, age-darkened, double wooden doors, hung with long iron strap hinges and decorated with brass studs and intricate carvings.

"Wow!" said Sean, his mouth round. "They're like old castles. If one of these fell down it'd smash us!" He ran his hand over the carving as we drew up in front of a door for a sliver of shade.

"How about a cold drink?" I asked, trying not to whine. I was hot and my head spun from jet lag.

"Yeah," said Sean, pulling his hand away from mine. "And you don't need to hold my hand. I'm not a baby!"

We continued down the narrow, cobbled street until we came to a T-junction. We turned left into a tight alley and walked for a few minutes before we heard a buzzing, followed by distinct shouts. Where was the noise coming from?

A group of ten or twelve young men exploded from around a corner ahead, some in white jellabiya, and some in red T-shirts, the color of the opposition party. Several men waved red pennants. The shouts grew louder as they ran fast, straight toward us, brandishing fists and flags. Without a word, we whirled to go the other way, back from where we'd come.

"Run," I shouted, as Jared and I each grabbed one of Sean's hands and raced for the junction. But before we reached it, three khaki-clad police materialized, clattering toward us and leaving us no way to move out of the path. Trapped, we flattened ourselves against the wall as the authorities and the young men overtook us from both sides, colliding where we stood.

The energized men threw stones, and police batons whizzed through the air. Crack! One of them connected with the shoulder of a man who couldn't have been more than eighteen, a few wisps of hair on his upper lip. He stumbled and toppled into the man next to him, and they both fell into us. Trapped in the melee, Sean yelled. Jared twisted in one direction, and I rotated in the other. Shouting, heart racing, I hung on to Sean with all my strength, but my slippery grip wasn't enough. I fell to the ground and lost sight of him. I saw Jared go down and terror seized me as I saw that he had no grasp on Sean either.

"Sean!" Jared roared.

I staggered to my feet searching right and left. Sticks and a few rocks flew through the air. "Get Sean!" I screamed at no one.

There he was! Sean's bright blue shirt peeked out from behind the white jellabiya of a wiry man bent over him. I rocketed toward them, yelling.

"Sean, are you all right? Sean!"

"He's okay, Mama, okay. The boy is okay," said the wiry fellow, looking up at me but still crouched and shielding Sean.

A bullhorn crackled with undecipherable words and, in an instant, the protestors turned and ran the other way. The man, his jellabiya rumpled and streaked with dirt, pulled Sean to his feet and pushed him gently toward me. "Take care of your son, Mama. This is not a place to wander."

He turned and dashed down the street after his compatriots, a blood stain on his upper back. The police chased close on his heels.

Sean, unsteady, turned to Jared, who was rising from his knees. He bent to hug Sean. The sole sign of what had just taken place were a few sticks and rocks and some torn pennants. The three of us remained alone in the middle of the alleyway, suddenly quiet and deserted. My chest was heaving too hard to allow speech.

Sean clung to Jared's waist. He looked up with huge eyes and a sniffle. After a minute he took a gulp of air.

We stood, shaky and disoriented, for several more minutes.

I calmed enough to speak. "Let's go back the way we came. We passed a hotel where we can buy a drink." I looked over at Jared, and our eyes connected. I smiled wanly. Sean walked between Jared and me, holding both our hands without complaint. We paused at every corner to peer down the street for young men.

At the hotel bar, I took a long drink of a heavily sweetened fruit juice, grateful for once for the sugar. "I don't get what that was about. This isn't an election year."

"No, but there've been arrests of opposition leaders in the past few months. Maybe these are protests over that." Jared shrugged. "The government promised to crack down on corruption — and they're using the chance to close down dissenting voices."

"I wish Mom was here," Sean blurted out of nowhere, his head bent over the straw in his juice. Jared scowled, his lips making a straight thin line as he reached out to rub

Sean's arm.

"I can take care of you, Sean."

"That man saved me. He was like the heroes in the airport museum. He was a hero, wasn't he, Dad?"

A muscle in Jared's jaw twitched.

"He was a hero, wasn't he?" Sean persisted, wonder creeping into his voice.

"Sure, Sean. He was a good man. But I wouldn't have let anything happen to you. I can be a hero, too."

I scooted over to put my arm around Sean's shoulders.

Jared took a long swallow of his drink. "Let's go back for a swim at the hotel. And how about some more of those prawns for dinner?"

We got up to leave.

"Heroes," Jared muttered over Sean's head, giving me an eye roll. "He's obsessed with heroes."

THE NEXT DAY — our last in Zanzibar — we agreed to skip the diving-with-dolphins trip.

"For once, I think lying on a beach sounds good," I said to Jared at breakfast. I'd awakened with stiff muscles and a couple of bruises in places I hadn't remembered bashing the day before. "I know you wanted to swim with dolphins, Sean, but honestly, there are so many boats out there. It's hectic and not good for the poor animals to be in the middle of the confusion."

Jared made a small face of disagreement at me — we'd debated this before, and he knew my opinion — but he didn't argue this time, and neither did a subdued Sean.

The beach turned out to be a good choice. There was almost no one on the stretch we found. Sean dashed back and forth in the surf — his first experience with tropical white sands and warm ocean water. We bought overpriced snacks from the few hawkers who were out, dressed in shirts made from colorful prints. We drew the line when a skinny, ragged boy with a runny nose, who looked about Sean's age, tried to interest us in a tortoise shell.

"Those are illegal, Sean," Jared said. "The species is endangered, and if people buy them, they'll harvest more."

"But the boy looks poor. I think he's hungry."

Jared and I exchanged glances. We'd both seen the boy gesture at Sean and make motions of putting food in his mouth. Sean was going to have some tough lessons on this trip. I squirmed at the uncomfortable reality that we were wealthy foreigners.

"Yeah, probably so, Sean. But we can't feed everyone," said Jared. I was glad Sean didn't pursue it. He shrugged and skipped off into the white surf.

"This trip'll be good for Sean," I said, spreading out a *kanga,* the ubiquitous, multi-functional two-meter length of cloth called by various names across Africa. I positioned mine to stretch out on and keep an eye on Sean. "Mom and Dad gave us great opportunities. I wish I believed they see us here now." I sighed. "I miss them."

A shadow passed across Jared's face. "Dad might've been here — if he'd wanted to be."

I let a slow breath escape. I didn't want to hear Jared's thoughts on this.

I turned my head to face him straight on. "Oh, Jared. They'd love seeing us here with Sean and be proud of what you're doing. If I can make a success of the GHI, there'll be opportunities for me to give the family I want the same great experiences we had growing up."

"Yeah." His face hardened. "Good luck with that. I

thought the same thing with my career, but it hasn't worked out that way. My work hasn't been enough to impress Beth. Building my non-profit was something she and I agreed on before we married. She helped me set it up — made personal donations." He threw his forearm up to shield his eyes as he watched Sean. "She used to like coming on the trips." His voice dropped, and I had to struggle to hear him. "I don't get why things are falling apart."

Finally. A crack in Jared's unwillingness to acknowledge his marriage failure. I avoided the temptation to point out that bringing his family along for short-term jaunts was not the same thing at all as raising children overseas. I bit the inside of my cheek, studying his face.

"She's gonna be amazed at what I can do with the non-profit on my own." He looked out over the water. "She'll see her mistake and come back." He turned back to face me. "Besides, she knows Sean needs a father in his life."

A vision of Beth and Paul in the bar swam into my mind. I swallowed and weighed my words. "I haven't wanted to say it, but I think you may be wrong on this. I'm afraid Beth is moving on."

Jared squinted out at Sean, playing in the surf. He scowled and stood up. "I'm going out to swim," he called over his shoulder, trotting away.

I lay back and tried to let the sound of gentle waves displace the unease filling my mind over Jared's denial. The inescapable smells — seaweed, sea water, and sea life — soothed me. All morning Jared and I traded off watching Sean, wandering the beach, and dog paddling in the warm, turquoise Indian Ocean.

"How about lunch?" asked Jared at noon, prodding me with a sandy foot. He pointed down the white sand. "I like the look of that yellow hotel beyond the big rock. Let's eat, then maybe visit the old slave market and museum?"

The boy with the tortoise shell sat on the far end of the white sand, beyond the rock. He might have been watching us. Narrowing my eyes, I saw guards at all the hotels along the beachfront. They'd make sure he didn't contact any more foreigners, but they wouldn't stop us from approaching him. When Jared and Sean were in the restroom I strolled over to the boy and gave him several small bills. Jared was right that we couldn't save every hungry kid, but I could feed this one today.

7

WEDNESDAY, AUGUST 23

Our trip back to the mainland by hovercraft the following morning was faster and rougher than the journey to Zanzibar. Sean was greenish when we stepped off the vessel. We rushed to grab a taxi to the airport for our flight to Kilimanjaro.

I nabbed a window seat on the right side of the small plane for Sean. He'd have a spectacular view of Mt. Kilimanjaro if the clouds cooperated, although they often didn't. Thirty minutes after takeoff, the Maasai Steppe stretched below us, brown in this dry season, with rare patches of green. Tin roofs flashed in the sun, a reminder that people lived in this harsh region. My eyes were drawn up into the foothills of the mountain, over the rich evergreen of the bananas, coffee, and tea planted there, but the huge cumulus clouds wiped out any higher view of the massive extinct volcano.

"It's there, Sean. You'll have to wait, but I promise it's there."

Jared was reading a magazine, but I was spellbound. In the same way that music transports someone to another time, this view took me back to my teenaged years in Moshi, the many times I'd flown in and out of this airport.

"Look toward the right side of the mountain, Sean. That's Rombo, where we're going next. The houses are stuck in among all those trees."

The plane landed with a few bounces and taxied to a stop in front of the domestic side of the terminal. We walked down the wobbly fold-out stairs onto the tarmac and I filled my lungs with the dry air, welcome after the humidity at the coast.

Our bags were the first to appear in the small claims area. Just outside, a smiling man held a sign for the tour company that would take Jared and Sean toward Arusha and the Tarangire game park.

I waved them off after back pats and hugs. "See you guys in a few days."

My reservation was on the outskirts of Moshi town. I chose a taxi from among the many vying for my attention and rattled off, enjoying a satisfying sense of purpose. I was finally starting the business that justified this trip.

The little guesthouse I'd booked was a couple of kilometers off the main road, in a hilly area with banana and coffee plants. The concrete-block cottages with thatched roofs were simple, but decorated with curtains, bedspreads, and pillows made from the same bright fabrics local women used for their *kangas*. A small shower, sink, and toilet took up the back quarter of my room, partitioned off by a modest woven grass screen. The peace and pace here soothed me after the hustle of Dar and Stone Town. I had a quick rinse-off, pleased to find that the instant hot water appliance here was grounded.

I identified the vague weight I'd carried around for the past day as springing from Jared's unrealistic talk about

Beth. Should I have said more about her relationship with Paul? Maybe that would help him accept the truth. But Beth must have already told him everything she'd told me.

I passed a quiet afternoon in the garden and little veranda of my cottage, reading material about programs I wanted to investigate. The clouds mounded up around Kili, and a brief sprinkle and light breeze brought the scent of rain on dry earth, making me dreamy. I found myself thinking about Mark. I glanced at my watch — 4 p.m. here meant 8 a.m. for him. Good time for a Skype call. I crossed my fingers for the internet connection and got lucky. Not good enough for video but the sound wasn't bad.

"My God, Ana. You say the business in Zanzibar happened on Monday? It's Wednesday evening there, right? Why didn't you tell me earlier? Are you sure you're okay?"

I was taken aback by the force of his concern. "I'm fine, Mark," I insisted. Maybe I should have told him before. But the time difference made it inconvenient to call. "I knew you'd be busy preparing for the conference. Don't worry so much. I can take care of myself. Besides, I was with Jared."

He didn't answer and the silence stretched. He finally spoke. "I'm glad you're okay. Please be careful." We talked about his upcoming meeting before saying goodbye.

Dinner alone — banana stew, a slightly tough piece of lean beef, and a fresh cabbage and carrot salad — satisfied me after the rich fare of the previous days.

Before I quit for the night, an email from Brad popped into my inbox. He'd be leaving for Mali in two days. *I'm optimistic about a women's microfinance project there, paired with family health outcomes. Great combo of research and a well-run program.*

I chewed my lower lip. I'd been in Tanzania for several

days and had nothing to show our boss for it yet. Meanwhile, Brad was moving along.

I pushed anxiety away and took in several deep breaths. In the morning, I'd check out the first possibility for work. A smile crept across my face.

8

THURSDAY, AUGUST 24

I woke early to crowing and barking, impossible to escape wherever people settled. Ever-present birdsong and insect noises filled the background, but they were white noise that rested easily in my head. The dogs and roosters were something else.

Nonetheless, a surge of satisfaction passed through me — I was ready to go to work.

I let myself lie in bed for a few minutes imagining interesting possibilities. After a good stretch, I sprang up and headed over to the dining room for breakfast.

I'd heard a lot of good buzz at an international global health meeting about the nurse training program at the university teaching hospital in Moshi.

Andrew, had spoken in glowing terms of the project. "There'll be major funding available from USAID for building on this, if we can get a foot in the door," was his assessment.

I had an appointment at the hospital that morning. A partnership would be a great start to a portfolio of projects for Honnelly.

A large European aid grant had funded the initial phase, a program to train general nurses with the special skills needed to treat critically ill children. Thirty nurses had completed training to staff the new pediatric intensive care unit in Moshi. An impressive building housing the ICU was a new addition to the hospital, constructed with a grant from the European Union. Andrew's pet project idea was to twin pediatric intensive care nurses from Honnelly with the Tanzanian nurses. It had potential. Most global health programs focused on opportunities for American medical personnel to travel, but I figured the learning could go both ways. I liked the idea of Tanzanian nurses coming to the US to share their knowledge and experiences.

I was eager to see what the hospital looked like now. My taxi driver chose a back route. I recalled it being dirt, pock-marked with axle-breaking holes. Now it was tarmac-covered, with concrete-lined drainage ditches on either side to carry the muddy water that flowed when the long rains started. The taxi looped around, and I got out at the front of the sprawling cement block hospital. It'd been re-painted a number of times since it was built, but forty-six years is a long time for a building to be assaulted by a tropical climate, and each successive paint job had to cover more warts and cracks than the last. The sky-blue trim was mottled from flaking. Many of the kids I'd been in school with at the International School in Moshi had parents who'd worked here, but I'd seldom had anything to do with the place.

I got turned around several times in the labyrinth of halls. I hated being late anywhere, whether it mattered or not, and now I had to race-walk. I was frazzled by the time I found the office of Professor Shirima, the head of pediatric care. My appointment was for 10 a.m. and I checked in with a secretary and plopped down in the waiting room chair, breathless and sweaty, a couple of minutes late. I needn't have worried — I was still sitting there at 10:30. I had plenty of time to catch my breath and look around the office. I'd plunked down in one of a set of six armchairs that had seen better days. The red upholstery was frayed and shiny with wear, and the padded seat wobbled on the metal frame. My probing little finger found an empty hole where the screw had fallen out of one of the armrests; I shifted my weight off the elbow I'd planted there.

Several framed photos of distinguished men were suspended against the wall by wires from a ceiling at least ten feet high. I recognized the center one as John Magufuli, the President for the past year. By all accounts, he'd followed through on some of his promises to clean up corruption, but he'd also cracked down on civil society. He criminalized homosexuality and insisted that schoolgirls who fell pregnant should be expelled. When criticized for the latter, he responded by instituting harsh punishments for the men responsible for the pregnancies. Many journalists were under arrest — always a bad sign.

I was mulling these unfortunate facts when, finally, at 10:45, a portly male in a white coat poked his head out of the inner office door.

"Dr. Lotman?" the rotund man said, walking toward me and sticking out his hand.

I rose from the seat, let down that he had my name wrong. I stuck my hand out and put a little extra emphasis on my name as I recited my part of the greetings.

Professor Shirima indulged me with a smile, led the way into his office, and gestured for me to sit on a lumpy armchair facing his desk. I avoided a spring sticking up on the front edge. I was determined not to make the American mistake of getting to the point of my visit before the obligatory small talk around my impressions of Tanzania. An attempt to avoid "wasting his time" would make me look rushed and impolite.

When he was ready, he smiled indulgently and rested his arms on the desk between us. "I have the proposal you sent me somewhere here." He shuffled through documents in front of him, picked one up, glanced at it for a few seconds, and cleared his throat. "Very interesting, yes. Remind me again, if you don't mind, about your project?"

"Thank you, Professor." I scooted forward on the chair, mindful of the spring. "First, congratulations on the new pediatric intensive care unit. I understand it's become a model for other hospitals."

The professor beamed.

"We'd like to build on the nurse training aspect."

"Oh yes. A fine program."

I listened to him wax enthusiastic about the success of the training program for several minutes before he asked, "And you'd like to sponsor more nurses for instruction?"

"Not exactly," I said, forcing myself to smile. He clearly was not familiar with the proposal nor prepared for our meeting. "We'd like to support a learning exchange between nurses here and some from our university." I wished he'd read the details. I'd outlined all this.

He picked up a pair of half glasses from his desktop and flipped through the document. He scrutinized the last pages — the budget, and the budget justification, describing the roles of the participants. I sat still, hoping to convey patience I didn't feel, as he ran a thick finger down the page.

He stroked his chin. "You need to add allowances for local counterparts."

I scanned my own copy, glad I had it in front of me.

"Those are included here in line five on page twenty-five, under 'Personnel.'"

Professor Shirima peered at me over his glasses. "You'll need a Principal Investigator here — someone from the Pediatric Department." He lowered his brows and compressed his lips. "I think forty or fifty percent of a full-time equivalent would be reasonable." He waggled his head. "I'd be willing to serve in that position."

Brad Hick's warnings at the reception came back to me. I swallowed. Professor Shirima had zeroed in on the budget like a hawk snatching a sunning snake. He hadn't even read the proposal, so didn't know what would be required of the P.I. The proportion of his time he was suggesting for the work was way out of line. How many other projects was he listed on at fifty percent effort?

I rubbed my brow and studied him, struggling for a response.

"Hmm. This is something we'll need to consider," was the best I managed, as I jotted notes on my copy. "This proposal is a draft. Most of my knowledge of the training comes from reading the final evaluations. It'd be helpful to talk to people who participated before we flesh out details. Is it possible for me to chat with a couple of the nurses who graduated from the program?"

"I don't see why not. We have three or four still on staff here."

"Is that all?" I couldn't hide my surprise. "What's happened to the others?"

"Many came from smaller district hospitals in the area, so of course they've returned there."

That made sense. I nodded my understanding at him.

"I'm sorry I can't take you over to show you the unit and introduce you myself." He shook his head. "So busy."

This was my cue to offer the Swahili condolence to recognize hard work. "*Pole na kazi.*"

He acknowledged the courtesy with a brief smile. "I'll have my secretary check the roster and tell you when she can set up a meeting with someone from the training. Would tomorrow or the day after be okay?"

"Sure," I said. "Thank you very much." He was getting up, so I did the same and we exchanged smiles again.

He'd think I was pushy, but visions of Brad making strides in Mali crowded into my mind, so I said it anyway. "Is there any chance for me to meet someone this afternoon? I'm sorry to rush you but..." I shrugged and gave my best self-deprecating grin.

He raised an eyebrow, stripped off his glasses, and laid them on the desk with a definite *thunk*. "My, my. You do expect things to move quickly." He blew out a breath. "Okay. Let's check right now."

He accompanied me to the outer office and spoke in rapid Swahili to the secretary.

"*Sawa. Sawa,*" she said, nodding her head smartly.

He turned to say goodbye, and I thanked him again. When he'd disappeared back into his office, she waved me over to the teetery armchair. She scrutinized her nails for a bit, then turned to her computer, leaving me fidgeting. After about ten minutes, she picked up her phone and called someone. She hung up and gave me a smile.

"You can meet Sister Mbeki in the pediatric intensive care unit this afternoon. You should be able to catch her about two."

THE NEW UNIT gleamed with stainless-steel equipment and bright shiny murals of children dancing and playing with friendly looking animals on the walls. Sister Mbeki and I exchanged greetings, and I liked her instantly for the way she looked me in the eye and spoke up, clearly and distinctly.

"Oh, yes, Dr. Lotner, I finished the training program last year. I was lucky to be posted to the unit afterward." She smiled broadly and stretched up to adjust the tiny nurse's cap perched on her short natural hairdo.

"I've heard so many good things about the training." I returned her smile. "Would you mind answering a few questions?" I reached into my bag for a list I'd prepared.

We sat on two stools in a quiet corner of the unit to talk, and I liked Sister Mbeki even more as we did. She was eager to help me.

"Oh, I love this work. We've saved so many children." She pulled a phone out of her pocket, scrolled to a picture, and thrust it at me. A beautiful young woman with a smile from ear to ear cradled a tiny child. "Mwaipopo nearly died of sepsis, but here he is on the day he was discharged." She bent forward and scrolled a bit further. "I'll never forget this one, Saidi, who survived cerebral malaria. His mother still comes around to visit."

She leaned in to answer my questions.

"On what basis was I selected for training?" she repeated, wrinkling her brow as she mulled my question. "Well, it was my turn. I guess that was true for all the other nurses who attended too. The matron made the decision, and she tries to be fair about providing opportunities."

"Sister, you said you were lucky to be posted to the unit after training. Weren't all the nurses who trained sent to intensive care units after they finished?"

"Oh, no. Most of the nurses came from district hospitals where there are no special pediatric units like this." She hesitated and adjusted her cap. Her face brightened. "But they got an upgrade and are making more money now. And several of the nurses were able to move up into administrative posts with the extra credential they got from the course." She smiled broadly. "And they got good per diems during the training year, which always helps — our salaries are low."

"Do you know how many of the graduates are working as pediatric intensive care nurses now?"

"Let's see." She rubbed her forehead. "There are three of us."

My eyebrows shot up before I thought. "Only three of thirty nurses who completed the one-year course are using their training now?"

"That's right."

The evaluation report heaped praise on this project, and I'd had high hopes for building on it. But the report was limited to interviews with nurses and instructors during and immediately after the course. It didn't include information on how the training had been used after they'd finished. Why didn't I think of that earlier?

There was no way to build on this program. I didn't want to embarrass the sister, so I struggled to smile and sound upbeat as I gathered my things and said goodbye.

Back at the guesthouse, fortified by a glass of wine, I worked to craft a detailed email to Andrew. The twinning scheme he was so keen on wouldn't work here.

It was still early back home and he replied just before I went to bed. *I'm sure you can develop something out of this. Give it more thought. The GHI needs you to show vision. The department needs this project to fulfill the expectations of large donors.*

I thought again about Brad Hicks — and imagined his microfinance and health project bounding forward. Frustrated, I crawled into bed with my Kindle, hoping I'd wake up in a better mood. I opened it and smiled to see the "new" notice at the top of my book list. Mark had surprised me with another present. I wouldn't have to wait till the next day for a better mood.

9

FRIDAY, AUGUST 25

I liked Ellen Mafwira the minute we met in her tiny office in Moshi the next day. To call her attractive was a considerable understatement. She was tall and willowy with beautiful, smooth, dark skin. Rather than a wig or an elaborate braided hairdo, she had closely cropped natural hair — and it showed off her gorgeous features to perfection. She and Beth would have understood each other's fashion sense on first sight. In comparison, I supposed I looked like a molting bird, but I put that out of my head.

After greetings, she came to the point. "So, Dr. Lotner, you want to talk about our key informant project," she said in a soft, clear voice. "What is it you want to know?"

Her directness startled me. I'd made this appointment with Ellen Mafwira on the advice of my friend, Grace, whom I'd be visiting in a few days. This was a fact-finding call, and I had no proposal to put in front of Ms. Mafwira. Jared had suggested it was a waste of time. "Stick with universities, Ana. More opportunities for publications and big projects. I've got doubts about those so-called community-based efforts. I mean, beyond pushing basic hygiene and nutrition, how much can they really do about disease?"

That was my surgeon brother speaking. I didn't remind him that basic hygiene and nutrition were still at the root of much disease. My gut feeling about this project was good and Grace understood community development better than Jared.

I smiled at Ms. Mafwira. "Please call me Ana."

"And I'm Ellen," replied the graceful woman.

"I'd like to learn more about the key informant projects you've developed. The ones for identifying kids with disabilities in villages. I've read a bit about them, but there's a lot I don't understand."

Ellen dipped her head to invite me to continue.

"Wouldn't it make sense to train the nurses who do immunization to look for these kids? Most children are vaccinated, so why not find the problems at that point?"

Ellen smiled. "Good question. Sometimes that works. But some of the problems only become apparent once the kid is past immunization age. And some of the problems are rare."

I cocked my head.

"Take pediatric cataract for example. You teach an immunization nurse to check if the pupil looks black. She can learn to do that." Ellen shrugged and threw out a hand, palm up. "But it takes time, and she'll need special equipment to do it right — and it's a rare condition. After training, when she doesn't find it in the next five-hundred or so kids she screens, she forgets or gives up checking."

I hadn't thought of that. Another example of something sounding good from afar that didn't fit local conditions.

"But," Ellen went on, "mothers are pretty good at knowing when there's something wrong with their kid, especially if it's not their first. Sadly, when it's a serious problem, the child may end up hidden away in the house — sometimes for their own safety and sometimes out of shame." She gazed out in the distance, and I wondered what she was thinking about. "We don't train the key informants — KIs — to diagnose problems or figure out what's wrong. We only want them to keep track of the mothers and organize them to show up with their little ones for a nearby scheduled screening. The screener is a specialist in disability — too specialized to be stationed at a health clinic or district hospital. She can decide who needs to go on to see the doctor."

"And who are these KIs?" I asked.

"Village women who are trusted and know the other women in their villages. They also have to be literate and be good communicators."

"Wow." I was impressed. "Sounds wonderful. Like that magic bullet we're always hoping to find."

"Ha!" Ellen had a tinkly laugh, brimming with real amusement. "There are no magic bullets. Would you like to hear about the mistakes we've made, the lessons we've learned?"

I loved this woman's honesty.

"The first time we tried this, we hadn't prepared well enough. We didn't have enough clipboards and pens — high value items to these women." She scratched her head. "Some women left, angry. And we hadn't thought about giving them cards with phone credit. They have to communicate, and it costs to make a call. Then we had to figure out how many homes each KI could visit, and in what time period."

"Yep. Makes sense. Do you pay them?"

"Coming to that," Ellen said with a wry grin. "We imagined these informal community leaders stepping up to do this work with joy in their hearts."

"And they didn't?"

Ellen raised an eyebrow. "Where you come from do a lot of poor people come out and offer their time for free? Volunteer to help in their communities in a regular reliable way?"

"Well...sometimes. Some people." But I was aware that volunteerism was most popular among people who weren't scrambling to pay the bills.

"And think about this, Ana. What if the community knows that a big organization from a wealthy country is paying for the project? They might want a little piece of that pie for their efforts, no? It's not as though village women have nothing else to do."

"So how have you resolved it?"

Ellen let loose that tinkly laugh again. "We haven't. It's a recurrent theme, and we debate it all the time. We want to be fair but we also hope to build a sense of caring and responsibility within the community."

"I guess it does sound a bit utopian."

"Sure. Among our mistakes have been instances when we *did* pay and had to cut back later. And there're the times village chiefs *assume* we'll pay and select themselves as KIs. Sticky issues."

"Okay. So maybe not a magic bullet yet."

Tinkly laugh.

"May I ask you, Ellen, why you do this work?"

She looked at me for several seconds. Her eyes moved to the window, and she rested her chin in her palm. "When I was a kid. I heard a story that made me angry. Our cook's aunt lived out on the Maasai Steppe. The aunt had a couple of kids, including a little girl. When the girl developed a lump on her face that didn't go away, the aunt took her to a health clinic. The first time she went, no one was there. Several weeks later, when the lump was larger, she made the hour-long walk to the clinic again, with the child tied to her back. The health worker on duty gave her some tablets and told her to come back if the problem didn't get better. When the lump was the size of an avocado, the woman sold her mattress for money to take the bus to the big hospital in Moshi. But it was too late. The tumor had spread. The doctor said there was nothing to do. He asked why she'd waited so long to bring the child to him." Ellen shook her head. "The child died a month later."

The injustice burned. I wanted to help people like the aunt, to stop such monumental failures of the health system. The balloon of indignation swelling in me popped, though, as I considered desperate friends who'd been denied care by the health insurance industry in the US. It'd happened exactly the way John Grisham described in one of his thrillers.

Ellen brought her gaze back to me. "I'll tell you, Ana, I still feel bad over that story. I was maybe eleven or twelve, but it wasn't right, and it stuck in my mind." She shook her head and shrugged. "I had the chance to go to university and study community development. I married a businessman who's done very well." She raised her eyebrows and smiled. "Lucky me, I can afford to work as a volunteer myself. I run a local organization to increase the use of KIs."

Excitement and admiration spread through me. "I'd love to find ways to work with you. Maybe we could study some of those sticky issues. Test ideas to find the best ways to engage with KIs. I believe we could find funding to expand it."

She smiled. "I'm willing to consider this, Ana, but I must

be frank. We have to be careful. Sometimes the smell of big money coming in from foreign institutions can ruin good community development. I've seen villagers start asking why they should dig their own wells without compensation, when other people are paid to come in and encourage them." She raised her hand, palm up. "But if they don't dig it themselves they don't have the same incentive to maintain it." She smiled. "As far as I know it's the same all over the world. Community development is hard."

"I believe you. That's part of what I'm here to learn about."

She eyed me for a few silent moments while she ran a finger under her lip. "We have another training coming up." She pulled a planner toward her and flipped a page forward. Let's see, there's one on Saturday September second and another two weeks later on the sixteenth. Both near Rombo. Would you like to join us to observe?"

"I'd love to." I opened my own calendar. "In fact, I was planning on being in Rombo on the second with Grace, so that's perfect."

She smiled. "Let me have your number and I'll text you the details early next week."

We said goodbye and I left humming with the feeling that I might have found a real possibility — a project that combined community development and service with interesting research potential. I couldn't wait to see it in just over a week.

10

SATURDAY, AUGUST 26

J ared and Sean were supposed to be at my guesthouse by 9:30 on Saturday morning. That meant they'd leave Tarangire at 6:30 — no problem since everyone got up early at game parks. We had plans for a hike that morning so I was annoyed when they hadn't shown by 10:30, but didn't start worrying until 11:00. My calls to Jared went directly to his voicemail. I told myself not to overreact and worked on a report for work. At noon, I called the lodge where they'd spent the previous night.

"Dr. Jared Lotner and his son checked out. Actually, they requested an early breakfast at 5:30 for departure at 6:00. Any earlier and they wouldn't have been able to see any animals." The hotelier chuckled.

"I don't suppose you know what their plans were?"

"Dr. Lotner mentioned they were driving to Moshi."

If they left at 6:00, they should have been here three hours ago. I tried to call Jared again, but, again, the phone went to voice mail. How annoying! I'd been looking forward to walking together through the nearby tea plantation in the foothills.

I got stuck on my report, gave up, and opened a book. Maybe the main park gate would have a record of cars entering and leaving. Sure they would. Park passes were issued for twenty-four hours, and I remembered being charged for an extra day when I'd been an hour and a half over time in the past.

I searched the internet for a number. All I found was the central office for National Parks in Dar. The phone rang and rang, but no one picked up. I hung up, but, with no better plan, I tried again fifteen minutes later. A tinny voice came through on a scratchy line.

"You want the number at the Tarangire front gate? For what reason?"

"I need to find out if my brother's car left there this morning. He's hours overdue returning from a trip." I ought to stay as clear and polite as possible. There'd be no hope if I let anxiety, which was starting to gnaw, turn to snippiness.

"Please hold," said the woman.

I waited, shifting my weight from one foot to the other on the veranda. A few minutes later the line went dead.

I sighed and punched in the number again, striving for good humor.

Someone else answered this time, and I had to start all over with explanations. The man on the other end cooperated but hope dimmed when he put me on hold again. Still, he was back in a couple of minutes with a number.

I called it, taking slow deep breaths, pacing on my little veranda.

"Hello," said a sleepy voice.

I started to respond. A loud and painful *crackle! phzzt!* hit my eardrum.

"Hello!...hear me?" I made out between the bursts of static. "... can't hear you!"

Damn! This was typical of about half the phone conversations I'd had in my early years in Tanzania. Cell phones were often better, but the front gate number was an unreliable landline.

The line suddenly cleared. I remembered to make my way through polite greetings before getting to the purpose of my call, hoping I wasn't wasting the few precious seconds of line clarity I'd be lucky to get.

"You say it's a private vehicle, not a regular safari company? What's the registration plate number?" asked the man, sounding sleepy again.

"I'm afraid I don't know. Do you have names in the log book? Can you please look for a Lotner? I'm his sister. That's L-O-T-N-E-R. He would have entered on Wednesday, the twenty-third, sometime before noon."

"Rotner?" I thought he said.

"A man and a boy aged nine."

"Okay. Please hold." *Crackle crackle.* "...log unavail... very busy this morning."

"*Pole sana* — sorry," I said, making a mighty effort to sound sincere. With no choice, I waited. In a series of small miracles, the connection held. I heard voices in the background, and at least I didn't have to endure any recorded music.

Thunk. Someone dropped the receiver. I nearly gave up, but I hung on, and my reward came a few seconds later when a man's voice reached me on a cleared line. "No, Madam. He is not listed in the log book as an exit. He's overstayed his pass."

"Okay. Can you please..." My luck expired and the line went dead.

I sat down and thought about it. Jared was overdue — missing in the park. I wondered if the National Parks offered a search service for missing people, until I realized I didn't need it. I'd find a safari company to go look for him if he didn't show up in two more hours. Someone was always willing to provide services for the right price. It was one of the things that made life in Africa easy for those with money. I went back to the internet to look at options.

My phone rang from an unknown number. I pounced on it.

"Ana?" It was Jared. "We're at the front gate of Tarangire, leaving now. A ranger recognized my name and said you'd called a few minutes ago. Sorry, my phone's dead. He let me use his. Is there some problem?"

"Yes. I expected you at 9:30." I wanted to shout. "Where've you been?"

"Sean wanted one last game drive this morning. And I don't recall saying...*crackle crackle*...there in a couple of hours."

JARED AND SEAN showed up at my guesthouse at 3:00 p.m. Sean was bug-eyed over the few days of safari at Tarangire. He was enthusiastically trying his voice at animal imitations — wild and domestic.

"The only thing more irritating than a rooster crowing at five a.m. is a boy imitating a rooster at five a.m.," said Jared, tousling his hair and smiling.

Sean was not discouraged. "We saw two lions stalking a warthog! And the little hog got away." He fished an expensive camera from his pack.

I'd had doubts about the wisdom of giving a nine-year-old such a gift, but Jared had insisted on it.

"Look at this!" Sean said, waving the shiny little silver

device at me with a fuzzy picture of the hind ends of three waterbuck on the screen.

The blurred, but distinctive, white horseshoe shaped pattern was the only way to identify the animal. "Looks like they sat on wet toilet seats," I said, squinting at the scene. Sean giggled and Jared smiled at the old joke.

"Show her more," he said, as Sean clicked ahead to a blurry image of a small herd of zebra, again recognizable only by their pattern.

I was careful in my comments. At age seven, I'd made a holiday card for my dad, with a horse under a sky dotted with puffy clouds. I'd outlined the cumuli with a black crayon, my latest artistic technique. Dad praised the lassoes in the sky until my quivering lip alerted him to his mistake. He managed to turn our mutual dismay into a laugh and a warm hug. At least he recognized the animal as a horse.

My stomach growled. Jared threw his arm around Sean's shoulder and gave him a good-old-boy squeeze. "Hey, maybe later, Sean. How about if we get a snack now? Didn't I hear you say you were starving about thirty minutes ago?"

"*I* certainly was — actually about two hours and thirty minutes ago," I said, glowering at Jared. He'd definitely said he'd be here earlier.

"Aww, Ana. No big deal." He threw an arm around my shoulders and shot me a huge grin. "We can go right now."

While we waited for a plate of chips, the only thing the little restaurant down the road could produce at that hour, Sean showed me more photos. His joy at capturing all he'd seen was infectious. Maybe Jared had been right about the camera, although a cheaper model would have sufficed. The extra effort to impress a nine-year-old seemed wasted.

"I wanna send this one to show Mom and Paul. He loves zebras."

I glanced up at Jared in time to see him swallow hard and scowl.

Sean prattled on. "Only one problem. I was trying so hard for a shot of a hyena with a dead buffalo, that I missed seeing the lion who sneaked in and chased him off."

"Yeah. Happens sometimes," I said, sympathetic, but unable to suppress a twinge of vindication — Sean had experienced one of the main reservations I'd had about giving him the camera. But my heart ached for Jared.

WE'D PROMISED Sean we'd take him to our old school in Moshi for a look around. It wasn't only for Sean — I was eager to see the place again myself. The driveway gate was locked, so we parked by a eucalyptus tree on the side of the road next to the school and walked through a small pedestrian entry. Off to our right, heading uphill, the peak of Kili stood above heavy clouds, suggesting that rain would drench the slopes in the late afternoon. But down where we were, the air was warm and dry. The branches of big eucalyptus shadowed the sun and dappled the gravel driveway we strolled on.

"Oh, Jare, do you remember Mr. Greer?"

That legendary mathematics and physics teacher had planned some ingenious games to entice us to his subject, including a model boat race in the school swimming pool.

"I still think mine was the best design," grumbled Jared, "and I'd have won if Joyce Malinga hadn't knocked it over."

I laughed, remembering only how much fun it had been. I took Sean's hand and swung him around. We were approaching the one-story classrooms and the cafeteria. The staff quarters stood out in the distance across the huge grassy playing field. Shrubs, sporting all shades of green, with splashes of yellow, encroached on the walkways.

I'd loved this place, the life, and the friends. I smiled, thinking of having kids with Mark and sending them to a school like this.

Sean barged ahead, peeking into empty classrooms and even bathrooms. "You and Ana both went here?" he asked, looking up at Jared with the curiosity of a child realizing that adults were once children. "How many kids were in your class?"

"Well it wasn't the same every year. Maybe twenty or thirty, max," said Jared.

"Did they speak English?"

I laughed. "It's a British school, so sure, classes were in English. But there were only a few Americans. Lots of the kids spoke other languages at home." I basked for a minute in the warm feelings I had for the twenty-two students from twelve countries who graduated with me. "We had some great school trips. Went to game parks, and climbed both Meru and Kilimanjaro."

"You climbed Kili, because you were here for several years. I didn't have a chance to do the pre-req climbs," Jared griped, shoving his hands in his pockets and looking away.

Something was eating him — probably Sean's earlier mention of Paul.

We rambled around the campus, toward the swimming pool and cracked cement tennis courts, places Jared and I had spent many hours. Little had changed, except for some new gates. It wasn't fancy by American standards — there was nothing sleek about the concrete-block buildings with their ill-fitted door frames and multiple layers of glossy paint, lumpy with drips. The noise on the tin roofs when it rained used to require students and teachers to shout to be heard. The jalousie windows were practical, but a few panes were cracked. Old, scarred, locally made wooden tables and chairs, worn smooth by years of use, still served as furnishings.

I liked the homey feel of it. "Hooray for the administration for not buying sleek modern junk from China. It's spilling out of the office supply stores in Arusha now."

"Not everyone's as detached from esthetics as you are, Ana," said Jared, with a significant glance at my baggy trousers. I grinned at this sign of better humor and slugged his arm.

Deeper into the campus, bougainvillea hedges, ready to impale the unwary or puncture a bike tire, bordered the gravel walkways and surrounded the grassy football pitch, now a riot of green after the rainy season. The old eucalyptus trees here, protected from people seeking firewood, had grown much taller than those outside the school's front gates. The water sucked up by the invasive species ensured that the leaves were glossy and thick. They displaced native plants and papered the ground with thin bark. An elderly guard, wearing the green uniform and peaked cap of Securicor, ambled toward us.

"*Habari za asubuji?*" Jared and I said, almost in unison.

"*Nzuri sana. Habari yako?*" he said. The polite words contrasted with his solemn face. He finally cracked a smile when we asked about a number of the former teachers and staff.

"Why all the new gates?" I asked. They'd block the people who took shortcuts across the campus in our day, on their way to work.

"The embassies in Dar told us to improve security," said the guard, drawing himself up straighter and resuming a stern face. He marched off without further comment.

"Well, he's got no problem letting us wander around," said Jared.

"Yeah. That doesn't seem right. It's power dynamics. We're foreigners who went to this school, rich by his standards. Wealth equals power."

"But we're not looking for power. We're here to help people."

Ellen Mafwira's comments ran through my head. "They may not see it that way."

11

SUNDAY, AUGUST 27

"I think that's the turn off," I said to Jared as he negotiated the curve of the rutted lane on the forested lower slopes of Kili. I almost missed it, admiring the above-ground roots of the massive fig trees en route to the waterfall in the small town of Marangu.

We came close to high-centering more than once, and finally stopped at a turnout to the path leading down to the pools below the falls.

Sean skipped ahead on the damp narrow forest trail, dappled by sunlight filtering through vine-covered tree branches overhead. Ferns of all sizes and shapes, as well as flowering plants, blanketed the ground. Chattering women with bundles of clothes on their heads overtook us several times, on the way down to the river at the foot of the falls. The distinct slap of their rubber flip flops, their laughter, calls, and shouts filtered back to us even after they vanished around the bends. The raucous cries of hornbills and jackdaws occasionally tore through an undercurrent of chirps and tweets from small birds.

Jared had been silent on the drive, and as Sean disappeared around a turn, he halted abruptly and faced me. "Look, Ana. I want to know. Is the thing with this guy Paul and Beth serious?"

I took a deep breath. This was really eating Jared. I kicked over a small toadstool.

"It bugs me to hear Sean mention him so casually — like he's part of his life now. And Sean acts like he's some kind of *Superman*." Jared's voice started to rise.

Against my will, the image of Paul and Beth together at the bar came into focus again in my mind's eye. Lying wasn't going to make this easier in the long run. I let out a deep breath. "I think Paul *is* part of Sean's life now. But how about focusing on the fact that Sean's here with you now?"

Jared narrowed his eyes. "I don't like the idea of losing my son."

"You don't have to lose your son." I took a step closer and hugged my brother hard.

WE GOT BACK from the waterfall early enough to relax and sip cold drinks next to the aquamarine pool at the guesthouse. Jared had a novel, but it was opened face-down over his eyes and nose. The Paul issue was, no doubt, still churning in his brain.

I had one eye on Sean, a few meters away in the water, and the other on a report I was writing about the nurse training project. I'd been a fool to count on it before seeing it for myself.

"I can't believe the evaluation was so positive," I grumbled.

"Well, what do you expect?" Jared mumbled under the book. "Everything in it was technically true, right?"

"Sure. Lots of quotes from happy nurses and instructors. The training may have been good but it was wasted on people who'd never use it." I took a long swallow from my drink, enjoying the clinking of the ice cubes and relishing the sugar I deserved after the morning hike. "The evaluation focused on the wrong endpoint. It was designed by European donors who made faulty assumptions about the health care system here. Was the goal to train nurses for the sake of training or was it to end up with well-staffed pediatric units?"

"What difference does it make? You've gotta satisfy the donors. No one wants to hear that a project wasted money."

"Damn it, Jared! That's the problem. We're supposed to learn from mistakes, not whitewash and repeat them."

I barely heard Jared from under his book. "You need to learn the art of spin. Don't be such a stickler for righteousness."

A moment later he was snoring. I wasn't going to get any help.

Sean splashed for another half hour before Jared jumped into the pool to race and rough-house with him. He was still small enough to be tossed around, but not for long. My chest constricted at the thought of children. Time wasn't on my side if I was going to get what I wanted.

I glanced at my watch. Three o'clock. We needed to change to go to the Walkers' house. I jumped up, shuffled my papers together, and switched my mind off thoughts of work and the future. "Sean! Time to get out. Come on! I've got a towel here," I yelled, flapping it like a bullfighter's cape. Sean charged, as I hoped he would. I wrapped him up, relishing the wiggling body in the nubby fabric as I rubbed him dry.

"WHO'RE THE WALKERS?" asked Sean, as we set out for their house. I was glad he hadn't whined about going to meet adults, and I'd reminded him to take a book along "just in case."

Geoffrey and Fiona Walker, now in their late seventies, had been my parents' closest friends, like godparents to us when we lived in Moshi. Geoffrey was an old-school type, as in old English public-school, but Fiona had made her way up from a life with an alcoholic mother in London's East End. They met while she was a bursary student at Cambridge. They'd attended the memorials for both of our parents, coming halfway around the world to be with us. On many occasions afterward, they'd assured Jared and me they'd always be there for us. When they retired, after working over twenty years for the World Bank, they settled in Moshi and we'd kept in touch.

"What's a world bank?" asked Sean. "It must be really big. My mom helped me set up a savings account at a bank at home."

I scratched my head. "It's not that kind of bank. The World Bank loans money to poor countries to build roads and dams and stuff like that," I said. Sheesh — that pretty much summed up my own knowledge of the institution. It was enough to satisfy Sean, though.

My parents had admired the Walkers hugely, and they stood in my mind as paragons of powerful do-gooders in developing countries. But if pressed, I couldn't expand much on what I'd told Sean. I'd been too young to understand what the Walkers did. Everything I knew about them was through my parents.

They lived five kilometers north of Moshi, near Kibosho,

on the lower slopes of Kilimanjaro. A high rock wall with broken glass embedded along the top shielded the property from the road. A guard opened the heavy iron gate to let us drive in. The house was set well back, a gracious old white-painted stone residence with a veranda encircling the perimeter. Orange and magenta bougainvillea climbed the sides of the porch and crept over the balustrade. It made me think of my mother's upset the first time the gardener "pruned" the beautiful tangled bougainvillea around our house in Rwanda.

"But he did it with an ax! He's destroyed the plant!"

It took a mere few months to grow back and we'd laughed for years over her unnecessary outrage.

Two dogs, of indeterminate lineage, large liver-colored hounds with similar wildly wagging tails, leaped toward us as we climbed out of the car.

The Walkers, looking older and smaller than I remembered, stood on the veranda. While Sean petted the animals, Jared and I mounted the few steps to greet Fiona with hugs.

"Oh my, it's been so long," she said, the lines around her eyes and mouth giving her face a look of aging dignity. I hugged her again — it *had* been too long.

"Must say, you look fit as ever, Jared," said Geoffrey, as the two of them exchanged back slaps.

Jared looked over at Sean. "Come on up and meet Mr. and Mrs. Walker."

Sean, accompanied by the frisky dogs, climbed the stone steps to the veranda. Fiona laughed as the hounds continued to give Sean their full attention, licking and sniffing, whacking his legs with their enthusiastic tails. "It's lovely to meet you, Sean," said Fiona. "Go ahead and scamper back into the yard with Ellie and Blu. They've not had someone your age to play with for a long time."

Pointing to the side of the house, Geoffrey added, "Run round to the back garden, lad. We'll join you there in a tick."

Sean bolted for the steps, and the dogs nearly knocked him over in pursuit. We stood on the south-facing veranda, taking in the view toward Moshi and the big hospital there for a minute or two before we went inside. The stone house was built to last and had withstood years of torrential rain storms and strong sunshine. It showed some wear, but good maintenance had paid off. The interior was neat, clean, and cool. We passed through the lounge and a formal dining room, then down a hall to the rear veranda.

As I stepped out through the back door, I gasped at the sight to the north. Fields of green coffee undulated gently upward, until they were met by an imposing wall of forest and the giant bulk of Mount Kilimanjaro. Late afternoon sun glanced off the snow-covered top. It was the view tourist agencies loved to show, along with herds of wildlife, which were not roaming the lower slopes of Kilimanjaro.

A man in white shirt and trousers, carrying a tray of freshly roasted cashews, came out to take beverage orders as Sean and the two dogs rounded the side of the house.

"Sean, would you like a cool drink?" called Fiona.

"What was that soda I had at the pool this afternoon?" asked Sean, skidding breathlessly to the edge of the veranda. "That strong fizzy thing? It made my nose tingle, but it was good!"

"He'll have a Tangawizi," Jared said, laughing, "and so will I."

"Make that three," I said. I'd rediscovered the delicious Tanzanian ginger beer earlier that afternoon.

We settled with drinks. Sean sat on the veranda steps, the snouts of both dogs in his lap. He politely answered questions about his safari in Tarangire, and I cheered inwardly that he didn't have his camera.

"Did you say you're going down to Mtwara Region to provide surgery?" Fiona asked Jared.

"Yeah, there's a small mission hospital there I've agreed to help. Ought to be able to do a lot of cataracts — I reckon on fifty or more, since they've never had any eye services in the area." Jared sat up straighter as he related the plans.

"Yes, I'm sure they'll be grateful." Fiona took a handful of cashews and chewed thoughtfully. "Your parents were always interested in the development of the natural gas fields there. They'd left Tanzania long before President Kikwete announced that the gas would transform Tanzania into a middle-income country. The people in Mtwara were supposed to get uninterrupted electricity, paved roads, schools, hospitals, and all sorts of other benefits."

"And jobs for all," interrupted Geoffrey, clearing his throat. "Don't forget jobs for all."

Fiona raised her voice. "About a year ago the pipeline carrying gas to Dar finally opened."

"Just before the election, of course," Geoffrey said, folding his arms across his chest. "Hmph. Fastest environmental and social impact assessment report you've ever seen round here!"

"Geoff, please!" said Fiona, with a subtle moue of irritation and an impatient exhalation. "The point I'm getting to is that there was trouble back in 2013 when they announced the pipeline was going to serve Dar instead of Mtwara. The government forces were heavy-handed in a couple of the villages after the fire-bombing at the marine park office." She lowered her brows in concentration. "I think it was in Msimbati — or maybe Mtandi. Several people were killed in the fray."

"There was even talk of secession from Tanzania," Geoffrey said, shaking his head.

"Huh," said Jared. "That's near where I'll be working."

"It quieted down eventually, but when the pipeline opened, anger broke out again. People believed the gas flame was poisoning the air and destroying ancient trees and crops."

"Recently there're also rumors about al-Shabaab in the area, but I don't think these have been confirmed." Geoffrey puffed his cheeks and blew out a sigh. "Bloody well don't need that."

"Geoffrey's become a bit of a cynic since he retired from the Bank," Fiona said, waving her hand dismissively. Geoffrey scowled at Fiona.

I figured they'd been through this before.

"Look, Fi. The World Bank's done some major damage." He grimaced and gave a half shrug in Jared's direction. "Back in the eighties, when they sent thirty-year-olds from New York and London, with no local political knowledge, to strong-arm governments to cut budgets, we saw internal upheavals go over the top — and tribalism reared its ugly head. Big boys in the capitals made out like the bandits they were. Civil servants at the bottom lost their livelihoods." He waved his hand with contempt. "Sure, bloated budgets needed to be cut, but it was done the wrong way." He leaned forward, warming to his subject. "Meanwhile, the folk back home were moaning that foreign aid was a waste and it all ought to be slashed."

Fiona sighed. "Okay, Geoffrey, I won't argue that mistakes — even big ones — were made. But the Bank has learned. Their support for the pipeline was important. Dar needs the energy."

They both sat back, almost simultaneously, as if they

suddenly remembered they had guests, and I relaxed. I hadn't realized what a sore spot this was between them. My father had always praised the World Bank. I wondered what he'd think about Geoffrey's attitude now.

Fiona sighed. "Well, the idea of helping countries develop is still a relatively new concept in the world's history. It's only recently that we're approaching it systematically, with scientific evidence for what works and what doesn't."

"And we won't mention how politics distorts it," grumped Geoffrey, getting in the last word.

The sky was turning to a deep dark blue, cloaking the green fields and the mountain behind them. It was cooling off quickly. "Anyway, you take care down there, Jared," Fiona said, standing up and shooting one more look of disapproval Geoffrey's way. "That's all we need say." She started toward the house, turning slightly before she spoke. "I saw Ahmed signaling me from inside. Shall we go to dinner?"

DINNER, in the stately dining room, turned out to be surprisingly fun after the awkward start on the veranda. I'd forgotten how witty both Fiona and Geoffrey were. Even Sean enjoyed it. Afterward, when Geoffrey took Jared and Sean out to look at a waterwheel he'd built in a stream, Fiona handed me a shawl, and we took a flask of tea out to the veranda. Cicadas, frogs, geckos, and nocturnal birds contributed their vocal selections to the ever-present rustling of an African night. A chunk of moon hung in the sky. The eruption of a hound's furious barking punctured the soothing background noise. I jumped.

"There's Blu," said Fiona. "Try to ignore him. Must have found a hedgehog out there."

I winced. Ugh! The carnage.

"Not to worry. The hedgehogs usually win." She chuckled, then turned serious. "What do you hope to get out of this trip, Ana?"

"Well, the years of graduate study I did in London convinced me I want a career in development in Africa. But I also wanted to have options in the US, to be closer to Jared's family." I leaned forward. "The Global Health Initiative is a fantastic opportunity for me. I've got to show my boss that I have the vision to develop good projects. I've barely started, but once Jared goes to Mtwara I'll be able to hustle around and check out possibilities. Sean can stay with my friend Grace."

She snugged her shawl around her shoulders. "I hope you don't let Geoffrey's attitudes about development bother you. Some of it is age. You look back and wonder if what you did made a lasting difference. It's so complicated with politics in both the donor and the recipient countries." Fiona leaned back in her wicker chair, with her face toward the mountain, now invisible in the cooling night.

"Yeah. I'm surprised he's so negative. All I ever heard from my parents was how great the World Bank was."

Fiona sighed. "Maybe development is easier to achieve in the health sector. I mean, at least there you can help individuals and see the results."

I snorted. "Maybe Jared can. But it falls to people in public health to establish the systems to allow people like Jared to do any work."

"Ah, yes. Establishing systems — management. That was part of what frustrated Geoff. It's particularly trying to get people to respect a chain of command here. You know the proverb: The path to the chief's hut should be well worn." She rolled her eyes. "Well, that concept makes it terribly difficult to define an organizational chart. Everyone wants to go straight to the 'big man' with their problems."

I sighed. "It seems way harder to change those issues than to operate on someone's eye. Westerners take health systems for granted. They imagine all Africa needs is more doctors and nurses."

Fiona laughed. "Well, Jared wouldn't be able to help a single person without a functioning hospital. Still, he's rather noble, isn't he? Surely he'd make a lot more money in his practice in the US."

I leaned forward with my teacup cradled in both hands for the comforting warmth. "Oh, yeah. He's deeply committed to helping people see. He's found his passion. His career and work have given him a sense of where he fits into the world."

"I'm so pleased to hear that. Your mother worried about him with all the moving around that always seemed to come at the wrong times in his life. Funny, how some children take to it — like you did — confident they belong every-where, while others are left feeling they fit in nowhere."

"I always felt like I belonged wherever Jared and Mom and Dad were."

"Ah, yes. The definition of a happy family." She moved to stand up. "I intentionally didn't prepare pudding for us tonight — trying to avoid taking in too much sugar, you know." She patted her stomach. "But now I want to see if I can find something sweet. Shall we look?"

It had grown cooler and the light shawl and my tea mug weren't enough to keep me warm. I gratefully followed her into the house, to the kitchen, which sat like an afterthought at the back of the dwelling. So many old colonial homes were like this. The kitchen *was* an afterthought, any modern appliances having been added years after the original construction, when a servant did the cooking over an open fire or coals out back. The smell of the roasted meat and vegetables we'd had for dinner still hung in the air. Fiona put the kettle on to brew more tea and rummaged up a box of imported chocolates.

Our conversation shifted to the inevitable as we cradled warm mugs over the soft worn wooden kitchen table,

"What about men, Ana? Anyone special in your life?"

"Yeah, in fact. I've been seeing a guy — Mark McElroy — for about six months." I looked down, and a glow of pleasure warmed me. "We have a lot of fun together. He's spent time in East Africa, working on sustainable energy projects and he gets what I want to do here. That makes him someone who'd consider living overseas with a family. And he's entrepreneurial, which gives him the kind of flexibility we'd need to carve out compatible career paths." I hesitated.

"And do you love him, Ana?"

"I do," I said slowly. "I like who I am with him."

Fiona raised an eyebrow. "Sounds good. What's the problem?"

"Something's holding me back, not sure what it is. And I wish Jared liked him more."

"Why does it matter what Jared thinks?"

"Well...he's all I've got left of family, and he's been my best friend, so his opinion matters. You know how it was, growing up like we did." I looked at Fiona's sympathetic face and took a deep breath. "I've made mistakes with guys in the past. And the way Dad disappeared tore a hole in me. It's hard to open myself to pain." I was surprised to feel tears welling. I'd buried this stuff well.

"Yes. Many of us have grieved your father, Ana. Fifteen years ago now. I'm sorry it's still raw."

"I just wish I knew what really happened with him." I used my index fingers to wipe under my eyes. "Fiona, how could he have made the choice to leave us?"

Fiona reached across the table, handing me a tissue, then twining my fingers with hers. Her voice was just loud enough to hear over the night sounds coming in through the kitchen window. "Ana, your father never prepared for the possibility your mother would go before he did. It was a terrible shock." She looked up and out the window, although all was black outside. What was she seeing in her mind? "Just remember we don't know for certain how he died. He was a strong swimmer but that lake was deep and cold. We don't know exactly how he died. We do know that he loved you."

IT WAS WELL after 10:00 p.m. when the guys returned from the waterwheel. Sean strutted in, no doubt awed at being treated as one of the men. I suppressed a giggle at his gait, wondering how long it would last, given the hour. Jared was holding forth on his plans to leave early in the morning. "I've got to meet Thomas, the resident I'm taking along for training. We'll fly together to Mtwara. If it's all set up the way I told them, we'll be able to start operating Monday morning."

Sean's eyelids were starting to droop, as were mine, and I cast a meaningful look at Jared. "We've all had a long day. We need to leave."

We managed goodbyes faster than I'd dared hope, thanks to the sensitive but efficient Fiona.

Even so, Jared was still talking as we exchanged final hugs at the door. "Check out the article in my hospital newsletter about my work with Thomas and the other residents. They love the chance to try out their skills and see how we do things in Africa." I pulled him out onto the veranda as he finished. "And, hey, you've got a good WiFi connection. You can watch the video I posted from my trip to Uganda three months ago. There's a link for donations to our work at the end."

12

MONDAY-TUESDAY, AUGUST 28-29

T he chance to take Sean on a safari, just the two of us, had buoyed me since Jared first mentioned a Tanzania trip. We'd started talking about Ngorongoro the moment Beth agreed he could come.

He stumbled over the name of the famous crater every time he said it. "It's not so hard," I told him. "Think of it as one short word, said twice. Then imagine the letter *i* in front of the *n* — just a little hint of *i* to get you started, like *ingoro*. *Ingoro-ingoro*. See, it's like sounding out anything." Since we arrived in Tanzania he'd been looking on billboards for other Swahili words that bumped an *n* up against a consonant.

"*Nzuri, ndiyo, ndovu!*" he shouted, looking at ads on signs as we sped along the road.

"Works every time," we agreed, high fiving each other. If I managed to have a kid, I wanted one like Sean.

Ngorongoro was a prime tourist destination, and it'd become ridiculously crowded. But it was unique in many ways. The larger Ngorongoro Conservation Area included grass plains, forests, lakes, rivers, and swamps. Sitting within it was the crater, a huge unbroken caldera containing vast herds of zebra, wildebeest, antelope, warthogs, elephant, a handful of rhinos, and more, plus the large cat predators. Missing were giraffe — the slopes were too steep for them to navigate. That was evident as we hung on to the sides of our Land Rover, making the bumpy journey down, unfortunately part of a long line of vehicles on the one road from the rim into the crater.

"Are those...*cows*?" Sean asked, pointing off a short distance from the car.

Our guide laughed. "Sure. *Ng'ombe.*"

I pulled a paper from my pack, scribbled out the word, and elbowed Sean, tapping on the *ng*. He grinned at me.

The guide continued. "These are ancestral lands of the Maasai, and they're still allowed to use the land for grazing." Indeed, men and young boys in colorful red and purple *shukas*, most carrying spears, watched over the cattle. Women on the crater's rim, wrapped in similar colored cloth, had been wearing and selling large elaborate beaded necklaces, bracelets, and earrings.

Now, deep in the crater, we saw that most of the roaming dots visible from above were herds of wildebeest and cape buffalo. While it was mostly grasslands down here on the floor, the rim and sloping sides included forested areas. Plumes of dust rose up as Land Rovers and other vehicles roamed around in search of the famed wildlife. The single road to the crater floor ended in three branches and I looked at the map our guide provided to figure out which one led to the hippo pools.

Sean was still puzzling over the cows. "Don't the lions eat them?" he asked.

I looked up from my map. I had no idea.

The guide, who was also our driver, glanced back at

Sean. "Sometimes," he said. He studied Sean through narrowed eyes. "It's the job of boys about your age to guard them." He smiled to diminish any menace in his words. At my suggestion, he headed straight toward the hippo pools where the road divided.

"Do the animals down here ruin people's farms?" Sean asked, his brow furrowed, apparently still not quite sure how the animal-human interaction played out. "Because we saw a place near Tarangire where people had killed an elephant. It was awful. The head was all bloody, and the legs were twisted up."

"Conflict between people and the animals is a problem," said the guide with a shrug. "But not down here in the crater. The Maasai don't farm, they just bring their cows here. They take them back to the *boma* up on the rim at night. You remember seeing that enclosure, before we started down?"

We both nodded. "I don't expect we'll see any dead animals down here, Sean — well, not unless they've been killed by predators," I said, and was rewarded when his forehead uncreased.

We saw no dead animals, and the live ones were spectacular. Herds of zebra scattered down the road ahead of us, then regrouped and turned to watch us pass. Elephants splashed in muddy pools, flapping their gigantic ears as they used their trunks to throw the cool ooze onto their heads and backs. An ancient bull rubbed against an old baobab. The confined space of the crater floor resulted in a density of animals impossible to match anywhere else in the world.

Sean hadn't exhausted his capacity for amazement at Tarangire. "Aww, do we have to leave already?" he asked, when our guide headed up the crater wall road in the late afternoon.

WE HAD reservations in a hotel on the rim. It was the kind of expensive touristy place I'd never have stayed if I didn't have Sean along. I had to admit it had its compensations. I'd regretted the decision to visit Ngorongoro several times that afternoon, due to the crowds, but now, high above the crater floor, relaxing on the expansive patio and eating multiple courses from the lavish buffet, I felt replenished. I loved watching Sean watch the entertainment — local acrobats and dancers performing reality-defying movements.

"Let's see what your dad's up to," I said before we went to bed. "He'd love to hear what you've done today."

"Yeah. I want to tell him about the hippos — and those dancers at dinner."

The connection was clearer than I'd feared, and Sean babbled for some time. "How's it going there?" I asked when I finally took the phone.

"Great," said Jared. "As I expected, there were dozens of cataract patients waiting. It's really busy. But I'm up for it."

SEAN WAS up at dawn the next morning. Good, since we wanted to descend into the crater early in hopes of seeing more animals, who took to the shade during the heat of the day.

We picnicked at a spot I remembered for having large numbers of black kites, a big bold bird of prey. They hung out here for the easy pickings.

"Watch your sandwich," I yelled, as a big one swooped down and snatched most of it from Sean's hand. He jumped, but I was glad to see him laugh, looking at the remaining ruined roll, as someone nearby whooped.

"They took my bow," a young girl screamed, grabbing at her hair. The thieving bird, dangling a bright red ribbon, soared off to a tall tree.

"Let's find another place to eat," I said, starting for the car. Sean didn't argue and followed right behind me. At the next site where we stopped, baboons were menacing a group of a dozen Germans, who were laughing and snapping photos. We didn't even leave the car.

Our driver glared. "They're much too close for safety, especially with kids. Their guide should know better."

As he spoke, a small monkey leaped from a tree onto the end of a family's picnic table and raced down the center, snatching food packets left and right as he ran.

It happened so fast the bandit was gone before the family, drop jawed, finished shrieking. Our guide shook his head. "Now all that plastic will be out in the bush to make other animals sick." It was true. Ripped packets and other rubbish festooned the nearby trees and brush.

"Looks like human-wildlife conflict to me," I muttered. We moved on, found a spot to pull off the road, and finished our lunch from the back of the car.

THAT EVENING, Sean and I stood out on the edge of the patio and looked into the black of the crater trying to differentiate sounds within the soup of night noises around us. I sniffed appreciatively at the dry, crisp, clean air. The clear sky was a gift, and above us were more stars than Sean had ever seen at one time. The Milky Way glowed as though someone had shaken a box of glittering crystals and thrown them across the heavens — hundreds of thousands of shiny stones skipped across a black sea.

"You and Dad love it here, don't you?" said Sean.

"Sure. Lucky people have good memories of places they spent time as kids."

"But do you think Dad would move back here?"

"You mean, come back here to live all the time?" I was astonished. Where was Sean getting this idea?

"Yeah. I just thought...since he doesn't live with us anymore. Maybe he'd want to move back here." The sadness in his voice twisted my heart.

I put my arm on his shoulder and turned him to face me. "Sean, listen. Your dad loves you. There is no way he'd ever move so far away from you. No way he'd ever leave you." I struggled to keep my voice calm and relaxed my grip on him. I couldn't let him imagine his father might abandon him. I knew how that felt.

I looked up at the glittering panorama and was swept back to a night when I was a twenty-two-year-old under-grad, under a similar sky in the mountains of southern California. I was slumped against Jared, the rough wool of his sweater scratching my cheek. We'd been devastated when cancer had taken our mother two years previously. Dad struggled to move beyond the pain, even as his passionate example of love for life and his work helped me through the loss. But that night, under the stars, I learned I'd lost Dad too. Jared had left his Boston medical school and flown out to California as soon as he heard from my father's lawyer, so he'd be the one to tell me. "Ana, Dad's gone. They say they don't know how it happened. They found his sailboat, but they haven't recovered his...body. It wasn't that far from shore. I don't know why he didn't swim to safety. I'm sure he could have. Unless...he didn't want to."

Jared's words, a decade and a half ago, knifed straight into my heart and lodged there, giving birth to the specter of abandonment.

He'd rubbed my back gently. "But I'll always be here for you, Ana," he whispered fiercely, his voice mingling with the sound, sensation, and smell of a scratchy wool sweater on my cheek. "Count on it."

I *had* counted on Jared. Standing on the edge of the vast Ngorongoro crater, a decade and a half later, I wondered if I'd let that specter of abandonment solidify, and built walls in my heart to contain it.

13

WEDNESDAY, AUGUST 30

W e left Ngorongoro crater early on Wednesday morning but still got caught in the steady stream of traffic honking and belching along the two-lane macadam road back through Arusha and on to Moshi. It could have been a beautiful drive; Mt. Meru, and later Kilimanjaro, rose in the distance to the north, and the plains on either side of us were unusually green. But the exhaust fumes were nauseating, and the traffic kept me on edge. Huge overloaded trucks and darting minibuses pulled in and out of the procession, passing without warning or common sense. Driving demanded full concentration, and hiring someone to do it for the Ngorongoro trip was a good decision. It was exhausting enough being a passenger.

Driving is generally on the left side of the road, stated a Tanzania tourist guidebook. Ha! What was that supposed to mean? But it was true, since cars veered often and widely to avoid the countless enormous potholes. The goal of many drivers was to push the vehicle as fast as possible and pass everything ahead. Never mind what might be approaching from the other direction. Tiny motorcycles *putt-putting* along without much power added to the hazards. Sean's eyes widened as we came right up behind one with two adults, a child, and a sheep on the back. He waved at the little kid, who lifted his hand to signal back. I was glad Beth couldn't see us. Visitors to sub-Saharan Africa worried about rare tropical diseases, but it was road traffic accidents that gave me nightmares.

"Eid's on the way," said the driver, careening around the little motorbike as the sheep bleated. "That's somebody's dinner."

Tanzania celebrated both the Christian and Muslim holy days, making for an astonishing number of official holidays. I'd once counted them for a study comparing productivity in the health systems of Tanzania and India. The Eid celebrations, like Easter, depended on the moon, and many businesses and offices didn't decide when to close until a Tanzanian Iman declared the date. The speculation sometimes lasted right up to the last minute and played havoc with planning.

Arusha was all hustle and bustle compared to Moshi. Diesel fumes made it impossible to lower the windows. In any between-town rivalry based on availability of goods, Arusha was the winner — but I preferred Moshi. Traffic made for slow going along the two-lane road. We passed a Maasai man, wrapped in a red and blue plaid *shuka*, laboring up a small incline on a heavy bicycle.

Four hours after leaving the crater we'd traveled through most of the Maasai Steppe, dotted with acacia trees and roofed over by a sky of multiple shades of blue, streaked with ragged gold-edged clouds. If I were dumped here, blindfolded, I'd know exactly where I was the minute I removed the covering. I hoped Sean was paying attention.

Just past a huge rock with *Bantu Unity* spray-painted on

the side —what I always counted as the beginning of Moshi — we pulled over at a little restaurant by the side of the road. Five plastic tables, all but one filled with patrons, crowded the small room. People looked up from their meals, and acknowledged us with small head gestures as we entered. Sean attracted the attention of several little children running around the place. The menu was limited: *kuku na wali* or *kuku na chips* — chicken with rice or with chips. We went for the fat golden chips.

"Wow, I have to chew this a long time!" mumbled Sean through a mouthful of chicken. He sucked grease off his fingers and I laughed.

"Yep. These poultry haven't been coddled or bulked up on steroids. They're tough and skinny. Your father used to refer to them as roadkill. I ordered you an entire quarter, and I'll bet you finish it by yourself."

We said goodbye to our vehicle and driver at a little car-hire business where I rented a small car to drive to Rombo, in the foothills of Mount Kilimanjaro. I didn't mind driving on these smaller roads with less traffic. At a thousand meters higher, it was cooler than Moshi, but provided the same daily doses of sunshine I loved.

"Who lives up here?" asked Sean. "Is she your friend or Dad's?"

I laughed. "Grace was in my class when I went to ISM. She and your dad and I hung around together."

"For the whole time you were a kid?"

"Well, for the years we shared at school. Most other students came and went a lot, after a year or two, when their parents' jobs changed. But Grace Ngassi got a scholarship and started ISM when I did. We were lucky to be there together for so long."

"What's a scholarship?"

"It's like a prize that pays for a kid to go to school."

Sean's eyebrows went up. "You mean it costs money to go to school here?"

"Yeah, and ISM is expensive. Not many local kids can afford to go there."

"But then where do they go to school?"

"Government schools are free — sort of." In fact, parents had to pay special fees for guards and groundkeepers, and some teachers wanted to be paid for giving good grades — but no need to get into that with Sean. "Free school for kids was one of the things the father of the country insisted on."

"How can a country have a father?"

"You ever heard of George Washington?" I said, pretending to glower.

"Of course!"

"Well, Tanzania became a country in 1964, and Julius Nyerere was *its* father."

GRACE HAD BEEN my best friend at ISM, and maybe the best I'd ever had. There was a deep satisfaction in finding so many feelings in common with someone from another culture and background. She used to talk a lot about her mother and her aunt, but she never mentioned her father. I learned the full story after we graduated. She came from Ndungu, an isolated rural hamlet over in Same District, hours from Moshi. A philanthropically inclined woman with roots in the community identified my bright friend in a village school at age fourteen and supported her at ISM. Grace graduated with honors and landed a university scholarship in Europe. I was thrilled when we enrolled in the same master's degree program in the UK, several years after undergraduate school. She'd been back in Tanzania now for several years.

The tarmac road to Rombo, in an advanced state of disrepair, cut through small-holder coffee plantations that carpeted the lower slopes of Kili. I crept along, following Grace's instructions until I found the turnoff onto a narrow drive. Loose rocks covered it to hold back erosion, but it was deeply rutted. A profusion of grasses and bushes lined the lane, attesting to the ever-present possibility of rain on these slopes.

Sean was young enough to think it was fun to bounce over the washboard. "Wow, my dad would really like to ride his bike on this!"

I wasn't so sure of that, but it could have been worse, so I held back my complaints. I was glad to see a little fuchsia-painted concrete-block house, surrounded by banana trees, at the end of the path. This had to be Grace's.

The grounds around the cottage were tended but not manicured like those at the school. Diverse plant species flowed into one another, creating a landscape worthy of a slick gardening magazine cover. No one had paid thousands of dollars to create this though — it had evolved over time, with patience, some encouragement, and lots of cutting back.

Sean and I climbed out of the car and started toward the house. The faint clatter of small machinery rattled through the air. On the side of the house, beyond the shrubbery, a half dozen chattering women pumped the treadles of sewing machines under a stand of bananas. "Hmm. Wonder what this is," I said to Sean, but I had no chance to check.

Grace, wearing a bright multicolored *kanga* over her dress, came flying out of the house, across the veranda, and down the steps, her arms spread wide in welcome.

"Finally! It's been too long." She enveloped me in a hug with her sturdy body before pulling back and turning toward Sean. "And who's this?" she asked, pretending a look of surprise with her round face.

He looked up at her from under his brow.

"I think you're Sean, right?" she said, her face opening into the wide grin I loved. "And Jared's your dad."

"Uh huh," Sean mumbled, still looking down. I blessed Grace for not making a fuss over Sean. My plan to have him spend a few days with her while I investigated potential projects down in Moshi depended on his being comfortable here.

"Ana, you sit on the veranda and relax. How about a cold drink?" She took Sean's hand and pulled him toward the car. "Sean and I'll take the bags in, then get you something."

The two of them fetched the gear from the car and disappeared through an open wooden door within a not-quite-perfect frame set in the fuchsia-colored house. I sank onto a wicker couch and looked around. The place was bigger than it had looked from the lane, and, in spite of the garish color, it was well made. None of the window frames was perfect, but they looked strong and held good jalousie windows. A tile roof topped the concrete-block walls.

A light breeze cooled me as I leaned back further on the couch, propping my feet on a low stool. The bright patterned cushions picked up the color of the house and blended into the lush garden of flowering bushes and trees surrounding the veranda. Artfully placed rocks made for interesting borders and mounds for greenery to spread over.

The rocks were large and heavy, but plants ruled the landscape. My eyes were drawn to a bougainvillea a stone's throw from the veranda. Its gnarly trunk must have been trained for decades, and it grew upward like a tree, supporting a massive profusion of paper-thin magenta flowers two meters over my head.

Grace emerged and stepped over the threshold, balancing a tray with three tall, sweating glasses. Sean followed her, carrying biscuits that threatened to slide off the plate. The tip of his tongue protruded as he set one cautious foot down ahead of the other. He put the treat on a low table and raised his eyebrows at me in a question.

"Sure, Sean, help yourself." He'd probably already done that in the house.

"And feel free to look around," said Grace, waving toward the garden. "There's an old tire swing over there."

Sean, with a handful of biscuits, hurtled down the veranda steps.

Grace and I settled down, glasses in hand. We'd seen each other through so much—standard adolescent outrage over our teachers; sneaked trips to corner groceries, where anyone with cash, regardless of age, could buy the local liquor; and commiseration in the ever-changing dance of teenage experiments with romance. I think Jared had had a crush on her for a while. I sat back, basking in the sweet satisfaction of being with someone who knew me almost as well as I knew myself.

"What's going on over there under the bananas?" I asked, leaning forward for a better look at the women I'd seen. But they were gone, and the sewing machines rested under custom-fitted tarpaulins.

"Ahh. The ladies. Right," said Grace taking a long sip of her lemonade before setting her glass down. "They've gone home for the day, but they'll be back in the morning. It's a project I started a couple of years ago. Local women wanted to make a little money. They asked me if I'd show them how to sew on machines, to make baby clothes to sell to tourists." She rolled her eyes. "Of course the market's flooded with those. So I suggested they make quilts out of pieced fabric. They're geniuses at piecing bits together — figuring out what goes with what. It's a good way to use cheap scraps." The corners of her mouth turned up. "I've managed to find them a few commissions. The large quilts are great as wall hangings to dampen echoes in big cement-walled office buildings." She sat back, and I felt that she and her surroundings suited each other perfectly.

I took a biscuit. It was sweet with a surprise peppery tingle. "There's fresh ginger in these! Your own recipe?"

Grace beamed. "Of course."

Sean thundered up the steps. "Look, Ana! Look what I caught." He opened his fist. I leaned in, and a gecko jumped off his palm. "No! He got away." He dived after the lizard.

Grace pointed up at the ceiling. "No shortage of those. Look up there."

Sean's eyes grew large as several of the little creatures zipped across the shady rafters and down the support posts. A minute later, with a new captive in one fist and a couple more biscuits in the other, he raced off the veranda again.

I scrunched the pillows at my back to fit better and looked at my friend. "I was surprised when you told me you'd left your job, Grace. That seemed like an ideal position."

"Yeah, Reproductive Rights International paid me very well. And I made great contacts and got to travel." She pursed her lips, leaning forward with her elbows on her thighs. "But when you work for those big international

NGOs, no matter how good their outcomes can be, you're at the mercy of politics — both within the organization and from the big funders."

"Sorry to hear you say that." I fidgeted inwardly. "My boss is expecting me to chase after some of those big funders."

Grace laughed, took another long drink, and munched a biscuit. "USAID gives some well-thought-out grants — but a change in president and administration in the US can mean a shift in attitude about females' reproductive choices. My old colleagues at RRI were devastated at the cuts that kicked in this year. A lot of women aren't going to be able to decide how many children they want." She shrugged half-heartedly. "Sorry to criticize your government, Ana."

I squirmed when people apologized for criticizing the US — as though I had any hand in making foreign aid policy

"Yeah. So do you think the fickle priorities of donors are the biggest problem?"

She took in a deep breath. "The *biggest* problem? Why fool around with small talk, huh?" She laughed again. "I don't know what the biggest problem is, but here are some of my pet peeves." She held out her hand, index finger up. "The priorities of funders like USAID can be misaligned with what the people in the country want." She unfolded another finger. "NGOs — local or foreign — learn the buzzwords the donor wants just to get money." She leaned forward in her chair and extended a third finger. "Grants require you to show results in two or three years, because that's the funding cycle. So we play games defining 'impact' and spend a ton of money proving it happened." She grimaced. "Consultants who don't know the local situation come over from 'beltway bandit' firms in DC to write evaluations."

"But don't you agree that donors need to make sure funds are spent properly?"

"Sure, but monitoring and evaluation has become its own industry, consuming a vast amount of the money out there for development."

The evaluation of the nurse training program, carefully crafted to show success, was a good example of Grace's point. She was someone who'd worked her way up in the development aid world and then rejected it. I blew out a puff of air. "So what's the answer?"

She gave a half smile. "Knew you'd ask that." She put her hand down and sank back in her chair. "Well, I'd like to cut out a lot of the middlemen. I wish big donors would listen to recipients instead of dictating." Her smile turned apologetic. "But it won't happen soon enough for me. I'm content to have left RRI. We're on good terms. I still do consulting for them when I want to and that helps keep me going financially. Meantime, I love my small-scale projects. I'm able to see big differences in these women's lives when they make a little money of their own." She looked out in the distance, then caught my gaze again and grinned. "Those women are also a captive audience for education on reproductive health. I found a small private development foundation to support the work."

My turn to laugh. How like Grace! "But..." How could I ask without offending her? "Is it enough to be helping only a few dozen women when before you were working on projects that helped hundreds or thousands?"

Grace laughed. "Oh. Ana. You're such an American! Expecting to change things quickly. You remember what I used to tell you? *Haraka haraka haina baraka* — hurry, hurry won't bring happiness. Swahili wisdom."

The sun had gone below the mountain when Sean galloped back up to the veranda again. His face fell when he saw the empty biscuit plate. "Are they all gone?"

Grace laughed and stood up. "No, but we've had enough for today. I can't believe we've been sitting out here talking so long. Let's go in. Sean's seen your room, but you haven't. Let me show you around."

The veranda stretched across the face of the house and opened into a spacious front room, which also extended the width of the house. A floor-to-ceiling bookcase covered one wall, and I laughed out loud with pleasure. A love of literature was one of the bonds Grace and I shared. She pulled me back as I started toward it.

"No you don't. You can look at that later. I've got more to show you." Sean and I followed her down a short hall, and she waved at doors opening onto a couple of rooms and a bath on the right. "These are mine. But come this way." She propelled me toward a door coming off the left side of the hall. "This, I'm rather pleased with," she said, a big grin spreading across her face.

"You must have designed it yourself," I said, surveying an unusually large kitchen, which was definitely not an afterthought. "Well done, Grace!" It was spare but spacious, with a polished, dark red-painted concrete floor. Ample tin-covered countertops, clean open shelving with a few pieces of neatly stacked cookware, and a big double sink marked this as a space a cook would love. A round table with four straight-backed chairs filled one corner. I pirouetted around, taking it in. "Great cooker — bigger than many." Modest Grace, one of the least materialistic people I knew, was proud of this kitchen.

"Some of the sewing ladies are starting to experiment with preserving veg from the garden. The extra space is useful."

Sean didn't care at all about the kitchen. He was tugging me out the open back door from this cook's dream into a small garden.

Grace followed us.

"Here it is. Here's where we'll be," Sean said, running down a small flower-bordered path to a tiny independent cottage and pulling me behind him. "I've already seen it." Indeed, my bag and Sean's were inside the door of the bungalow.

"I had it built hoping my aunt would live here," said Grace. "I'm still working on that. She visits often but prefers to stay in the main house with me. Freshen up and unpack, then come back to the kitchen, and we'll rummage up some dinner."

Sean found his camera at the bottom of his bag. "Hmm...wonder what I can take pictures of around here," he muttered.

"Well, when you get your stuff put on that shelf over there, you can go back to the living room and look for geckos. Might be fun to try snapping closeups."

A shower and a change of clothes were exactly what I needed. Sean was gone when I emerged, and I took a couple of minutes to check email. I sent a quick reply to Mark and opened a message from Andrew. I wished I hadn't. He wanted an update as soon as possible. How was I going to tap into the nurse training program? I still had no idea.

GRACE WAS BUSTLING around the kitchen when I entered. She put me to work chopping some tough unidentifiable green she called spinach. The tender leaves I ate at home wouldn't survive the heat and abundant insects here.

"So, Ana, you haven't said much about this guy, Mark. How serious is it?"

I laid the knife down and turned to face her. "Serious, I think. But I need to be careful. I don't want to rush it." I explained why Mark couldn't come with me. I was less forthright about voicing my worry that Jared didn't like him than I'd been when I talked to Fiona. I didn't want to defend my feelings to someone I suspected didn't fully appreciate Jared.

"What do you like about him?"

"Besides the fact that he's fun and easy to be around, we laugh at the same things. We both want to stay engaged with work in Africa so we might be able to build a life together. Family matters to him, and he wants kids."

The last I added gently. Grace wasn't going to bear children. We'd been in graduate school when doctors discovered her uterine cancer. I'd admired her philosophic approach back when she'd been diagnosed.

"Ana, first of all, thanks to being in the UK, I received treatment to save my life. That might not have happened in Tanzania. And, besides, birthing my own child isn't so important to me. There're plenty of children and women at home to nurture."

True, but I remembered the wistful look on her face as she said it.

I stepped over to give Grace a hug, and she spoke in my ear. "Don't be so afraid, Ana. Give this guy a chance. I want to celebrate your wedding."

"GREAT PHOTOS, SEAN," said Grace after dinner. "Look at the eye on that one! I can't believe you got so close. Those little guys are skittish."

"Yeah. I had to be really still. This button here lets me zoom."

"Are you okay getting to bed by yourself, Sean?" I asked. "You can use the small bed. I'm sure you'll figure out the shower, but shout if you need any help. I'll be in the front room with Grace and come to bed later."

He didn't argue, and went off hugging his camera to his chest. I figured I'd find him reading in bed under the mosquito net when I finally retired. I headed to Grace's bookcase as she stretched out on a low couch. The shelves were a treat. Grace was an eclectic reader, leaning toward the same fiction I liked. I'd probably read or intended to read half the books here. Much as I loved using a Kindle, I was glad she didn't. Perusing someone's book collection was a great source of entertainment and a way to learn about them. I hated to think it might become obsolete and that I'd be part of the reason it did.

I pulled *Three Cups of Tea* off the shelf. "Haven't you read that?" asked Grace, wrinkling her nose. "The author spent a few childhood years in Moshi. He claims his parents started ISM and the big hospital there." She laughed. "That'd be news to them! And there's some follow up on that book..."

But she didn't finish because Sean appeared at the door. He wanted help with the shower. I put the book back and didn't think of it for days.

We stayed up late talking that night. Grace lay on her back on the couch and listened to my complaints about the discouraging nurse training.

"I thought I knew something about human resource policy. My PhD compared licensing requirements for midwives across the EU."

"Mmm. And I'm sure you learned from that work. But training in African countries has different challenges — and every country is different. Sometimes projects that sound good in theory, developed from afar, miss issues that are obvious in the field."

"Maybe the project was just too big."

She bit the inside of her cheek. "Big isn't always bad. Remember that scandal here over the bogus malaria medicine from the Ministry of Health? When counterfeit malaria tablets were all over the country? I got involved through Imani Moyo, the woman in the Ministry of Education who got me the scholarship to ISM. She encouraged me to apply to work for a program aimed at improving the quality of medicines in Africa. That big project was all funded by USAID. I hate to think how many more children might have died without it."

She rolled over to her side and propped her head on an elbow to look at me. "How funny that Jared wound up in the health field," she said, pouring another glass from a bottle of South African wine I'd brought from Moshi. "Helping people that way, it's not what I imagined he'd do."

I laughed. "Coming from our family, a passion for social justice was expected. Jared and I used to plan how we'd build an orphanage — he'd run it, of course. Now I suspect he'd resent a description of himself as being 'in the health field.' He'd be the first to let you know he's a *surgeon*." I took on a deep voice to imitate Jared. "The most important member of the team." Grace chuckled, and I felt a twinge of guilt, hoping she wouldn't think I was mocking my brother. I was uncomfortably aware that Grace might consider Jared as a "surgi-tourist," a doctor who made occasional forays to poor but exotic locations to enjoy the natural wonders, with a little aid work on the side. I sipped my wine. "What did you imagine he'd do?"

"I'm not sure," she said. "Something with status. Something where he'd be in charge and in control for sure." She laughed. "The way you put it, I guess that's what he's done."

14

THURSDAY, AUGUST 31

I slept like a rock, exhausted from the trip the day before. Not all of the women's quilts ended up on walls in office buildings — a pile of them on my bed kept me warm during the cool night. In the morning light, Sean slumbered under a similar heap across the room. I loved the care Grace had put into making this room cozy. The furniture was locally made and, although not finely crafted, items fit the space. Large quilts covered two of the walls, and pieced squares formed curtains and cushions. They looked familiar. Grace's women's group must have also made the soft furnishings in the guesthouse I'd stayed in several nights ago outside Moshi. Colors and mixed prints I'd never combine back home created works of art here.

I lay in bed, luxuriating under the weight of the quilts, as warm and comforting as Grace herself. Her steady good nature was pure pleasure to be around. I'd often asked myself how much of it was a product of the culture she grew up in. Tanzanians, in general, didn't "let it all hang out," the way American society encouraged people to do. There was something about the assumptions Americans made about their place in the world. Grace didn't expect automatic respect or privileges based on her nationality. She approached each day as though she needed to contribute to the welfare of everyone around her, rather than wondering what the day would offer her.

I pulled open the curtains above my bed, and sunlight flooded the room. Full of energy from a great night's sleep, I jumped up and showered. When I emerged, Sean was gone. I headed over to the kitchen for breakfast.

"He bolted toast and peanut butter," Grace said. "He's right out that window, digging in the dirt."

I looked around the uncluttered room, admiring it again. She had what she needed — but not more. I pictured friends' kitchens, drawers and cupboards crammed with rarely used pots, dishes, and appliances that served one purpose alone. The clutter drove me crazy, and the gross excess, migrating from garages to thrift stores, and finally to landfills, depressed me.

She rose as I entered, wished me a good morning, and handed me a small box of matches to light the cooker. I groaned — the dreaded Lucky brand. They had two problems: thin irregular sticks that broke with the slightest pressure and poorly coated heads, which either failed completely or flared belatedly. Many times I'd seen one snap, sending the business end cartwheeling through the air while I waited in suspense to see if it would flare and land on something flammable. This time, a tiny jolt of success ran through me when I got a flame out of the fourth stick. I twisted the knob on the little propane-powered stove and waved the match at the burner as fast as I could, unable to control my yelp and backward leap as the gas caught fire. When I looked up, Grace was laughing.

"I hope I'm not blown to Kingdom Come in the next few days," I muttered.

We boiled water for tea and toasted bread in the broiler, then sat in the sunny kitchen eating fresh fruit and grilled toast with avocado. I scrutinized a jar of local peanut butter on the table, thinking I might lick a dollop right off a spoon. I looked around, saw what I wanted instead, and reached over for a small banana. "Fresh peanut butter and a good banana. Can't wait."

Grace laughed. "I remember my shock in the US to find I had to pay extra for 'natural' peanut butter."

I laughed. I'd never been to an African country where I couldn't buy cheap, delicious, locally made peanut butter — just peanuts and salt, sometimes still warm from the mill. I smeared some of the pure stuff on a perfectly ripe little banana and savored it.

She stood up. "Let's see what Sean's up to."

Sean was squatting under a couple of forlorn papaya trees, digging with a stick. He'd managed to find three enormous, but harmless, millipedes, about the size of my middle finger, and he'd poked them so they'd rolled into neat spirals. Two boys who looked about Sean's age were watching him from a few feet away, giggling. Grace spoke to them in Swahili, and they came toward me with outstretched hands. I loved the way African children were expected to follow the simple courtesy of introducing themselves and shaking hands with adults.

"*Shikamoo*," they said, offering the polite greeting for an older person as they inclined their little heads.

"*Marahaba,*" I responded solemnly.

With one more sentence from Grace, they turned and walked toward Sean with big eyes. This time, it was just a slangy "*mambo,*" but it was enough. They giggled at the millipedes, pointed and motioned, drew with sticks in the dirt, and soon all ran away together.

"Sean, stay within shouting distance," I called to his back.

"They're good boys," said Grace. "They come sometimes with their mothers." She gestured at a path in the opposite direction, down which the boys frisked in the sun like small antelope kicking up their heels. "Would you like to see the *shamba*?"

"I'd love to see what you've got growing. I have a little patch for veggies in a community plot at home, but this trip means I'll miss out on some of my harvest."

Grace chuckled. "Most of what I grow is edible. Any good Tanzanian with a piece of land will have maize and beans — and I do." She waved at the typical neat rows of the *shamba*. "But I'm also experimenting with some types of intercropping — those are sweet potato growing on the ridges between the bananas. And notice how much space we've left between the fruit plants?"

Now that she mentioned it, I realized why this field looked different from what I was used to seeing.

"I use it as a training project for local women, teaching them basic accounting, money management, and marketing, along with the farming. A woman named Joy Mollel, who works for a non-profit organization in Moshi, comes up once a week and teaches nutrition. She's terrific, and I was lucky to find her." She lingered to examine a brown spot on a leaf. "Actually, it was Imani who introduced me to her. That woman has had her hand in so many good things for this country. She crossed paths with Joy some years ago in Ndungu when Joy's daughter was ill there. Imani kept in touch with Joy and told me about her. I plan for Joy to train someone here to do the teaching."

I smiled at my hard-working friend, wishing our lives intersected more often.

"I go to bed most nights satisfied, Ana, and that matters to me more every day. I'm so lucky. By living in a simple way, I can afford to spend my time on things I know for sure make a difference to women here. I used to worry about that all the time." She stooped and plucked a caterpillar off a leaf. "By the way. Where's Jared? You haven't said exactly why he's here."

"Right now, he's down in Mtwara doing surgery for a mission hospital. He spends a lot of time making trips to developing countries and raising money for the work. His non-profit's getting a reputation." Grace didn't say anything, and I continued. "In fact, Jared's own reputation is growing. He puts his charm to good use."

Grace glanced away at that.

"I'm a tiny bit surprised he comes back to Tanzania to do good," I said.

"Oh?" said Grace, looking back at me and lifting an eyebrow. "Why do you say that?"

"I think you know that he wasn't always happy here. I mean, those couple of years at ISM weren't the best in his life." I produced a shrug of apology. "It wasn't Tanzania that was the problem. He hated the moving around when we were kids." I stooped and pulled an obvious weed from between two bean plants. "That's why I'm surprised he wants to travel as much as he does these days. I thought he'd be more of a homebody."

"Oh, Ana," Grace said with something like a grunt, "surely you can see the difference in being forced to be here as a kid and what he's doing now?"

I drew back. "What do you mean?"

She glanced at me sideways, giving a small one-shoul-dered shrug. "It was no secret that he didn't like it here." She started to say something else but seemed to think better of it. After a few silent seconds, she put her hand on my arm. "Sorry, I don't want to sound critical of him. He is a charmer, and it's nice he's been so successful."

"Yes, it is." I said, disliking the tiny note of defensiveness in my voice. "He teaches residents and uses his private prac-tice to fund a lot of his work overseas. *And* he's the director of a non-profit that raises money from many places for all the good stuff he does." I was gaining steam. "His work's been written up in several publications and he's featured on news shows."

"Sure, I can see why you're proud of him." Grace inclined her head in assent, but she didn't offer any more comments on Jared.

We'd reached the edge of the garden. The laughter of members of the sewing group emerging from a path into the *shamba* made us both look up.

"Ah. Here come the women," said Grace, her face bright-ening. "I need to start them on a new project this morning." She waved in their direction. "Sorry, but can you excuse me, Ana?"

She hurried off.

I HELPED Grace set out an early lunch on the veranda while Sean recounted his morning explorations with the boys. He gobbled a sandwich and looked up at me, a tomato skin clinging to his lower lip. "'Scuse me, please? My friends are waiting."

Grace and I exchanged smiles.

"Okay." A vision of Beth materialized in my head. "But be careful, Sean."

Grace laughed as Sean dashed out the door. "He'll be fine, Ana. I know those boys' mothers, and the boys know the land around here. They'll be out playing in the dirt this afternoon like kids should. They'll not get into any trouble."

I settled back with an after-lunch cup of tea. "I'm going to observe a screening program at one of the primary schools near here this afternoon. Want to come?"

"I might. What kind of screening?" Grace took up a ball of yarn and her knitting needles. She was casting on, and she counted stitches under her breath.

"It's a project Jared advises. There's a group of volunteers running screenings for eye diseases in schools in several regions. Happens to be one up here at Sokoine Primary." I tested my tea, shocked at its heat, and added more milk. "It's only a kilometer or so from here, right?"

"Sure. You can drive, but the road from this direction's awfully rough now. You can walk it in about twenty minutes. I didn't know you were interested in eye care projects."

"I'm not — at least not necessarily. But I'm keeping open to opportunities for our program. Naturally, Jared's pushing me toward some in his field."

"And are you keen to join forces with him?" Her needles were flying.

"Yes — maybe." I scratched my head. "On the one hand, he's got useful connections. And it might be fun to work together. But..."

"Go on," urged Grace. "I'm still interested in public health — I just come at it from a less academic viewpoint now."

"Well, I'm afraid Jared often dismisses public health

approaches. Like, with this mission he's on right now, which he's touting as an effort to rid Mtwara District of cataract blindness. I suggested that he should have an advance team go first, to tell people about the service, find cases."

"Yeah," said Grace, laying her knitting — already a dozen rows — on the table. She leaned back and steepled her fingers. "Publicity's essential. Showing up and expecting patients to flood the gates won't get you far."

"Jared's non-profit pushes this narrative that needy people will flock to the hospital when they hear an eye surgeon's coming. I think it's more complicated than that."

"Of course it is." Grace chuckled. "Many older people with cataract don't trust the system. They believe the doctor will take their eye out and replace it with one from a goat." She picked up the knitting and eyed it critically. "Wonder where that idea started."

I shrugged. "I think he also tends to exaggerate the prevalence of the problem to market his work." I blew out a breath and shifted on the wicker couch. "Granted it's the major cause of blindness across Africa, but, sheesh." I leaned back.

"Will he be working with a Tanzanian doctor or student?"

"I don't think so." I shifted again. "In fact, he's brought along an American trainee."

"Oh." Grace raised her eyebrows, just a bit.

I swallowed the last of my tea. "Anyway, he was enthusiastic about this school screening project, so I'm going to check it out."

Grace rubbed her forehead, looking down at the floor for several seconds. "You know, I think I *would* like to come. Not sure if you remember what I told you about my mother, but among her many problems was congenital cataract. Of course, she never got an operation."

"Mmm, Grace. I'm sorry. I didn't know about the cataract." I looked down at the floor too.

Sitting next to Grace's hospital bed in the UK, I'd learned about her mother, who had died before Grace came to ISM. Severely disabled with multiple problems from birth, she had been raped by an unknown assailant at age twelve — and Grace was conceived. In the ensuing family crisis, Grace's aunt rebelled against her parents' attitude, and provided shelter for her disabled sister and baby. To everyone's surprise, Grace grew to be physically sound, bright, and cheerful. Her childless aunt loved Grace as fiercely as she loathed men.

"Yeah. In hindsight, I think my mother had congenital rubella syndrome. I've sometimes imagined how a project like Ellen Mafwiri's could have helped her." She shook her head, then looked up. "Sure, I'd like to come with you."

Grace and I walked to the screening, leaving Sean under the watchful eyes of the sewing ladies. The early afternoon sun cast gentle shadows over the hard-packed earth pathway through the forests of banana trees on either side, and the fresh air was perfect. The shouts of children reached us as we approached the cement block, tin-roofed school. Blue paint still covered most of the walls, but it was flaking in large patches. The surrounding grounds, although dirt, were swept clean. A banner reading *Sight for the World* stretched across the front of the building. A young, tall, blond man in a white coat bounded up to us.

"Welcome!" he said, with a huge grin that showed

perfect white teeth. He stuck out his hand to me but ignored Grace. "I'm Dr. Steve. We're here from Macarry Medical School in New York. We're looking for visually impaired children we can help."

On the playground, groups of youngsters joshed and milled around, kept from serious chaos by someone I presumed was a teacher. A slender red-haired woman in a white coat strode back and forth, arranging old wood benches. On two of these rickety seats, which showed signs of multiple repairs, several adults sat silently in a row, while a third white-coated young woman with nose pink from sunburn moved methodically along the line, peering at their eyes with a small light. Even from this distance, many of the eyes looked red and sore. An old man appeared to be arguing with her through a translator. She shrugged, handed him a pair of spectacles and a bottle of eye drops from a satchel she carried over her shoulder and moved to the next person. I turned back to Steve.

"We've come to observe," I said. "This is Grace Ngassi and I'm Ana Lotner. Wasn't this supposed to be a screening for school children?"

"Yes. But adults are also showing up. We can't ignore them."

"So, are you doctors?" I asked.

Steve shifted from one foot to the other before he spoke. "Well, we're final year medical students. We've all taken a two-week rotation in ophthalmology, learning to examine the eye. Maybe you know that childhood blindness is a big problem in Africa? We have to find the kids early to have any hope of improvement."

Medical students with two weeks of ophthalmology training? I studied Steve, but he seemed serious. How much did Jared actually know about this program?

Grace and I exchanged glances. She smiled faintly at the young man and narrowed her eyes. "Is the district medical officer around? Or someone from his office?" she asked.

"Uh, no. We couldn't find him this morning, so we decided to get started and talk to him later."

"How about the head teacher for the school? Have you met with him?" asked Grace.

The young man glanced at his watch. "He was supposed to be here at twelve-thirty. We figured we ought to begin when he wasn't here at one. A couple of other teachers agreed to help us."

As he spoke, a tall Tanzanian man dressed in a jacket and tie ambled up the path to the school. Grace's face brightened, and she walked toward him, extending her hand.

"Titus. *Habari za mchana*?"

They exchanged greetings and several more sentences — I thought she asked about his mother — then she turned and gestured toward me. "Ana, this is Mr. Titus Ndossi, the head teacher here and my neighbor." Her smile broadened. "Titus, Ana's an old friend — and she's also involved in public health. We hoped to observe the eye screening."

"You're most welcome," he said, including me with his eyes. He asked me about my visit, unhurried, then turned to Grace and furrowed his brow. "What eye screening are you speaking of?" He looked around, taking in the scene of children, adults, teachers, and foreigners in white coats. "I'm not sure what's going on here."

At this, the medical student stepped forward, flashed his gleaming smile, and stuck out a hand. "Good afternoon, sir. I'm Dr. Steve," he said. He swept his hand toward the other students. "My colleagues and I are from Macarry Medical

School. I'm leading the eye screening that our university contacted you about."

Mr. Ndossi pinched the bridge of his nose and used his index finger to push his glasses into better position on his face, all the time eyeing Steve. "I'm sorry. I don't believe I've heard about a screening." He cocked an eyebrow. "Grace, are you or Ana part of this team?"

"No, we aren't," Grace said with a small shake of her head. "We learned about it through Ana's brother. He's an eye specialist, working down in Mtwara right now."

"Well, perhaps there's been a misunderstanding. Why don't we go inside and discuss it," said Mr. Ndossi, as the corners of his mouth began to droop. He turned to Steve. "Please ask your team to come in so we can talk."

Steve's mouth turned down too. His shoulders slumped in his white coat as he walked over to speak to the two women.

"Why don't you come in as well, Grace. And Ana. Maybe we can sort this out together."

His office was dim, weak light filtering through two small jalousie windows. A battered armchair with a small wooden table served as his desk, and a rickety bookcase overflowing with files and papers leaned against one wall. Two straight-backed chairs completed the furnishings.

"Heri!" he called though the window, clapping his hands together. "Bring one of those benches into my office please." A boy in school uniform, who looked about twelve, hurried into the room a minute later lugging a piece of the patched-up furniture he'd probably dragged in the other direction earlier.

"Please, take a seat," Mr. Ndossi said to the medical students, waving toward the bench. A half dozen children clustered at the windows, their small faces lit up with curiosity. "*Phhht!*" He flapped his hand at them and they scattered.

Over the next ten minutes, Steve described a project that involved several medical schools in the US from which volunteer students visited village schools in Africa looking for children who needed glasses or eye surgery. He insisted that his mentor from Macarry had been in touch with a hospital in Moshi, which had organized screenings at schools in Kilimanjaro Region.

"Do you have a letter from the Ministry of Health or Education?" Mr. Ndossi asked.

Steve demurred. "Uh, no, I didn't know I needed a letter." The other two medical students shifted on the hard bench.

The headmaster's features progressed from curiosity to consternation before hardening into frank displeasure in the silence.

Steve cleared his throat.

After a few seconds Mr. Ndossi spoke. "Did you meet with the district medical officer? I'm sure you went to see him since he's responsible for health care in this district."

I cringed while Steve repeated his excuse.

Mr. Ndossi produced a tight smile that conveyed neither mirth nor warmth. "It's highly irregular to carry out an activity like this without a letter from the district medical officer. I'm sure the same would be true in your country, no? We do have procedures to be followed here." He stood up and glanced at the windows. A couple of faces that had reappeared there vanished in a flash. "I'm afraid I must ask you to cease your activities, collect your things, and leave now."

The three students looked at each other. In a heavy silence they rose, grim faced, and filed out of the room. Mr.

Ndossi turned to Grace, and they exchanged some words I didn't understand. As we got up to go, Mr. Ndossi took my hand. "I'm sorry to disappoint the doctors," he said. "We are grateful for donations and volunteers but I have a responsibility for my school and students."

I wilted inside, imagining that Mr. Ndossi assumed I had something to do with this. I held my tongue though, except to say farewell.

Outside, the students were gathering their supplies. Steve reached up and released both ends of the banner, which crumpled onto the ground.

Grace and I started walking back down the pathway. I fumed. "I can hardly believe the arrogance of those students."

"Yes. It's bad." She nodded. "I'm surprised the teachers allowed the screening to move ahead, but I guess they didn't want to question foreign doctors."

"Or medical students pretending to be doctors," I said, twisting my mouth and throwing up my hands. "I hope the teachers don't get into too much trouble from the headmaster. My God, what a screwup."

My irritation grew as we picked our way along the rutted road back toward Grace's house. It was impossible to appreciate the same lush scenery I'd enjoyed walking the other direction.

"What were the students going to do if they found a kid who needed referral? Did they make any arrangements for that?"

Grace sighed. "Honestly, Ana, this whole project is ill-conceived. Most children with serious eye problems don't go to school, so it's not a great place to screen. But it appeals to donors in western countries who don't know any better. I wish I could say I'd never seen anything like it."

I was going to have a solemn conversation with Jared about this program, planned from the US, with little, if any, collaboration with Tanzanians. How could he be championing these activities? Did he know what the students were doing? And how was I going to tell Andrew that another project — this one Jared's suggestion — was a dead end?

15

FRIDAY, SEPTEMBER 1

O n our third day in Rombo, Sean and I filled our water bottles and started down a narrow footpath, winding through banana trees bearing heavy loads under huge protective leaves. We emerged on the far side of Grace's *shamba* and made our way up into a dense forest of towering trees through which direct sun rarely touched the ground. In spite of the apparent seclusion, voices filtered through the thick growth on both sides of the path. This land was far more inhabited than it appeared. The view from a hundred meters up would be solid green, not a single person or home visible. We heard the rush of water ahead and the track forked.

"This way!" shouted Sean, darting down to the right.

I slowed for a second to avoid tripping on a thick root, then hurried after him. I caught up to find him kneeling, looking down into a small gorge, where water cascaded, sending up a white spray. A crude bridge, constructed from long bamboo poles, spanned the rushing water.

"Wow! I wouldn't want to have to cross *that*," said a wide-eyed Sean.

"Me neither." I shuddered. "There's almost nothing to hang on to, and I don't trust those rickety sticks. I wonder who uses this."

"Let's go back and try the other way," said Sean, turning around.

We hadn't traveled more than a few meters on the left fork when we met the same gorge, this time with a satisfying difference. Strong, broad, rough-hewn wood planks were braced with stone and mortar abutments at either end to form a sturdy bridge. Stout branches lashed with nylon cord formed handrails on both sides. It looked well taken care of and well used. Water several feet deep rushed below.

Sean grabbed a handful of sticks, ran out to the middle of the bridge, and started throwing them upstream. What was it about running water and children? I smiled at his obvious pleasure in watching them dance on the water before disappearing in the froth. We lost the shade of the trees, and the sun warmed my back. Sean played on the bridge and I lounged on the bank for a pleasant half hour reminiscing about trips to Rombo with friends as a teenager. I tried to place Jared in these, but he was never there. Life seemed less complicated then, although perhaps that was an illusion of time.

When my stomach started to growl, I stood up, hoping Sean would hear me above the rushing water. "Time to go! Sean!"

I learned more about the bridge, preparing lunch with Grace an hour later.

"Ah, yes," she said, a smile spreading across her face. "The sewing ladies made that happen."

"The sewing ladies?" I raised my brows as I spread peanut butter on bread for sandwiches.

"Yep. Many people need to cross that gorge each day for

work, including some of the women who sew. They all dreaded it. There were always accidents, and when Mary's young sister slipped last year and broke her leg, her friends decided to do something. They called a meeting and planned. Using some of the money they'd earned, they purchased cement and nylon cord. I agreed to pitch in a little if they supplied all the labor. They got husbands and children to collect the required stones and convinced a couple of men to prepare the wood planks. I got a friend from Moshi to come up and advise on construction, and the result was that beautiful bridge. It makes a difference every single day for the people — especially the women and children."

Having seen the previous structure, I could imagine. I mulled over the enterprises Grace ran, with clear and simple benefits. On such a small scale they'd never be of interest to big donors. But could they be scaled up to serve as springboards for larger health initiatives?

Grace took a chair at the kitchen table and was about to bite into the sandwich when she stopped. "What's most satisfying is seeing how everyone feels this bridge belongs to them. They organized a small group to inspect and maintain it."

I sat across from her, thinking how little actions led to big changes in people's lives — and how Grace glowed talking about her work. I think I was a tiny bit envious.

I ALMOST DIDN'T HEAR the text message alert on my phone through the whistling of the kettle. I was boiling water in the kitchen with the mobile on the table when I caught the sound and glanced over, noting that it was half past one. I turned off the flame, picked up the phone, and opened the message.

I don't know how long I stared at the phone in my hand, as if it were an explosive device from which I needed to protect myself. I opened my mouth but no sound came out.

We have your brother. I blinked and shook my head, as if I could clear the words away. What? Who's got my brother? Where? Was this a joke? But I looked again, and that was what the text said. *We have your brother. Contact no one.* The message came from Jared's number.

I reached out and grabbed the edge of the table as the concrete floor heaved in slow motion. My heart hammered my ribcage. I sank onto a chair, my eyes fixed on the screen. My shoulders tensed, and I tried to make my body relax, to take stock, but my insides were filled with ice. I laid the phone down, put my hands flat on the table, and looked around the tidy kitchen, reminding myself to blink.

My eyes came back to the phone. I picked it up, found Jared's number at the top of the recent calls list and tried to connect. It rang, every *bdrrrr* sounding like it came through a heavy fog. After what seemed like ages, voice mail took over. *Hi. This is Jared. Leave a message and I'll get back to you.*

"Jared?" I spoke into the tiny microphone. "Jared, are you okay? I just got a ridiculous text saying someone had you. What's going on? Call me now!" I hung up. For good measure I went back to the message and texted. *Call me now!* But the phone lay silently in my hand, and the only movement was my thumping heart. My mind a black sea.

After what might have been one minute, two minutes, or even five, I stood up and went outside to find Grace.

The buzzing of unseen insects was deafening. The midday sun blasted out through a clear blue sky, nearly blinding me for a moment. A fuzzy Grace was bending over, showing something to Sean by the bean poles in the garden.

Sean! I couldn't tell him about this.

Through my haze, Grace looked up, wiped sweat from her brow, and beckoned me over. I forced the corners of my mouth up and waved at Sean, willing my legs to propel me forward.

"Hey, Sean, hang on out here for a sec, will you? I need to show Grace something inside."

I fixed my face in a rigid grin. I stepped toward Grace, took her hand and, without asking, pulled her toward the house, ignoring the startled look on her face.

"What's going..." she tried to ask as I tugged her through the backdoor into the kitchen.

"Look. This just came from Jared," I said in a voice so low and rapid that she took a moment to process the words. I thrust the phone into her hands.

She took it as if it might be infected, but looked at the screen. "This is from Jared?"

"Yes. It came a few moments ago. When I called back there was no answer." I took the phone back and tried again in case something had changed.

It hadn't. There was nothing but ringing, followed by his voice message.

I ran my hands through my hair and pulled hard on it, just to feel something besides fear. When I let it go, I found my fists clenched again. I paced in a small circle.

"What am I supposed to do?" I flung up my hands. My throat ached with tension.

A frown creased Grace's face, and she spoke firmly. "Ana, sit down. Let's think about this." She pulled a chair from the table and pushed me into it. "You sent a text back to this number?"

"Yes. No response."

"He doesn't have another phone he might use?"

I shook my head, tearing at the nail on my little finger with my teeth. I needed to get out of the chair. I jumped up and resumed pacing. Then I sat again, and slumped, my head in my hands.

"Do you have a number for the hospital in Mtwara? Maybe we could contact them," suggested Grace, rubbing the back of her neck.

"Maybe, I guess. But the message said not to contact anyone. I'm afraid to call the hospital." I chewed at the inside of my mouth. "Wait!" I shot out of the chair. "Maybe I can reach Thomas, the resident who was with him down there. Lemme see." I bit my lower lip. "He's not in my phone contacts, but he was copied on an email Jared sent about his itinerary." I scrolled through my emails with shaking fingers, cursing because Jared never started new threads for new subjects. "Found it!"

Thomas, I entered, *need to talk. Call asap.* I tapped in my phone number, hit send, and put the device on the table. The order to contact no one popped into my mind. Surely Thomas wouldn't count.

Grace had turned the kettle on again and was getting out tea makings. Thank God, Sean was still out in the garden. I collapsed in the chair and tried calling Jared again. I groaned when his answering voice invited me to leave a message. My stomach churned and I jumped up to pace.

Grace put a cup of tea on the table and, without asking, added milk and two teaspoons of sugar. "I know you don't usually sweeten it, Ana, but do it this time. It'll be good for you." She sat down and added sugar to her own mug. I was reaching for the scalding liquid when my phone rang. I grabbed it to answer the call from an unknown number.

"Hi. Dr. Ana? It's Thomas."

"Thomas! Where are you?"

"I'm on my way to...uh...to Ngorongoro," he said, stumbling over the unfamiliar syllables. "What's wrong?"

"Where's Jared?" I asked, the hoarseness painful in my tight throat. I rubbed my forehead. Slow down, Ana, and take deep breaths. But I could barely think straight.

"I guess he's still down in Mtwara. At least that's where he was when I left yesterday morning. What's the matter?"

The text appeared in my mind: *Contact no one.* But what did that mean? Did it mean Thomas too? I breathed in and tried harder to think. I forced myself to slow my speech. "He was at the hospital when you left yesterday?"

"Yeah. Sure. What's the problem?"

"Just bear with me, please. What time did you leave?"

"A driver picked me up at six-thirty in the morning as planned, to take me to Dar. I saw Jared before going, but we didn't talk for more than a few minutes."

"Was he okay?"

"Sure. He thanked me for being there and wished me a *safari njema*. You know, a good trip."

"Yes, I know," I snapped, incredulous to be getting a Swahili lesson at that point. But Thomas didn't know about the text message. I tried to unclench my teeth and draw in a few deep breaths.

"What's the problem?" asked Thomas again.

I ignored his question and plowed right on with my own, glancing out the window to be sure Sean was still occupied. "How did things go in Mtwara?" I laid the phone on the table and switched it to speaker mode for Grace to hear.

"Yeah, it was pretty cool. I enjoyed it." He hesitated. "We didn't quite have as many patients as I expected. I mean, I thought they'd be lined up for miles since Jared said there's been no surgeon there for a couple of years. There must be hundreds of blind down there, but only a dozen or so showed up."

"Okay, Thomas, I understand." My mind was whirling. I wasn't surprised at the low turnout, but I took no satisfaction in being right at that moment. I pulled at my hair again and started walking around the table. Could Thomas tell me anything useful? I needed to think.

I wanted to talk it over with Grace. "Thomas, can I call you back in a couple of minutes?"

"Sure, but I'd like to know what's going on."

"Call you in five," I said, hanging up.

Grace stood up, pushed me down into the chair again, and slid the cup of tea toward my trembling hands. "First, drink it. Then we talk."

I took a deep breath and swallowed the beverage, now cooled. Reflexively, I tried Jared's phone again. There was no ringing this time; voice mail kicked in directly. Somebody had turned it off — or it had gone dead. Tears welled in my eyes.

"Stay calm, Ana." Grace stood up and leaned over the back of my chair to hug me. I wiped under my eyes and reached up to put my arms on hers. Her warmth felt good. She laid her head on mine for a few seconds before moving away to take a seat across from me. "Let's think it through." Her face was serious but calm. "First, do you think we must keep this secret? To not contact the hospital or the US Embassy?"

"That's what the message said." I sniffed up a few tears. She reached for a tissue on a counter behind and handed it to me. I blew my nose and looked at her. "I need to be careful if Jared's been...abducted."

There. I'd said the word out loud. An icy chill ran down

my back, and tears pooled in my eyes again. "People get killed when they don't follow instructions." I was rigid, willing my voice and body to be steady. My clenched jaw ached with the effort at control.

Grace sat across from me again and fixed her eyes on mine while a deep vertical crease formed between her brows. "I understand that. You're right. But even if you aren't going to contact the authorities or the hospital, we have to decide what to do next — what to do about Sean. We need a plan." She drank her tea and got up to make more. "Can you think of anything that might have gone wrong down there? Even if you aren't going to tell Thomas what's happened, you need to find out from him exactly what went on during the week they were there. Getting a day-by-day picture of their activities might shed some light, provide a clue."

I reached for the crumb of control. She was right. I had to pull myself together and do something to use what power I had. "I'll call Thomas back and ask him to tell me everything that went on. Every detail he can think of, in case one of them matters."

Grace nodded encouragement. "I'll go keep Sean out of the way."

Thomas was waiting for my call and eager to give me lots of details, although he was clearly uneasy that I wouldn't tell him why I wanted to know. He and Jared had spent the first day they arrived, Sunday, talking to the Catholic sisters who ran the hospital. Jared was disappointed that there weren't any patients waiting for surgery for Monday, but the nuns explained that no one would come until the word got out that the doctor was really there.

"Can you believe that scheduled doctors sometimes haven't shown up?" asked Thomas.

It wasn't such a stretch to imagine. I kept silent and let Thomas continue.

The nuns had apologized for the delay, but it was outside their control. Once Jared got there, they sent several boys out to nearby villages to spread the word that the doctor had arrived.

I focused on Thomas's story, difficult due to a crackling connection. I switched to speaker mode and the noise filled the room. "And there was a disagreement about asking patients to pay for surgery. Jared insisted people were too poor and the service had to be free. The donors supporting his trip had made that a condition."

Again, I wasn't surprised, but Thomas wanted to talk about it. I forced myself to listen.

"I read a couple of research papers on the advantages of asking patients to contribute a small amount for elective surgeries, like cataract. Jared still didn't buy it. The nuns insisted they had a system in place to cover anyone who couldn't pay the ten-dollar charge. They work hard to keep themselves afloat and the bit they collect from fees helps. They don't turn away truly needy patients."

"Okay, Thomas, I get that." My God, did I really have to hear all this right now? "Sorry, I don't have a lot of time," I drummed the fingers of one hand on the table while I used the other to try to stop them. Anxiety from me would only add to his curiosity. I had to let him tell the story. "So you started operating on Monday or Tuesday?"

"Tuesday morning. Jared tried to push the staff to start Monday afternoon, but they balked."

"Did all the surgeries go well?" It was unlikely, but a disgruntled patient or his family might have something to do with this.

"Oh sure. Jared's a great surgeon! It was fantastic to see

sight restored to people who'd been blind. We never see cataracts that advanced at home. I learned a lot and even got to do a case on my own."

"How many surgeries did you do in the end?" I was on a fishing expedition, casting as wide a net as possible.

"Oh. Well." His enthusiasm dropped a few levels. "Over the two days, we did twelve cataracts. Plus a few minor cases — you know, enucleations and a couple of lids."

"And there were no complications at the time you left on Thursday morning?"

"Nope. All good. I was a bit sick on Wednesday night so Jared went out to dinner without me. He was going to do a few more cases Thursday, then leave today — on Friday. Why are you asking me all these questions? Is something wrong?"

"Nothing wrong, Thomas. How long will you be in Ngorongoro?"

"Two days there, then a couple of days in Tarangire. I've heard it's relaxing there. Have you ever done their walking tour?"

I couldn't stand any more of this conversation, nor think of other things to ask Thomas without telling him what was going on. "I've gotta go. Nice talking to you, Thomas. Keep your phone handy will you?" I said. I hung up before he could ask me anything else. I stood up, sat down, and stood up again.

Grace came back into the kitchen. "Sean's with the boys. Did you learn anything from Thomas?"

"I don't think so." I rubbed my head and repeated most of my conversation with Thomas. "I talked to Jared on Monday night when Sean and I were in Ngorongoro. He said they had dozens of patients then, which isn't exactly what Thomas said, but I guess that doesn't mean anything."

I shook my head, hoping to rattle new ideas free. "No helpful information."

Conflicting urges battled inside me. I wanted to rush out and do something but had no idea what. I wanted to fold over into a fetal position and wail or flail out and scream. A hot white light of urgency illuminated everything.

Grace brought me back to earth again, putting her strong arms around me in a full body hug. "Ana. Let's focus. We've got to plan the next steps, for the sake of Sean if nothing else."

Sean. The thought of him summoned the discipline I needed to calm myself. I was responsible for him. I sat down.

"Okay, here's what we've got. As of yesterday, Thursday at six-thirty a.m., Jared was at the hospital and all was well. As of today, at half one, thirty-one hours later, I have a message from Jared's phone saying he's been taken by someone. We can't reach him. We've been warned not to contact anyone. We can't call the hospital to ask about him. We can't fill in those thirty hours. Maybe I shouldn't have even talked to Thomas. I can't imagine what he's thinking."

"Let that go, Ana. You've spoken to him, and he'll be busy with his game park trip the next few days. He probably won't think much about your call and doesn't know about the abduction, right? But I agree that calling the hospital would be a bad idea." She tapped her extended fingers lightly over her lips, letting her eyes roam over the room. "I think it's important not to alert anyone, even if it limits our options."

Abduction. The word was taking root in my brain. Jared had been abducted. Grace and I both knew of kidnappings of foreigners in other countries that ended badly when the authorities got involved. Maybe not in Tanzania, but it was still frightening. Losing Jared would be like spinning out into space forever to a place where nothing existed.

An idea hit me. "Maybe I should talk to the Walkers. They'd keep it quiet. I'd like their advice."

"Hmm. Sounds good. But it'll be dark before you reach there. It's foolhardy to drive down the narrow road to Moshi on a Friday night. How about calling them?"

"Don't want to do that. I can't tell them this over a sputtering phone line. I need to see them face-to-face."

She tapped her lips again. "At least send a text to let them know you're coming. You can go first thing in the morning. It's a good idea."

"Let's not say anything to Sean, okay?"

She agreed.

Thank God I was with Grace.

GRACE SET OUT A SIMPLE SUPPER, and we tried to convince Sean an early bedtime was a good idea. "Sorry, Sean, but we need to go back to Moshi tomorrow, to see the Walkers. Please go pack up your gear."

"Aww," he groaned. "I was having a good time here." He looked at me sideways. "Besides, I had stuff planned with the guys tomorrow."

I blinked. The kid had picked up from the successful adults around him a notion that plans were important and inviolable. Another time, I might have laughed.

"You'll be able to play with the Walkers' dogs. And who knows, we may be back here soon," I said, injecting hope into my voice, as though that might displace the fear gnawing at me.

After I said goodnight to him later and closed the door

to our room, I remembered that I, too, had made plans for tomorrow. I was supposed to observe the KI training. I'd have to call Ellen Mafwiri and cancel. Too bad, but nothing compared to what I faced with Jared.

GRACE and I stayed up late into the night talking. We couldn't solve anything, but at least it kept me from being alone with my terrors.

"Who'd do this?" I asked, sick of repeating the question. "Jared doesn't have enemies here." I took in a deep breath. "I know there's anti-American sentiment everywhere — and it's worse since the 2016 US elections, but why go after someone like Jared?"

But hostage-taking wasn't about the hostage. Hapless Americans made good targets.

Grace made soothing noises and poured brandy into our tea. I finally brought myself to ask her about something the Walkers had said a few days ago, something I'd struggled to keep below consciousness since I first said the word "abduction."

"Is it true al-Shabaab has made its way to Mtwara?"

Grace sighed. "Those stories haven't been verified." She hesitated. "Other rumors of political abductions along the coast are unproven."

I remembered a movie Jared had watched on one of our flights. "How about those Somali pirates that were in the news a few years ago?"

"No. They're north of here, and I've not heard of them working off the Tanzanian coast." She rubbed her crossed forearms. "This is all speculation."

She was right, but what else did we have?

I punched in Jared's number again and screamed. "It's ringing this time, Grace!" And it was, several times, just before it switched to voice mail. "There's activity! Whoever has the phone is doing something with it." In my exhaustion, it seemed like a hopeful sign.

Five minutes later, though, the phone once again went directly to voice mail.

Grace rose and came to give me a hug. "We don't know what it means, Ana. I'm going to tuck you up in bed. Would you like me to stay in your room tonight with you?"

I warmed at her kindness. "Thanks, Grace, but it's not necessary. You go to bed. I'll be fine."

But I wasn't. Once in bed, the walls around my feelings cracked. I sobbed quietly under the covers, worried about waking Sean. A full-throated wail would have felt better, but it also might have brought me to the edge of the abyss where uncontrolled terror dwelt. The nighttime cacophony of insects, dogs, and roosters was tension-filled tonight and it tangled with the jumble of thoughts in my head. Who had Jared's phone? What were they doing to Jared? I looked at my watch. Two fifty-five. Next time I looked it was 3:10. Then 3:17. The night went on forever.

16

SATURDAY, SEPTEMBER 2

I was grateful Sean wasn't old enough to recognize what red eyes at breakfast meant. Keeping him in the dark about his dad was going to be hard.

"Do we have to leave this morning?" he whined. "You said I was gonna stay here while you went to Moshi to do your work." He crossed his arms on his chest and hunched his shoulders.

"Things've changed," I snapped. Shame washed over me. Where did stressed-out parents find the energy to cope with kids?

Grace was hustling around the kitchen slicing fruit and making us toast. We'd discussed leaving Sean here with her while I went to talk to the Walkers, but I nixed it. I had no idea what I might need to do next or where I might have to go on short notice, and I didn't want him left behind. For now, he needed to stay with me. I looked down at my plate of untouched fruit, hoping his whine was finished.

"Since you said we'd come back, why not just leave my stuff here?" he asked, upping the challenge with a fierce scowl.

I hesitated and pretended I was considering his suggestion. "Naw, let's both take our bags. They're small and not much trouble to carry. We're ready to stay the night anywhere." I gave what I hoped he'd take as a chummy smile. "See why we travel light?" I forked a piece of mango into my mouth, hardly tasting it as it slid down. "Why don't you put your bag in the car?" He trudged out of the room, shoulders now slumped instead of hunched. It was an improvement.

My lip quivered as Grace wrapped me in her warm embrace. "I'm ready to help you any way I can, Ana. Just let me know."

Sean and I drove down the rutted road as Grace waved from the veranda. Time had become peculiarly elastic, and it seemed like a lifetime ago that we'd driven up this way.

It was just after mid-morning when we pulled up at the metal gate in the high wall that protected the Walkers' house. The entrance guard peeked out through a little window and, after a few seconds, opened the iron entrance. It creaked, sending shivers up my tense spine. The gracious old white-painted stone house stood before us, and we rolled onto the property. Fiona was on the porch reading a book. She rose as I parked the car at the side of the gravel drive.

"Welcome," she said, coming down the veranda steps. "We were surprised by your text. I hope there's nothing wrong?"

It was almost impossible not to pour out the whole story immediately, but Sean was standing by my side. I turned to him as the dogs sprang around the corner of the house. "Hey, your friends are here. Why don't you run with them?" I forced my face into the broadest smile I could muster.

As he raced off, I turned to Fiona. "I need to talk to you about something important. Is Geoffrey around?"

"He's in the house." She knit her brow. "Is everything all right?"

"Not exactly," I said, willing my lower lip not to tremble. "Can you please get Geoffrey so I can speak to both of you?"

"Of course," she said, the furrows deepening on her forehead. She stepped toward the door. "I'll fetch him right now. Shall I ask Ahmed to bring coffee? Or tea?"

"Thanks. Tea please." How could I hurry her along? Now that I was here, I ached to unburden myself quickly.

At last, Fiona, Geoffrey, and I sat together on the porch. Sean was in view but out of earshot.

I pulled up the text message on my phone and passed it to Geoffrey. "This came yesterday afternoon, at one-thirty."

Geoffrey retrieved reading glasses from his shirt pocket. His eyes grew large behind them as he read. He handed the phone to Fiona and removed the spectacles.

She broke the silence. "What on earth...?"

Geoffrey extended his index finger across his upper lip and shook his head slowly. "My God, Ana. I can't get my head around this. It's terrible. What's going on?"

I shrugged. As though I knew.

Perhaps realizing his question was unanswerable, Geoffrey tried another. "What have you done since you got this?"

I described my call to Thomas and what I'd learned from him while Geoffrey got to his feet, pacing the porch and running his hands through his hair. Fiona sat upright in her chair, ashen, her gaze fixed on me. I imagined gears turning in her head. They let me talk. I stuck to the facts and finished in ten minutes. Geoffrey collapsed on the settee, and we all looked at each other.

None of us knew what to make of the fact that, once in a

while, irregularly, my calls to his phone rang before going to voice mail.

"But I think some activity is better than no activity," Geoffrey said, echoing my thoughts of the night before.

"We've got to decide what to do — consider every one of our options," said the ever-practical Fiona. "Brainstorm. No matter how silly or stupid it may appear at first."

"Okay," said Geoffrey leaning in, elbows resting on his thighs. "We could call the hospital in Mtwara."

"We could drive to Mtwara," suggested Fiona. "Better to talk in person."

"Or fly to Mtwara through Dar. Maybe fly to Dar and drive from there," said Geoffrey. "But either way we spend about two days."

"How about calling the American Embassy in Dar? They have standard procedures when citizens go missing."

"Trouble is, all those ideas fall into the 'contact someone' category," I reminded them, chewing a ragged edge of thumbnail.

Geoffrey huffed out a breath and fell back on his seat, lips compressed in a thin line. Fiona put her hand over her own closed mouth and looked at me. They were waiting for me to continue.

"First, do you both agree it's important not to contact anyone?" I half wanted them to disagree.

They exchanged a look, and I longed to believe they would reveal some hidden wisdom.

Geoffrey shifted his gaze to me and spoke. "Yes, I think that's imperative — at least for a while."

"So, are we saying we merely wait here and see what happens?" Fiona asked. "Take it hour by hour? We don't inform anyone?"

They weren't hiding any wisdom. They didn't know

what to do either. A deep hollowness filled my gut and carved its way up into my chest. They were as afraid as I was.

Fiona reached over and laid her hand on my arm. "I guess this is as good a place to wait as any. Of course you and Sean should stay with us. You'll be safe here."

Sean. With the mention of his name, a new worry blossomed. I flicked my eyes around to find him. It took a few seconds before I heard him shouting at a dog in the side garden. "I don't want Sean to know what's happening. How do we make sure of that?"

Geoffrey, who'd been silent for several minutes, leaned forward again, chin cradled in the sling between his thumb and forefinger, and looked up at me. He raised an eyebrow. "Look, I have to ask, Ana. Are the two of you actually safe here? Are you safe in this country at all, considering what's happened? We have no bloody idea what's going on. Since we're clueless about Jared, how can we be sure you and Sean are safe?"

I met his gaze and my worries exploded. Why shouldn't Sean be just as much a target as Jared?

Fiona's face went rigid. She moved over and wrapped her arms around me. I put my head on her shoulder. It helped. In those few minutes — or maybe it was seconds — the whirling pieces of my mind coalesced back into a thinking brain, a center from which I could function. The hazy path I was on didn't stretch far, and I had no idea where it led, but at least I wasn't on it alone.

"Thank you. We'll stay here tonight and rethink our next moves tomorrow."

Ahmed came out to the porch to call us to lunch. I was glad to be with the Walkers. It forced me to act like a human, to talk and react and pay attention to other people.

I called Sean, and he came bounding up the steps with

the dogs, which brought me a whisper of pleasure. We went inside and sat around the table for a meal. Sean's presence kept us from talking about Jared, asking questions with no answers, and speculating on his current and future prospects.

After lunch, Sean went back out to the garden. I watched out the dining room window as he disappeared among the trees. I couldn't stand to be alone with my thoughts, sitting around doing nothing, waiting for who-knew-what. I was back in limbo, struggling in a fog of unreality. I hadn't done anything constructive. The complete inability to make progress maddened me. What do you do when there's nothing to do?

"Would you like to help me in the garden, dear?" asked Fiona, laying a hand on my shoulder. Geoffrey announced he was going to check some online news and information sources, so Fiona and I went out to dig in the dirt. It was sunny but not too hot, and Fiona, intelligent and competent manager that she'd been for many years, gave me specific tasks to do, along with a sun hat. "Can you prepare the ground for those lettuce transplants over there?" She pointed toward a rickety table with an assortment of old plastic containers cut down to make flats for seedlings. We'll plant them directly behind that row of marigolds — so good for keeping off the insects that would devour the tender leaves."

I plowed onward like an automaton, grateful to have something physical to do. Fiona wasn't given to chatter, but she made a valiant effort to fill my mind with distractions.

"We'll need to put up shade cloth if we're going to have any nice salads. These European varieties are soft and delicious, but they need lots of help to survive the African ecosystem."

I tried to focus on lettuce — better than sitting in the house waiting for something to happen. I felt for my phone in a pocket and checked for the thousandth time that it was charged. I called Jared's number again. Directly to voicemail now.

Around four, Ahmed stuck his head out the door. "Tea, Madam. Shall I bring it to the veranda?"

"Ah, yes," said Fiona, groaning her way from her knees to her feet. "Why don't we take a rest, Ana?" She clapped dirt off her hands, removed her gloves, and rubbed her lower back. "Oh, if your mother could see me now. She wasn't a gardener, and she always laughed at me for working like this when it would be so easy to hire someone else."

She was right about my mother. I loved Fiona for reminding me of a happier time.

AHMED BROUGHT out lemonade for Sean, and he gulped it down. Geoffrey, Fiona, and I sipped milky tea and ate biscuits, measuring our words until Sean ran back into the orchard, leaping alongside the hounds.

Geoffrey cleared his throat. "I rang a few friends earlier this afternoon."

My alarm must have shown.

He continued hastily. "No. I didn't tell them anything about Jared's disappearance. I wanted a better sense for what might be going on in Mtwara with al-Shabaab."

My heart thumped, and I took in a sharp breath. "And...?"

"As you might imagine, reliable news is hard to come by." He waggled his outstretched palm. "But there have been a few indications of activity. There's at least one sighting of a man reputed to be a leader in the movement." He stuck out his lower lip. "I don't want to cause undue alarm, but anti-American sentiment has increased since America's ban on Muslims entering your country."

I wanted to approach this calmly and rationally, but I guess my face gave away my true state. I set my tea cup down. My shaking hand upended the lip of the saucer, and the cup rocked with an unnerving clatter. Fiona stood up and came over to sit next to me, wrapping her arms around my shoulders again. I fought hopelessness as images of blindfolded, shackled hostages crowded into my mind.

"Ana, we need to learn all we can about what's happening there, but we have no evidence al-Shabaab is operating in Mtwara, let alone that they have anything to do with Jared's situation. Let's not jump to conclusions or imagine the worst. That won't help."

Geoffrey nodded his agreement. "I want to propose something. An idea I've been thinking about."

I resisted the urge to grab at this statement like the straw it was. Any more emotional upheaval and I'd crumble. I folded my hands and listened, with Fiona's arm gently resting on my shoulders.

"There's a Tanzanian journalist. Name of Haamed Hassan. Don't guess you've heard of him?"

I drew a blank, and shook my head.

"He's from Dar, and I've followed him for a couple of years. He's gotten himself in a spot of trouble with the government here — not his fault at all. The chap's a straight shooter, and he's dead clever. He's a strong critic of the World Bank — finds it undemocratic. Reading his stuff has changed my mind about a number of issues. He's a thorough investigator, which is one reason he got into difficulty with the current government. I met him a couple of years ago — liked him. Close friends of mine who know him well, people I absolutely trust, vouch for his integrity."

I played with my earring and willed myself to be patient, shoring up my precarious composure.

"Here's something I learned this afternoon: Haamed's from Mtwara Region. Actually grew up around Msimbati."

I took hold of the straw. Msimbati was a village close to the hospital where Jared was working. I leaned forward.

"He's done some investigation and reporting on the gas field development down there." Geoffrey used his hands to make a tamping down movement. "That might be helpful. It's something." He studied my face. "I'd like to see if he'd help us look into this."

"But..." The text words, *Contact no one,* flashed in my mind. "But, what..."

"I know." Geoffrey made the tamping down motion with his hands again. "We agreed not to tell anyone, fair enough. But, if we trust Haamed — and everything I know indicates we can — and if we convince him to get involved, he might be able to help us. I believe he'll be discreet."

"But why would he want to help us?" Fiona said, reading my mind.

Geoffrey crossed his arms over his chest and leaned back. "It's not so much that he might want to help us, Fi. It's that he might want to get to the bottom of something going on in his old neighborhood. I believe he's a moral man — one who cares about justice."

"But, a *journalist*?" I croaked. "What's to keep him from telling the world?"

"As I said, we'd be banking on his integrity — and his desire to learn the truth. He'd have a vested interest in seeing Jared emerge safely from this situation." He shrugged. "Of course, he might want to tell the story once it's over."

Over. Whatever that meant. The three of us looked at one another as I twisted my hands.

"Let's think about this," said the reasonable Fiona. "Geoffrey, can you reach him and see if he'd help, without giving up too much information?" She reached out to touch my arm. "Meanwhile, Ana, have you had any more ideas about Sean? It's going to become harder to keep him in the dark."

"Yeah — you're right." I sagged. The kid was smart. More unexplained or sudden changes in plans would increase the sense he must have that something was off. I was on edge every minute, waiting for him to suggest calling his dad.

"It was only yesterday, wasn't it?" I asked Fiona, in wonder. It felt like years since I got the text message. "And I'm going to have to let Beth know too." But did that mean today? Or tomorrow, or when?

"Let's think about things," said Fiona, glancing out at the sky, intensifying into a deeper blue as the sun dropped. "Why don't you have a lie down. I've asked Ahmed to serve an early dinner." She got up. "I'm going to call Sean in and have him bathe." She made gentle shooing motions with her hands. "You've got at least two hours. Go."

Exhaustion was making it hard to make the simplest decisions. But napping never worked for me. If I couldn't sleep maybe I could learn something about the journalist Geoffrey mentioned. I stacked several pillows against the wall at the head of my bed and leaned back with my laptop for some online research.

I found dozens of reports from Haamed Rashid Hassan in *The East African*, as well as Tanzania's *The Citizen*. He'd written for Swahili newspapers too, where several articles, starting in 2004, headlined Mtwara. He'd been around for over twenty years, and quick calculations told me he must be a year or two older than Jared. He had international credits, and I got caught up in a distressing story in *The Christian Science Monitor*. He'd interviewed dozens of returnees and detailed the ostracism faced by Senegalese immigrants returning from Europe when they failed to make it in France. "The young men fled crushing poverty only to find themselves oppressed by slavers and forced to pay thousands to smugglers. They question whether they should ever have left home, but now home doesn't welcome them." He'd reported from other Francophone countries in West Africa, too, often about the downtrodden, the victims of sex trafficking, corrupt politicians, and counterfeit medicine. Huh. For the past ten years his reports came from both West and East Africa. He'd been crisscrossing the continent.

I must have dozed. When my mobile's message alert *pinged* at 6:30 p.m., I came to like I'd been slammed in the chest. I smacked the bedside table as I groped for the phone and sat up to read the screen.

I had a straight-to-voicemail message from Jared's number.

My shaking fingers missed the icons twice before I got it to play. I inhaled sharply as Jared's voice, modulated and unnaturally distinct, spoke to me.

"Ana, it's Jared. This is important. I'm okay now but won't be unless you can raise one hundred-twenty-five-thousand dollars cash. Stay calm. We have a week. This is doable. Call the Loubets. Remember their son. Do not contact anyone else. *No* authorities." There was a brief scuffling sound, then silence.

I breathed out. I did a slow deep breath in and carefully tapped the replay option and the speaker icon.

The voice, unquestionably Jared's, spoke exactly the same sentences. I listened once more before I rushed out to find Fiona and Geoffrey.

I found Geoffrey first, in his office on the computer, having a pre-dinner drink.

I shoved my phone at him, tapping the icons as I did. "Listen. Just got this."

He held the device to his ear and jumped as the hollow speaker voice came through. His eyes widened. As Jared's voice mentioned "authorities," he blew out a long breath. He looked at the screen and fumbled. "Let's hear it again," he said, handing me back the phone. We listened together. He took the phone, rose, and hurried out of the room, waving the device and calling, "Fi! Fi! Can you come hear this?"

I was right behind him.

We found Fiona in the kitchen, showing Sean how to use a pastry bag to add little curlicues of whipped cream to the top of a fancy layer cake. She looked up in alarm, and Geoffrey and I skidded to a stop like cartoon characters as we took in the scene with Sean. She had the presence of mind not to gasp or demand an explanation. Instead, with a flourish, she stuck her finger right into Sean's latest dollop and licked it off.

"Hey," he protested. I held my breath for a moment, then relaxed when he laughed.

"Better do that one again, my boy," she said with a wicked grin. "You might want to taste a few yourself! Now, keep at it for a second, and I'll be right back."

The three of us got out the door before Sean had a chance to ask any questions. Another time I'd have hooted at the look on his face. Now I was weak with relief that he didn't follow us.

"What's happened?" Fiona demanded, once we were out of earshot, hurrying through the door into Geoffrey's office.

"Listen!" We huddled on chairs, and I held the phone in the middle of our little circle. I played the message once again. The new reality was starting to take shape in my mind: Jared was okay, but bad people had him. I needed money to get him back.

"So, we're talking about a ransom demand," said Geoffrey, leaning back in his chair.

"Wait," said Fiona, quirking an eyebrow. "Are we sure that's Jared speaking?"

"It's Jared's voice," I said flatly. "It just came."

Geoffrey leaned back into the circle. "Although I suppose a recording might have been made earlier?"

We looked at each other in silence for several seconds. The ticking of the wall clock filled the room. Fiona scraped a hand through her hair.

I fidgeted with my earlobe. "Let's not second guess. Let's act as though it was just made and it means exactly what it says."

We stared at one another for several more seconds until Geoffrey broke the silence.

"One-hundred-twenty-five-thousand. That's an odd amount. Not enough for most groups to justify an abduction, but a large sum around here — and not easy to come up with quickly in US dollars."

"Who are the Loubets?" asked Fiona.

Sean appeared at the office door. "Ahmed said to tell you dinner's on the table. And the cake's done." He narrowed his eyes at us. "What's going on?"

Fiona jumped up and gave Sean a light clap on his shoulder. "What's going on is we're going to eat. You ready?"

At the dinner table, once again, Sean's presence forced

me into behavior that taxed me, but I was glad for it. I worked on keeping my hands steady and forked small even bites into my mouth. Fiona deserved an award for her acting, making normal conversation, even getting laughs from Sean a few times. Everyone made special efforts to *ooh* and *ahh* at the cake.

Dinner seemed to go on forever, but finally it was time for Sean to be excused and go to bed. I'd never exercised such self-control as I did in our guest room. He insisted on telling me about the latest chapter in the *Redwall* series book he was reading. I clenched my jaw to keep from exploding as he described in excruciating detail the relationships among swashbuckling small mammals decked out in little boots, caps, and jackets. I'd learned to set a time limit on these cozy bedtimes, and when we were finished, I flew to Geoffrey's office, where he and Fiona were speaking in low tones.

I was numb with exhaustion, but the latest events had me grinding my teeth as I sank into an easy chair.

"So, who are the Loubets?" asked Geoffrey.

I touched my forehead. Right. I hadn't had a chance yet to think about the Loubets, and I started to pull up shadowy memories.

The Loubets had been *Tante* Giselle and *Oncle* Luc to Jared and me. They were friends of my parents, from international work they'd shared when I was too young to pay attention. I couldn't remember the last time I'd seen them, but it must have been at least fifteen years before, right after I graduated from ISM. Jared had spent several summers living with them in Paris so knew them better than I did. They were immensely wealthy, with old family money, and I always thought he loved the options that came along with so much affluence. I guess anyone would.

A hazy memory dwelt in the back of my mind in which my parents helped them in some crisis, and they had been terribly grateful. They had one son, who was at least a decade older than Jared — maybe a journalist? I'd met him once or twice.

Now, I spilled out this information to Fi and Geoffrey.

Geoffrey interrupted politely. "So," he said, leaning forward and propping his elbows on his wide-spread knees. "These are wealthy people who owe your family a favor? Have I got that right?"

"Yeah, I guess so." I chewed at my lower lip. "I think that's fair to say. That's got to be why Jared mentioned them. He knows them well."

"Oh dear," said Fiona, breathing out so her words sounded more like a sigh. "We're talking about paying a ransom. Shouldn't we consult with someone? What about your embassy?"

Geoffrey stuck out his lower lip and slowly shook his head. "I still don't think we should involve them." He looked pained. "Okay, here's some more of what I learned this afternoon." He ran his hand through his hair. "You remember a year or two ago? An American journalist in Syria?"

An incident I'd been trying not to think about stood now like an enormous elephant in the office. The young man in question had been abducted in Syria. The US government had refused to negotiate, and he was killed.

Geoffrey continued. "In 2015, in response to pressure from his family, the US set up an interagency body called the Hostage Recovery Fusion Cell. It's supposed to make sure all intel is shared and used in abduction cases. It reaches up to the highest levels in the FBI, State Department, National Security Council — all the big ones. But," he shifted in his chair and leaned forward to make his point, "it doesn't change the basic policy of the US, which is to refuse to negotiate or to pay ransom to terrorists with American hostages." He ran his hand through his hair again. "And here's something else — the family says they were threatened with prosecution by the US government if they paid."

"No wonder Jared's adamant about keeping this quiet," I said.

"I think you need to contact the Loubets," said Geoffrey, leaning back. "Find out if they'll see you. You'd need to leave very early tomorrow and go through Nairobi, but there's a new daytime flight to Europe you can likely get on."

A flicker of hope flared somewhere inside me. Something constructive to do. I could contact the Loubets.

"And what about this," said Fiona, cradling her chin. "Take Sean with you. If Beth will meet you, you can take him out of here."

"Yeahhh." I nodded, first slowly then faster. "That makes sense." The flicker grew into a small flame. We were moving forward. I looked at my watch. Nearly 10:00 p.m. That made it 2:00 p.m. for Beth and 9:00 p.m. in Paris. Perfect!

My activities depended on the Loubets, so I called them first. I sank back in the chair when Luc answered the phone. I didn't go into details with him, but I made sure he knew it was important. Thank God he didn't press me for information. He agreed to meet me on Monday morning, which was as soon as I could arrive there, after — I hoped — seeing Beth and reuniting her with Sean on Sunday night. I signaled a thumbs up to Fiona, who'd watched me pace as I spoke into my phone.

The conversation with Beth was more difficult, and my hands shook as I called. She was in a meeting. I hated to do it, but there was no way to avoid alarming her when I told her secretary it was urgent. I remembered to insist she start by telling Beth that Sean was fine, but it didn't help much. Beth was on the line in a few seconds.

"Ana? What's happened to Sean?" Fear throbbed in her voice.

"Sean's fine, absolutely fine. I promise. He's asleep in bed or I'd put him on the phone." I heard her exhale, and I kept going. "But, he needs to return to the US. The problem is Jared."

"Jared?" The tension disappeared and her voice went flat. "What's Jared done?"

I was a wounded animal pulled between two predatory birds. I took a deep breath even as she rephrased her words.

"I mean, what's happened to him?"

I swallowed. "He's been abducted, Beth. It occurred yesterday."

"Abducted! Yesterday? Where's Sean? Why am I only hearing about this now?"

"Sean is with me here in Moshi with friends. And, like I said, he's fine. Asleep right now in bed. He doesn't even know about Jared." I took another deep breath. "Look, Beth, this isn't easy. I'll give you all the details when we see you. Let's organize travel first. I'd like to bring Sean up to Paris. I think I can get us on a flight tomorrow, which would put us into Paris in the evening. We can meet you there. It's best if he's out of this country." I heard her sharp intake of breath before her rapid-fire response.

"Why Paris? What about you? Does the Embassy know?"

"Beth — wait. Listen. I haven't contacted the Embassy, and I don't want to do that. I've been advised specifically *not* to let anyone know." My throat was tight, strangling my voice. "Please trust me on this. Trust me and don't talk to anyone about Jared. Come meet Sean. I'll tell you everything when I see you."

"Okay, Ana. Okay." She took in a long breath. "Call me back when you have your tickets. I can book a flight out of here tonight. I'll do it as soon as we hang up." She exhaled.

I pictured her running her hands over her face.

"I'm sorry, but I'm in shock. This'll take some time to understand." Her voice became softer. "I appreciate your taking care of Sean. Don't let anything happen to him."

17

SUNDAY, SEPTEMBER 3

I'd managed to lie down for two hours after my last conversation with Beth — and it had taken several calls to arrange everything. She'd cancelled all her afternoon appointments and found a flight leaving Detroit that evening. She'd be in Paris before we were. I figured she liked it that way, and I didn't blame her. She'd want to grab Sean the minute he stepped into the arrival hall.

"Why are we going to the airport? Why isn't Dad going back with us?" were among the whiney questions Sean had when I woke him at 5:00 a.m. He rubbed his eyes with his fists.

An hour earlier, tossing around sleepless in bed, I'd decided not to tell him the truth. "Your dad's been delayed by a sick patient and he has to stay in Mtwara," I said without a shred of shame for lying. "I've got to spend more time looking at projects here, but, guess what? Your mom's going to meet us on the way back."

As we sped toward the airport, dawn breaking, featuring silhouettes of acacia against a pinky-orange sky that belonged on postcards. A lone Maasai child herding goats waved at us with his entire arm and shoulder.

I turned my attention from the view to check email on my phone. Andrew again. *Brad's developing good ideas. I need to hear more from you about project possibilities.* The knot in my stomach tightened and I hit my thigh with my fist, suppressing a mild curse as Sean looked up at me with curiosity. Drawing in a slow breath I reminded myself how important it was to make this trip as smooth as possible. I assumed a cheerful expression. Andrew would have to wait for now.

During the flight north, Sean blasted away at space aliens on the entertainment system while I watched dumb romcoms. I lost count of the miniature bags of Smarties and airplane-shaped Goldfish crackers I ate. I didn't even look at what Sean consumed. With the obliviousness of a nine-year-old in front of a screen, placated with packets of junk food, he was uncon-cerned by changes in plans he hadn't made. He asked no more questions about Jared. He'd had a good time in Tanzania and was soon to see his mom. I feigned nonchalance.

Ten hours after boarding in Nairobi we descended into a darkening Paris. Crushed into the plane's aisle with passen-gers pulling down their overhead luggage and jockeying for position to deboard, I texted Grace to catch her up on progress and answered a couple of messages on my phone from students. Andrew would be starting a new workday and there was nothing else from him. I'd need to send some reassurance soon. Ellen Mafwiri had responded that it was too bad I couldn't make the KI training.

A minor sense of accomplishment buoyed me as Sean and I stepped off the jetway. At least I'd got him this far. We sailed through the efficient immigration system and retrieved our bags without problems. No one stopped us at customs and my heart leaped to find Beth peering around in the arrival hall, next to the "Meeting Point" sign. A sliver of hope penetrated my dark mood as Sean flew into his mother's arms.

BETH KNOCKED on the door of my connecting room at our airport hotel later, after she got Sean into bed. She got right to the point. "Tell me exactly what happened."

I showed her the first text, filled in the events after that, and activated the voice message for her to hear. "It's Jared's voice, isn't it?" I said, studying her eyes.

Her head barely moved in assent. "No question. What are you going to do?" She crossed her legs at the knee and a stiletto dangled elegantly on one foot.

"I'm meeting the Loubets tomorrow morning."

"Jared truly could be in danger, couldn't he?" I heard less angst in her voice than I expected. She might have been describing anyone. I glared at her.

"Look, Ana, this *is* terrible. Of course it is. And I'm worried about Jared. I'm also concerned about Sean. What does he know?"

I sighed and kept my eyes locked on hers. "I told him Jared had a problem with a patient, which was delaying his return. I thought you should figure out what more to tell him — if anything."

"Okay. Thank you for that." She let the dangling shoe drop, removed the other one, curled her legs up, and rubbed her feet. After a few seconds she stood and walked barefoot to the mini bar to pour us mineral water. For the first time since landing I took a good look at her standing figure —

and then a second look. With her slim build it was obvious. Beth was pregnant.

"When?" I stammered in shock.

She sat back down in an armchair with her back straight and rubbed her belly gently. Her face glowed. "You met Paul. The baby's due in February."

"Does Jared know?"

Beth sighed. "Yes. Jared knows." Her voice softened. "But it's not Jared's business. Our marriage is over." She narrowed her eyes. "I told Jared I wanted a divorce many months ago."

Blood drain from my face.

She put down her water and slipped over onto the couch to put an arm around me. "I'm sorry, Ana. I thought Jared would have told you."

He hadn't. He'd never mentioned divorce. My mind flew back to the conversation we'd had on the beach in Zanzibar. Deception? Or was he lying to himself too? I broke away from her embrace. "How long has he known about the baby?"

"Only since a few days ago, on Wednesday morning — Wednesday afternoon in Tanzania. I told him then." Her voice hardened. "I hoped the pregnancy might force him to be more realistic about divorce."

"I haven't spoken to Jared since then. He's been talking this whole time like he thinks the two of you will reconcile." I tore into a packet of nuts from the flight and chewed without tasting. Swallowing wasn't easy. "How'd he take the news of the baby?"

"Badly. He's angry, among other things." She narrowed her eyes. "Frankly, it's harder and harder to maintain civility. We've done it so far, for Sean's sake, but I'm fed up with him." She took in a deep breath and produced a loud, slow exhalation. "Another thing, unrelated. One of the corporations I work with — one that I introduced Jared to several years ago — is having to reduce their support to his non-profit. I guess they won't tell him officially until he's back home. I told Jared to give him a heads up. Maybe I shouldn't have. I feel bad about it now."

We sat in awkward silence for a few seconds. Beth reached out to put her hand on my arm again. "I am sorry. Sorry about the failed marriage and the way Jared's taking it, and sorry he's gone missing now." She paused. "I'll help you any way I can."

I studied her face. "Thank you, Beth. You've been a dear friend, and I don't want that to change."

"I don't either." She gave me another squeeze and moved back to the armchair.

I took a deep breath. "I don't want to pry. But I'm searching for anything now to help me understand what's happened. He must have been distraught on Wednesday when you talked to him, but the resident, Thomas, didn't notice anything unusual on Thursday. And he didn't disappear until Friday."

She cocked her head and kept her eyes on mine.

"Was there anything else going on in his life, anything that could explain this? I never understood what went wrong with the two of you."

Beth looked down and produced an explosive breath. "Oh, Ana. You know him as an older brother — you don't see him as I do. He's supported you over the years, but he also likes the influence he has over you." She rubbed her brow. "He's deeply insecure."

I opened my mouth to protest

"Oh, not about his work, which is technical. It's about his personal worth. He compensates by trying to control people. You must have noticed his attitude about Mark?"

She gave me no chance to answer.

"Mark's impervious to his efforts and it maddens Jared. He resents the influence he thinks Mark has on you. I tried to talk to Jared about it, but he clams up, insists Mark's not the right guy for you."

I frowned. There were obviously things Beth didn't understand. Jared would never begrudge me the chance of a good relationship.

She stood up and slipped her shoes back on. "I want to go check on Sean. And I imagine we both need to sleep. Are you going to be okay here?" She moved our empty glasses and the water bottle over to the bar. "Sean and I are scheduled for a ten-thirty a.m. flight back to Detroit. Can we have a quick breakfast at seven?"

"Sure. I'm fine. I'll see you downstairs tomorrow."

Beth and I hugged good night, and I changed and fell into bed, dreading another long fitful night. I was more alone than I'd ever been in my life.

18

MONDAY, SEPTEMBER 4

Breakfast was a rushed affair. Beth managed to pull me aside as we hurried through a buffet. "I decided not to tell Sean about Jared. I worried about it all night, but I'm going to let him believe what you told him. He hasn't asked, so I haven't had to tell an outright lie — yet."

I piled scrambled eggs on my plate, took a piece of bacon for good measure, and smiled wanly at Beth. "I know it's hard. I'll keep you updated when I learn more."

"Sean, watch that cinnamon roll! And can you go save that small table for us, please?" Beth gestured toward a corner of the busy room. With Sean out of earshot, she turned to me. "I forgot to mention something. I saw Mark for a couple of minutes after you called me about Jared." She lifted the cover of a chafing dish and made a face at the contents. "I ran into him in the lobby of my office building. I didn't say anything about Jared or meeting here. Figured you'd do that yourself." She met my eyes. "He's a good man, Ana. I hope you'll let him help you through this. And don't let Jared's opinions about him color yours."

"I won't. And I'll talk to Mark soon."

We hurried over to join Sean and wolfed our food. Beth wiped her mouth, draped her used napkin elegantly on her clean plate, and nudged Sean. "Gotta go, buddy. Planes don't wait."

I hugged Sean, grateful he couldn't see my face, which I feared would be streaming with tears any second. "See you back home," I said, with all the false cheer I could muster.

Thank God for the detachment of a nine-year-old boy.

I GOT a text from Mark on my phone as I returned to my hotel room after breakfast. *Ready for bed. Wish you were here. What's up? Haven't heard much. Tell me all is okay.* I closed my eyes. I didn't want to see this. Not because Mark's message was out of line, or bad in any way — it was characteristic of the good guy Beth recommended. Part of me desperately wanted to tell him what was up, but I couldn't square it with the warning to tell no one. But Mark wasn't "no one" was he? Telling Mark might be disloyal to Jared, but it was disloyalty to Mark that made me feel sick as I texted back. *All good. Just busy. More soon.*

Another message, from Geoffrey, followed immediately, and made my pulse bound. *Reached Haamed. Call me.*

"Geoffrey?" I burst out, giving him no chance to say hello. "What did you learn?"

"Are you all right?" His calm, reasonable voice soothed me. "Is Sean safely back with his mother?"

"Yes." I twiddled my earring. "What happened with Haamed?"

"Okay. I did reach him by phone. He's reluctant to become involved, but he didn't say no either."

I slumped. I'd been pinning a lot of hope on this.

"I asked him to think it over. There's a chance he'll come around. When do you see the Loubets?"

"I was just reminding myself how to navigate the Metro. I'm supposed to meet them at eleven this morning." I glanced at my watch. "I need to run. Thanks for your help with Haamed — and everything else," I added, my voice threatening to dissolve in tears.

"Chin up, Ana. Go get it sorted with the Loubets and keep us informed. We're here for you."

I WAS SOMETIMES CLAUSTROPHOBIC, but that morning the confined tunnels of the Metro on the journey calmed me, kept me from flying apart in a million directions. I got off the line at Alma-Marceau and found the Loubets' home near Avenue Montaigne in the 8th Arrondissement just before 11:00.

It had been years since I'd been there, and it wasn't as big as I remembered, but their ground floor flat was still an impressive upper-class home. I rang the bell with a fresh sense of determination. I was moving ahead. Jared had his reasons for instructing me to come here.

Luc, in a neat linen shirt and summer-weight wool slacks, answered the door himself.

"Ana!" He ushered me into the house, embraced me, and kissed both my cheeks, all in one fluid movement. His silver hair gleamed from a light pomade, giving off a faint odor that reminded me of my father. "We were so surprised by your call — and frankly, worried."

"I know. I'm sorry." I'd been too self-absorbed to consider how the Loubets might feel.

Luc patted my arm. "No worry, Ana. Giselle's in the garden waiting now."

We walked through an elegant foyer and hallway where dark eastern African carvings and basketry hung in lighted recesses in the smooth white walls. At the back of the hall, tall glass doors opened onto a small summer garden just past its prime, but beautiful in the still-cool morning air. We stepped through the doors as Giselle limped up a pathway to meet us. I was shocked to see her hobbling gait. She was about my size but managed to envelop me within her light cashmere shawl and the silk scarves draped artfully around her neck.

"Ana. You're the image of your mother. How good it is to see you! Come, sit down." She led me to a set of wicker armchairs around a table, and the three of us sat. I sniffed jasmine from trellises thick with it a few meters away.

A young woman in trim trousers and a simple cotton shirt appeared to confer with Giselle.

"*Merci*, Claudette," said Giselle before she turned to me. "Would you like a coffee?" When I hesitated, she smiled. "Or perhaps a *tisane* of mint or verbena?"

I wanted to cradle something in my hands so I accepted a cup of mint tea.

Luc cleared his throat. "Please, let us know why you're here. We assume it's a matter of some urgency." He dipped his distinguished head formally.

"Yes, I'm sorry to be rushed and blunt. Thank you for understanding the need for that."

Giselle's smile faded and she raised her eyebrows in encouragement.

"You know I've come from Tanzania. Jared and I were there on a visit." I swallowed. "He was abducted in the

Mtwara Region three days ago — Friday. He's being held for a ransom." The bare words sounded unreal in my ears.

Giselle lifted her chin and her subtly made-up eyes grew wide.

Luc leaned forward, took off his glasses and tapped the table top with them. "*Alors*. Tell us everything, starting with why both of you were in Tanzania and what happened once you arrived there."

I told the story as succinctly as possible, using my phone at the appropriate points to let them see and hear the messages. Luc caught his breath when he heard Jared suggest I contact his family. Giselle turned white. She and Luc exchanged a long look.

I swallowed and plunged forward. "I don't understand why, but I believe Jared suggested I contact you to ask for the money."

"*D'accord*," said Luc, laying his glasses down and leaning back in his chair as Giselle slumped in hers. "I expect that is correct." He studied me in silence for many seconds. He closed his eyes for some moments, opened them, and spoke. "I should tell you a story we rarely speak about, and one I think you don't know.

"Perhaps you remember Giselle and I worked with your parents back in 1995," began Luc. "We'd left Tanzania then, and we lived in Nairobi. You wouldn't have paid a lot of attention to our son, Alain, since he's about fifteen years older than you."

That was true. I would have been starting school at ISM around then.

Luc took several sips of his coffee, pursed his lips, and continued. "Alain was a journalist working in Tanzania, based in Dar. He was investigating a Tanzanian business-man, John Ntabaye. Alain had evidence Ntabaye was embezzling from a large aid project." Luc shook his head. "With the enthusiasm of youth and the righteous, he was determined to expose him. But before he succeeded, he was abducted."

A shock went through me. I was hypersensitive to any mention of abduction. Luc's matter-of-fact way of talking made the tale more chilling and not less.

"A ransom was demanded, but it wasn't clear who was behind it. No group claimed credit."

Giselle took up the story, twisting her arthritic hands in her lap as she spoke. "The French government had a different attitude about ransoms than the Americans. They were willing to negotiate with the abductors — and we were definitely prepared to pay for Alain's safety." Her voice threatened to break with sadness and Luc took over again.

"No one had as much experience dealing with kidnappings then as they do now. We agreed to the first demand they made."

Luc shook his head and looked away. A muscle in Giselle's cheek jumped as she clenched her jaw. It was costing them to re-live this.

Luc looked back, straight at me. "Then they raised the ultimatum."

"It was unbearable," said Giselle. "How much would we pay for our son? We'd pay anything. But we weren't prepared for the emotional devastation of a back and forth. I've never been in such agony."

Luc patted her arm, keeping his eyes fixed on me. "It was your parents, Ana, who stepped in and saved us. They knew us, they knew our situation, and your father was a brilliant strategist and diplomat. He offered to take over, and we stood back."

"It was the worst sort of torture. I don't think I'd have survived another hour of it at that point," said Giselle.

I shivered. This lovely dignified couple knew the same terrors that gripped me.

"I still don't know everything that was said — by your father or by those with whom he negotiated," said Luc. "In truth, I only wanted it to be finished. And, in time, it was. He arranged a deal, the money was handed over, and Alain was released. We owe him for our son's life."

"Did you ever find out who was responsible?"

"No one ever proved Ntabaye was behind it — the deed went unpunished, as did the embezzlement of which I'm sure he was guilty."

I was drained. This was all new to me. I remembered my mother talking about the Loubet family being fed up, bitter about Tanzania, but some people became disillusioned with work in Africa, and I didn't ask for any details back then. My parents worked in the human rights arena, and it seemed to me they were involved in dramatic incidents all the time.

Looking at it now, I wasn't surprised I was ignorant of the situation at fourteen. Jared, a couple of years older, and closer to the Loubets than I, had obviously learned the details. I tried to imagine the family's ordeal. No wonder they wanted nothing more to do with Tanzania. Now I was pulling them back in.

My tea was cold, and I hadn't moved a muscle for several minutes. The oxygen had been pulled out of the air. A bird's trilling sounded from miles away.

Giselle shifted in her chair and spoke. "But this happened twenty years ago. Hasn't the US changed their policy about paying ransoms? I mean, since that American journalist was killed?" She looked at the ground and shook her head. "Ah, the poor family."

"The change is to say they won't prosecute citizens who choose to pay criminal groups," said Luc. "The US government still won't negotiate. They've taken an intractable stand on this in spite of the lack of evidence that paying ransom does harm." He smoothed his hand, trembling slightly, over his coiffed hair. "France and Spain both negotiate, and they have a significantly higher rate of returned captives than does the US. Of course, it's true that hostages have no value to kidnappers if they know there'll be no payout. But does that result in fewer abductions or in more killings of those taken? It's an old debate, and a complicated one, without a clear answer."

He shifted, frowning so that vertical lines, delineating three distinct sections, emerged on his forehead. He moved agitated fingers through his hair, leaving it in disarray. "In Jared's case now, I think you're right not to involve the Embassy or the officials. We'll provide the money."

I sagged in the chair. I'd been holding my breath. "Thank you," I said. It was wholly inadequate. I bowed my head, as if I were in a church.

But we still had a hurdle to cross.

"Getting this much cash to you in Tanzania is going to be difficult," Luc said, "and we don't have a lot of time." He stroked his chin. "Transferring this sum from my accounts in Europe is possible, but you can't simply walk into a bank and withdraw this much money in Tanzania, even if you had an account. We have a number of contacts we can call on for help in the private sector, but it's still going to be tough." He continued to rub his chin. "Giselle, what do you think?"

"We'll struggle to come up with anyone who can produce even twenty-five-thousand dollars in a hurry —

and we need five times that. Do you have any way to access US cash in Tanzania yourself, Ana?"

I shook my head. Foreign currency was hard to come by.

"We'll have to rely on friends of mine and some of the private Bureaux de Change — and we need to start right now." Giselle was transformed, looking nothing like the sweet older lady who'd hobbled up the path earlier.

I recalled her career had been in international finance and banking. There was more than one reason Jared had suggested I contact the Loubets.

Luc glanced at his watch. "We haven't got any time to waste," he said, rising. "I don't think there's anything you can do to help with this, Ana. Can you excuse us to make some calls?"

We weren't in the clear yet, but events were moving in the right direction. I pressed my hand to my chest. I was exhausted, as though a plug had been pulled and everything that had held me up was draining out.

"You'll have lunch with us, and we'll take you back to your hotel," said Giselle, getting up herself. "Why don't you enjoy the garden for a bit — or would you rather take a short nap? Shall I ask Claudette to bring you more tea? Are your reservations made to go back to Tanzania tomorrow?"

They were, but now I'd do an online check-in with a sense of accomplishment before lunch at 2:00.

"EXCUSE GISELLE, please. She's on the phone," said Luc as he and I sat down to eat together.

I went back to the garden after lunch, where I tried to distract myself with an early Sue Grafton novel. I'd enjoyed a couple of these for Kinsey Millhone's irreverent attitude toward conventional femininity, but she couldn't make me laugh, or even keep my attention, this time. After I had started the same paragraph three times, I put my Kindle down and paced in the garden.

At 4:30, Giselle emerged through the tall glass doors. Luc followed her out with a bottle of mineral water and three glasses.

"I think we're set," she said. "I've got five people in Dar who can each come up with twenty-five thousand in cash." She dropped into a chair.

Luc poured water, and I took a seat at the little round table.

"Three of these parties prefer to bring the cash to you at your hotel. The other two want you to pick it up from them. I can verify your identity by phone if they desire before they hand funds over. That's no problem. But it'll need to be carefully coordinated. They'll try to obtain it as hundred-dollar bills — new ones — to keep the bulk down, but they all can't guarantee that."

A vision of the dirty, rumpled paper money in Tanzania flitted through my mind. "Thank you, Giselle." I struggled to find more meaningful words but only shook my head as tears seeped into the corners of my eyes.

Luc reached across the table and laid his hand on my arm. "It's good to be able to repay your parents."

THEY INSISTED on taking me back to the hotel, and I was in my room by 7:00 p.m., feeling a lifetime had passed since I'd said goodbye to Sean and Beth that morning.

I ordered dinner from room service and texted Geoffrey. *All good. Loubets arranging money. See you tomorrow night.*

The phone *pinged* a reply. *Good. Will meet your flight. Safe trip.*

I sent a short message to Grace and considered calling Mark and telling him everything. I convinced myself I didn't want to worry him.

In the fuzzy land between sleep and wakefulness, about 10:30 p.m., my phone rang.

It was Luc. "Sorry, Ana. One of the contacts we were counting on has fallen through. You'll have to carry some cash yourself."

"That doesn't sound too bad. I've got a money belt I feel secure with."

"The problem is that the legal limit you can take out of France is ten thousand Euro, and you'll have double that. Charles de Gaulle Airport installed body scanners in the past year. Not only can they detect bulk under clothes, but the metallic strips on US bills show up. They can estimate how much cash you have."

"Oh." I was suddenly wide awake, anxiety building. Would our painstaking plans fall through now?

"I'd be willing to fly down myself with half of it, but heart disease doesn't allow me the long-haul flights anymore. Giselle doesn't fly either. Let us give it more thought tonight. Can we meet at eight tomorrow morning in your room?"

I did a quick calculation. I'd do an online hotel check-out, meet Luc, and still clear security and be at my gate by 10:00 a.m. "That'll work. Thank you."

I tossed and turned through a long night. I had to get the money.

19

TUESDAY, SEPTEMBER 5

L uc called from the lobby at 8:00 the next morning. I'd been trying unsuccessfully to distract myself with a book since 5:30 a.m., and I was ready for him. The stack of bills he pulled from his coat in my room was an inch thick. "This is twenty-five thousand, Ana. I'm afraid you'll have to carry it all yourself."

I shivered at the sight of the currency I'd have to carry illegally through customs.

"There's a small risk." Luc took my hand. "If you're caught the money will be confiscated, but you'll most likely be allowed to proceed if you have an excuse ready. Maybe some benevolent but naïve hope that you could just carry money into a country to support a school or a clinic?" He looked straight at me. "I'm willing to risk the money."

I swallowed and picked up the thick stack of bills. My gut tightened at the thought of trying to lie in the face of law enforcement. If caught, I'd probably fall apart and start crying. But I had to do it. I lifted my money belt from the bed.

Luc shook his head. "I don't want you to use that. The

scanners will show the belt, and then you'll have to take it off, and they'll examine it and ask questions. I believe the best option is for you to take the legal limit — roughly half of this — through security in your carry on, spread out in several compartments. The rest of it is going to have to go into a checked bag."

"Money in a checked bag?" He must be kidding.

"I know it's risky, but I see no alternative. Scanners can detect American bills, but not the denomination. Scatter the dollars in two or three wads, in clothes and shoes and books. A lock on the bag will provide some protection against a casual thief. Customs agents will break into it if they want to." He paced the room as he spoke. "Call when you pass through security at Charles de Gaulle and again when you arrive at your friend's house tonight. And take care."

My lower lip trembled as I returned his gentle embrace.

THE FLIGHT ATTENDANTS slammed galley doors and hurried to their jump seats as the plane rolled down the runway and gathered speed. I'd had four days in an emotional pressure cooker, punctuated by brief releases when hope crept in. I'd been jittery for the previous two hours. Every time the airport's public address system crackled into action I expected to hear my name, and to be hauled before a customs agent to explain why I was leaving France with twenty-five thousand US dollars.

But I wasn't paged, nor stopped. Now all I had to worry about was someone breaking into the checked bag, not a rare event in Tanzania. I was worn into brittleness.

I settled in for a ten-hour lull, a daytime flight alone

across the Sahara, where I was protected, insulated from any news, good or bad. Everything was out of my hands. The seat next to me was empty, always a welcome occurrence. I planned to pull out my laptop and make headway on a progress report for work. Anything for distraction from the real issue.

I'd watch a movie first. I selected *Atonement* because I'd loved the book, then decided against it because I'd loved the book so much — movies were never as satisfying. I changed my mind and turned it on again. Two hours later, I admitted it was good — almost as good as the book. I finished it with a great gush of grief and a streaming nose. It was the first good cry I'd had in days — since I learned Jared was in trouble — and, even trying to hold down the noise under a blanket, it eased the tension wrapped like a band around my mind. Whoever said crying doesn't help must not have tried it. I finally gave a last shudder, wrung out, and came out from under the blanket. I couldn't help looking around, but no one was watching me.

I needed to do something about work. Clear as I'd made it that I was using vacation days on this trip, Andrew would expect to hear from me. As far as he was concerned, I was in Tanzania to look into business for the GHI. I'd received another email from him about the nurse training program, this time proposing I might draft an editorial of the "what-can-we-learn-from-this" genre.

I pictured Brad at the reception, chomping samosas, suggesting that the man's main goal was to build up a list of publications. Still, Andrew had a point — and I was the one who'd railed at Jared about learning from mistakes.

I needed to discipline myself, put my immediate fears away long enough to write a report. But it wasn't coming easily. What had I seen? The nurse training project, which offered important lessons, but wasn't something the GHI could build on. A so-called school eye screening, recommended by Jared, which had American medical students masquerading as doctors. The possibility I was most interested in — the key informants — I'd had no chance to investigate fully, due to Jared's situation.

I thought uneasily about the work Jared did in Africa. It wasn't a long-term solution to the problem of blindness in eastern Africa, regardless of how he tried to pitch it. A platoon of foreign volunteer surgeons couldn't eliminate blindness from cataract. The public health strategy — educating villagers to seek help for failing vision and establishing a network of affordable services staffed by local doctors — was slow hard work and it didn't excite people. Jared wasn't even training local people, but his approach got donors to open their wallets. Why was I thinking about this now, with his life in danger? My head hurt.

I shut the laptop and tried to stretch over into the empty seat. I wasn't going to get any work done. My work — my whole life — was on hold.

I spent the remainder of the flight flicking from one movie to another, trying to find something distracting. I pulled my feet up under me one minute and itched to unfold my legs the next. The seats had never felt so small.

The moment the plane touched the ground at the Kilimanjaro airport, I checked my phone for messages.

Nothing.

I hurried across the tarmac at the bottom of the stairs and was the second person through the visa line. I rushed to the baggage carousel and wormed my way forward, chewing my lower lip as I watched the belt lumber to life. My knees nearly buckled with relief when my bag emerged through the flaps onto the conveyor belt. It looked untouched, the lock intact.

A crowd of men stood outside the arrivals building, waving signs from Arusha hotels and safari companies. Two men approached, grinning broadly. "Taxi? Taxi, Madam?" yelled the one in a multicolored knit cap. The other made a lunge for my bag. I jerked it back and shook my head, and they pivoted to try their luck with someone else.

Thank God, the Walkers stood at the back of the crowd, craning their necks.

They saw me, and we headed toward each other. Fiona pulled me into an embrace. "Flight okay, Ana?"

Geoffrey, behind her, threw an arm around my shoulders. "You all right then?" he said, hearty as always, but with a warm smile. "I talked to Haamed again earlier this afternoon. No promises, but he's willing to meet you tomorrow." He took my bag and started toward his car, out in the lot. "I've booked you on a flight to Dar in the morning. I expect you can use a quiet night now."

"I can. But I won't rest until I check that my bag's not been opened." I took it from him at the car and laid it in the back. Digging through folded clothes, unzipping inner compartments and toiletry bags, and poking my hand into shoes and socks, I retrieved thirteen thousand dollars. Fi and Geoffrey watched with open mouths.

"That was a hell of a risk, Ana."

"I know. I had no choice." I told them the whole story as we drove to the house.

20

WEDNESDAY, SEPTEMBER 6

Resentment washed over me as the alarm split the air at 5:00 the next morning. First time I'd been asleep at that time in days, so the disruption was doubly offensive. The guy who'd dumped me in London used to laugh about the insomniac's prayer: to dream, perchance to sleep. Not funny then or now. No one who didn't suffer from it understood the injustice of insomnia. The more exhausted I was, the more difficult it was to relax into slumber. The day following a bad night was often a complete write-off, and angst over that made me grind my teeth as I flopped back and forth through long, dark nights.

Now I dragged myself, with heavy head, leaden limbs, and bleary eyes, from the bed, feeling like I'd been hit by a train. Ahmed had tea and toast ready for me, and I blessed him for this kindness.

Geoffrey tossed my bag in the car and drove me along the all-too-familiar road to the airport, where I arrived with all twenty-five-thousand dollars on my person and plenty of time to spare. The small domestic flights were known to leave ahead of schedule sometimes — although not as often as they left behind — so it didn't pay to cut it too close. The crystal-clear view of Kilimanjaro as we banked eastward was a treat, but I found it difficult to enjoy.

Forty-five minutes after we took off in the cool morning air of Kilimanjaro, I was in Dar, sweltering in a taxi on my way to a downtown hotel, shedding the scarf I'd needed around my neck earlier. I planned to meet Haamed Hassan at ten o'clock.

I was savoring a cup of strong tea with plenty of milk from a thick mug in the lobby of my hotel when a man appeared from behind me, graceful as a big cat. I jumped, sloshing a khaki-colored stain on my clean white shirt.

"I'm sorry. I didn't mean to startle you," he said, his face serious but with a hint of a smile. "I believe you're Ana Lotner, aren't you?" He was tall, over six feet, and slender. He looked at me with dark caramel brown eyes, from behind square tortoiseshell spectacles that skimmed his cheek bones. He had the high forehead and straight, narrow nose I associated with people from the Horn of Africa. His hair was carefully coiffed, top longer than sides, and he was dressed in smart, well-cut linen slacks of a pale green that was picked up perfectly in the small pattern of the African print shirt he wore. A gold chain glinted out of the open neck. Definitely a handsome man. "May I?" he asked as he melted into the armchair across from me, and crossed his legs. "I'm going to have a coffee. And samosas. Would you like something?"

I watched him as he swept his gaze over the entire room. In spite of his polish there was something in him that looked slightly vulnerable. I sort of wanted to reach out and adjust his collar, although it was likely in better position than mine.

Wariness weighed on me. I was about to take an

irrevocable step, confiding in him the details of Jared's
disappearance. I had Geoffrey's reassurances about this guy,
but I needed to pay attention to my own gut responses.

"I'd like another pot of tea, with a small pitcher of milk,
please."

He beckoned a waiter with hands twice the size of mine,
the ringless fingers long and slender with neatly trimmed
nails. The way he signaled the server made me think of the
graceful movements of an Indian dancer.

I scooted my chair a bit closer to him and plunged
ahead. Telling the story this time took far longer. Haamed
wanted background on my family, information the Walkers
and Loubets already knew.

"Your parents were Robert and Alicia Lotner?" he asked
with raised eyebrows, looking up from writing in a little
notebook he took from his shirt pocket. "Who worked for
the tribunal in Arusha? I was sorry about their passing.
Their work helped to bring some justice in a terrible
situation."

I acknowledged the kindness with a nod.

He sat up straighter and looked at me, eyes half closed.
He wanted dozens of other details. He listened to the voice
message from Jared over and over. "Sound like the ocean in
the background to you?" he asked.

"No, at least I don't think so," I said. But I hadn't noticed
it before.

I shouldn't have been surprised at all the questions. He
was a journalist, and details were his business.

"Your brother's never worked at this hospital in Mtwara
before, but what about other hospitals in Tanzania?" He
wanted to know Jared's opinions about the current government. Would he be likely to talk politics with locals? Did he

have colleagues in the country? Who paid him to do this work? Why would he leave a successful practice in the US to volunteer in Tanzania? How did it benefit him?

"Everything isn't about money," I said, giving him a hard smile. "Jared wants to make the world a better place, to help people. It's the way we were brought up."

"Okay," he said, with a small shrug before continuing. "So he isn't paid for this work. What do his American colleagues think of it?"

"Actually, lots of people admire him for it." I hoped I didn't sound defensive. "He's received several awards and been interviewed on radio and TV programs. He inspires people."

"Ahh. He gets good publicity from this. Good press. It helps his image."

What kind of cynic was this man? My early impression that he looked vulnerable evaporated. He knew how to ask questions, and he paid attention to every detail of my answers. But why did I need to defend Jared?

By the time we got around to the issue of the ransom, discouragement was heavy on me. This guy was sure to have some strong opinion on whether I should pay it and plenty of doubts about my ability to get the cash. I explained that friends had agreed to provide the money. "I organized it in Paris, and I'll be collecting it here in Dar tomorrow," I said with a tiny thrill of pride.

"Why are the friends doing this?" he said, eyebrows raised and pencil poised over his little notebook.

I was back on defense again, this time because I had connections with this kind of money. "They're close family friends. French. My parents helped them out some years back." I considered for a second how much I wanted to tell him before pushing on. "In fact, their own son was abducted in Tanzania over twenty years ago."

Haamed stopped his furious scribbling, sat straight up, and leaned forward, narrowing his gaze. "What's their name?" His abruptness startled me.

"Luc and Giselle Loubet," I said. Should I have told him this sooner?

His eyes widened. "Alain Loubet," he breathed, running his cupped hand over his hair. "I was too young to know him myself, but we all know that story." He raised his eyebrows and bit his lower lip. "John Ntabaye. Always thought he was behind it." He took a deep breath and leaned back, staring up at the ceiling for a few moments before he glanced at me and started writing again.

"So why is this so important? What are you thinking?"

He looked up with the ghost of a frown. "I don't know, Ana. But John Ntabaye is still around. In fact, he's rumored to be in the Mtwara area. Definitely worth checking out."

He came back to the ransom amount. "Only a hundred-twenty-five-thousand? You realize that's unusual? These days, most terrorists start in the millions, prepared to negotiate their way down. I take it Jared had no kidnap insurance, or you wouldn't be talking to me."

By 11:45, I was slumped in my chair, wrung out. The five o'clock alarm and Haamed's probing were both taking tolls, in spite of attempts to revive myself with cups of tea.

Haamed took some time reviewing the notes in his little book, then closed it deliberately and slipped it back in his pocket. "Okay," he said, leaning toward me, forearms on the crisp creases of his trousers. He produced the first warm smile I'd seen, and his eyes gleamed. "Okay, Ana Lotner, I'm going to help you. I cannot resist this story." He picked up his cup and swallowed the last bit, then made a face. "Ugh, I hate cold coffee."

I almost laughed. What did he expect? We'd been sitting here for nearly two hours. He stood up and stretched, hands on hips, rolling his shoulders in a fluid motion. It was my cue to stand too.

"I want to spend the afternoon checking out several of the leads you've given me," he said. "You say Jared worked at Good Shepherd Hospital here in Dar two years back. How about if you go there this afternoon and talk to them? Try to learn about their previous interactions and whether he's been in touch recently. Don't tell them he's your brother, but maybe you can come up with some pretext and mention him. Just find out what you can."

I got to my feet, gathering my scarf and little backpack. "Well...I guess I can try."

I didn't like this idea. I was no Sam Spade, but time was short, and I needed Haamed's help. How could I say no? I twiddled my earring with one hand and ran the other down my trouser leg. Maybe no harm would come of it — at least if I didn't use my name.

Haamed stuck out his hand. "Let's meet back here for dinner. Say seven thirty?"

I shook his smooth hand. "Yes. And, please. This has to remain confidential."

He nodded solemnly.

I PLANNED my strategy while I worked on a sandwich and dallied with a plate of greasy chips. I abandoned them without regret half way through. I was buoyed by my instinct that Haamed was someone who knew what he was doing. His mannerisms made me think he was gay and I wondered where that left him in the current homophobic political culture of Tanzania.

The facility where Jared had volunteered was a medium-sized Lutheran hospital, which I knew nothing about. Jared had said little about his trip there two years ago. I used my phone and the shaky internet connection in the hotel to look them up. Ophthalmology was one of their biggest departments, so no surprise that Jared knew about them. Their list of research publications was impressive and many of them focused on the public health aspects of eye care.

A dart of annoyance shot through me to realize he hadn't suggested this place when I made plans for my trip. I might have discussed potential collaborative projects with them. Now I'd have to go there pretending to be someone else. I had no appointment and only a slim hope someone would see me on short notice.

I took a taxi to the hospital. It looked to be a decade old, but it was well maintained, not easy in the tropical climate. Open-work cinder block walls allowed fresh air flow in corridors and administrative offices, the paint was new, and there were even some live plants in big pots along the open hallways. Someone made an effort to keep this place up.

I found my way to the right secretary's office by 1:30. Introducing myself as Dr. Ana Folker, I asked if I might have a word with the department head about "collaborative projects with my university." I was prepared to provide a made-up name for the institution — and the efficient woman asked for one. She looked sulky over the lack of appointment but stepped into an inner office and reappeared after a minute.

"Dr. Nganga will meet you for a few minutes if you can wait a short time. Please have a seat."

I sat and tried some deep breathing. I pulled out the few notes I'd made during lunch and looked for ways to embellish my strategy. This cloak-and-dagger stuff didn't suit me at all. After forty minutes, the secretary spoke on her intercom phone and waved me toward the inner office.

"*Habari za mchana*," said an attractive older man, graying at the temple, rising from behind a massive dark wooden desk and reaching out to shake my hand. Light glinted off his wire-framed spectacles. I hoped he wouldn't notice my sweaty palm. I was grateful for the comfort of the formal greetings.

"Thanks for agreeing to talk to me. I know you're busy so I won't take too much of your time."

Especially since I don't know where I'm going with this, added a voice in my head.

He smiled indulgently and gestured for me to be seated. "Please tell me why you're here."

"I'm from Barnes University, outside Detroit. We've recently been awarded global health funding to put in place collaborative programs with East African ophthalmology departments. Yours got our attention, of course."

Dr. Nganga raised his eyebrows, and leaned back, folding his hands on his belly. "Please, tell me what you have in mind. We're interested in collaborations. What are you proposing?"

So far, so good. I was encouraged that he hadn't asked for my card, and I stuck my toe deeper in the water. "Well, for starters, we're hoping to set up exchanges between students or faculty."

Dr. Nganga bobbed his head in agreement, so I continued speaking, eager to imply broad possibilities.

"These would be learning experiences in the beginning,

but could develop into mutually beneficial research projects with time."

He leaned forward and rested his chin on his folded hands.

I wished I'd had more time to think about this. I plunged ahead, rolling out a few of the phrases and buzz words I'd included in the proposal to the foundation, remembering to make them relevant to the field of eye care. Somehow this had to lead to asking about Jared.

He sank back into his chair again.

Something I said hit home and his brows shot up. He took off his spectacles and dangled them by the temple, twirling them slowly, as he kept his eyes on mine.

"Oh. *Reciprocity. Equity.* Sure, I appreciate those ideas," he said. "It's all possible of course. American medical students are keen to come to Africa for short rotations. I'm told it looks good on their CVs. But, if I may speak candidly, many of these exchanges are one way — unbalanced, if you understand me. And sometimes not realistic at all."

He leaned forward and put his spectacles back on. His smile became guarded. "Last year I was asked to guarantee that an ophthalmology resident visiting here for two weeks could do work leading to a scientific paper." He sat back, shaking his head and *tsk-tsking.* "That institution seemed to believe it was our mission to cobble together opportunities for foreign students. I had to tell him we'd have to charge a fee for such an opportunity." He chuckled without mirth. "Didn't hear back after that."

I cringed. I'd heard the accusations that university "global health initiatives" were often one-sided affairs, with most of the benefit going to the institutions in the high-income country. Visa requirements and licensing — not to mention the costs of travel and housing in the US — made a joke out of some "exchange" programs. I was determined to avoid those mistakes in the projects I developed.

But I wasn't here for a philosophic discussion of the issues, and now I'd annoyed Dr. Nganga. Thank God I hadn't mentioned Honnelly or given my real name. Our conversation might leave a lasting impression. Maybe I should forget the subterfuge and come right out and ask about Jared. There wasn't much to lose.

I swallowed and leaped in. "I understand your feelings. Have you worked with Dr. Jared Lotner?"

Dr. Nganga took a sharp breath. He narrowed his eyes and a vein in his forehead throbbed. He took off his spectacles and polished the lenses as the question hung for several seconds. He didn't smile when he replaced them and looked at me. "What is your interest in Dr. Lotner? Our association with him ended two years ago. Is he part of one of your projects?"

My heart skipped a beat, and the sweat that had collected under my arms trickled down under my thin cotton blouse. I couldn't think fast enough to pull off this kind of brazen deception. A flare of resentment at Haamed for suggesting it shot through me. I itched to leave that office. I forced words out of my dry mouth.

"No. I don't actually know him. I heard him mentioned by a colleague."

"To be clear, we're not interested in another project with him." He used his hand like a knife, cutting through the air. "Will there be anything else today?"

The meeting was over. I looked like a fool and there was no point in asking further questions. He stood, with the barest attempt to maintain a pleasant face. It was the most dismissive move I'd ever seen from a Tanzanian professional.

My face grew hot as I struggled to my feet and tried to recover some dignity; I stretched out my hand for a parting shake. "Thank you so much for your time, Doctor," I offered, my insides shrinking. I turned to leave, shivering under his cold eyes on my back.

Dr. Nganga's frankness — unusual in a culture where a high value was put on courtesy and one didn't speak ill of others, at least not directly — shook me. What had happened to cause such dislike for Jared?

I CHECKED in with the Walkers before dinner.

"Ah, so glad Haamed is willing. Fi will be reassured you've got him helping you. Let us know if there's anything at all we can do — and we'll be keen to hear what's happening."

When I spoke to Grace, her warm voice provided a reassurance not possible in text messages. "I know of Haamed Hassan — not personally, but at least by reputation. Getting his help is a good idea. What has Mark said about all this?"

"I haven't told him."

The silence from her end grew.

I jumped in to fill it. "I don't want to worry him." I could guess what Grace thought of that, but she knew enough not to give unasked for advice.

"Be careful, Ana," she finally said, slowly. "I'll be thinking of you constantly. Call me any time you need to talk."

I WAS WAITING for Haamed at 7:30 that evening. I didn't plan to tell him too much about my idiotic performance earlier in the day. I should have been more reserved, but, unsettled by my afternoon, when he came through the hotel dining room doorway, looking cool and smart, he was my new best friend. He raised his hand, palm up, in a gracious "after you" signal, and I walked ahead to our table. Like a student hoping for approval, as soon as we sat down, I spilled out all that happened in Dr. Nganga's office.

"Hmm. Interesting. Is that all you got? No idea what actually took place with Jared?"

I shook my head and felt foolish all over again for the afternoon's interview. "I did come away with the sense that the hospital and the Ophthalmology Department are respectable and well run, though."

"Never mind," he said, studying me. "I may be able to learn more from someone I know there." He must have sensed my embarrassment, and he leaned over and gave my arm a pat. "Don't worry about it, Ana. I didn't expect you to be Sherlock Holmes." He picked up his phone and tapped in a text message while I watched, then he signaled for a server.

A waiter arrived at the table, and Haamed raised his eyebrows at me in a question as he asked for a wine list. He perused it and quizzed me for a moment about my preferences, but I didn't know any of these wines. He'd have been better off with Jared as a dinner partner than with me.

His phone rang. He looked at the incoming message and smiled. "Ah, good. I'll meet a nurse friend of mine at the Good Shepherd later tonight. Maybe I can collect more information about Jared's activities there."

"So, what did you learn this afternoon?" I asked.

"Okay, the easiest part first. When Alain Loubet was

kidnapped, most people believed John Ntabaye was behind it, but it was never proven. What I've confirmed is that Ntabaye is still very active. In fact, he's got a high position in the Tanzania Investment Company, an organization that provides opportunities for foreigners, as well as Tanzanian citizens, to invest in large infrastructure projects here. One of those is the Mtwara gas fields."

My eyes widened. "Really? Do you think he might be connected again to an abduction?"

Haamed put up a hand to stop me. "Not so fast, Ana. What would be the point? These days, from what I know, he appears to be involved in legitimate business. Our President's restricted human rights and civil society, but he's also stopped a fair amount of corruption. I just don't know about Ntabaye. The ransom demand is smaller than I'd expect from him."

"Okay," I said slowly. "So that's open."

The waiter appeared with our bottle. Haamed swirled, examined, tasted, and approved it with a head nod. We ordered dinner and I pushed onward.

"What else did you learn?"

"How much do you know about the Mtwara gas fields?" asked Haamed.

"Not much. What's important?"

"A lot, for the people who were affected," he said, compressing his lips. "Like my family." His eyes darted around the room before he lowered his voice and leaned in over the table. "Here it is in a nutshell. The natural gas reserves were discovered in the seventies. In 2004, President Kikwete made a big deal about how the people of Mtwara would benefit — you know, electricity, factory jobs, roads, hospitals, schools — all the stuff that comes with development. The World Bank was involved. Things moved along bit by bit and, in 2013 — just before an election, of course — the Minister for Energy and Minerals announced that the gas would be transported by pipeline to Dar. That angered everyone in Mtwara and gave a big boost to the resistance. Violence erupted."

Our grilled snapper arrived. Haamed arranged his napkin, buttered a roll, and kept going.

"One night, someone firebombed a government office near the pipeline. The army moved in. My mother, who lived alone, ran to the forest, helping a neighbor carry her children. Several people were killed, many were beaten, and property was destroyed. It was ugly. My uncle was one of the people who perished."

He looked down, bowing his head slightly, and stroking the stem of his wineglass. "I was living in West Africa then. I wasn't here to protect my mother." He shook his head and looked back up. "After things calmed down, she moved north to Lindi, wanting to distance herself from the place. She knew she'd never see justice." He took a few more bites, laid his knife and fork down, took a sip of wine, and wiped his lips. "The resistance movement, which I was somewhat involved with, grew stronger. But now I wonder if it's gone over the top. They've been accused of some bad acts in the service of raising money. One-hundred-twenty-five-thou-sand US would be significant to them."

I'd never heard any of this. Quite a contrast to the picture Geoffrey Walker had painted. There's an African proverb: when the elephants fight, the grass gets trampled. It applied here, and Haamed's family were not the elephants.

"This afternoon," he continued, "I talked to a friend of mine from down there. He and a couple of other guys are meeting in Dar the day after tomorrow, and I convinced him to let me join. I've not mentioned Jared's abduction to him, but I want to see if I can learn anything about activities that might be related to it."

I was impressed. No wonder Geoffrey had suggested Haamed. He had connections, and he didn't mess around. A needle of hope shot through me. I was lucky to have this man on my side. Still, I wanted to be doing something.

"Should I come with you? I'd like to hear what they say."

His eyes widened, and he suppressed a grin. "Don't be ridiculous, Ana. How's your Swahili? Anyway, I had to push the guy to let *me* come on Friday morning. They're not going to say a word if they see you."

I half expected him to roll his eyes. He didn't need to. I was chastened and I didn't argue. I had enough to worry about with picking up the ransom cash on Thursday.

But there was one more question I needed to ask before we parted. "Haamed, I've heard rumors about al-Shabaab in that area. Think there's any chance they might be involved?"

He removed his spectacles and bit gently on the tortoise shell temple with his perfect white teeth. Had I made myself look stupid again?

But he didn't laugh. His face grew somber, and he beetled his eyebrows. "I'm not surprised you've heard that, since there're all kinds of rumors out there. There've been reports of terrorists in northern Mozambique. But I'd expect the Somali al-Shabaab to claim responsibility if they were behind this."

"So, you don't believe it's al-Shabaab?" I searched his face. "The ruthlessness of those extremists scares the hell out of me."

Haamed glanced down at the table and spoke with patience. "Look Ana. That's not what I said. It's not the al-Shabaab you're thinking of from Somalia — *al shabaab* just means 'the youth' — but there is a group in Mozambique that uses the name, and the border with Tanzania is porous." He settled his spectacles back on his face. "All jihad is local. Recruits are motivated by anti-government senti-ment — and there's plenty of that down there."

21

THURSDAY, SEPTEMBER 7

The *muezzin* woke me at 5:00 the next morning with his sonorous call to prayer. I took out my partially-effective earplugs and got an instant demonstration that they were better than I gave them credit for. Street noises rose from below, audible even through the closed windows and my humming air conditioner. I tried and failed to go back to sleep, so I attempted some basic meditation in the hope it might help me. Not that it ever had before, but I gave it twenty minutes before I quit and opened my book. Nothing was going to free me from the blanket of anxiety that had overlaid every waking moment since that first text message nearly a week ago. But I understood now what people meant when they advised the bereaved to "go through the motions of living." Even if I couldn't lose myself in a book, I could try for distraction. *A Gentleman in Moscow* was compelling. Relentless cheerfulness annoyed me, but Count Rostov was a sophisticated, resourceful version of Pollyanna who gave me hope. He also gave me something to think about for an hour before I got up and showered.

By 7:45, I'd had breakfast and returned to the room. According to plan, my phone rang at 8:00.

"Ana?" came the lightly accented voice of Giselle Loubet. "How are you? Is everything on track?"

"Yeah, it's all good. I met the journalist yesterday, and he'll help me. I think he'll make a good ally."

"Excellent. Now, Mr. Jonas Shija asked me to confirm that you'll be in your room in fifteen minutes. He'll ring from the front desk, where you'll find him. Is that okay?"

"Yes. I'm in my room now. Thank you, Giselle."

"When you finish with Jonas, send me a text. Then you'll need to leave to meet Mr. Oscar James. His office is on the third floor of the Moto building, next to the Equity Bank on Uhuru. He'll expect you between eleven thirty and twelve. He's very punctual. The other contacts will come to your hotel after lunch, so go back there as soon as you're finished."

"Got it, Giselle. Thanks again." I hung up and rubbed the back of my neck. I picked up my water bottle and quenched my dry mouth.

The room phone rang a few minutes later. "Gentleman at reception asking for you, Madam."

"I'll be right down."

A middle-aged man in a suit approached me as soon as I stepped off the elevator into the lobby. Jonas Shija could have been drawn with a series of circles — round face, round cheeks, round wire-framed glasses, and a large round belly. His short stature added to the illusion.

"Excuse me, Mama. You are...?"

"Ana Lotner," I said, extending my hand. I wasn't sure of the etiquette here, but if he had qualms, he didn't show them.

He shook my hand, scrutinizing me with eyes set back in fleshy folds. He loosened a button on his jacket, reached into the inner breast pocket, and drew out an envelope, about an inch thick. He handed it to me. "You have very good friends, Mama," he said, arching his eyebrows like new moons.

I'd wondered earlier if I should ask him to come to the room to count the cash, but before I could ask, he gave a brisk nod, turned on his heel, and hurried out the entryway. I took the elevator to my room, counted the money, and put the envelope in the safe. The whole deal had taken about twenty minutes, most of which I spent counting the bills.

I texted Giselle. *Got it!* One down and three to go.

The Moto building was three-quarters of a mile away, according to Google Maps, but Dar traffic was a mess. I'd considered hiring a car and driver, but I only needed to make one trip out of the hotel to collect money, and I figured ordinary transport — a private taxi — ought to be good enough. I'd planned for thirty minutes, more than enough travel time. At 10:50, I snatched up my little backpack, strapped on an empty money belt, and walked downstairs and out to the street.

Taxicabs crowded bumper to bumper in front of the hotel and I grabbed the nearest. I soon wished I'd searched for something higher class. The back seat springs were shot, but the real problem was the stifling heat and lack of air conditioning. I rolled down the window. The driver turned and gestured for me to roll it up. "Thieves," he said, grimacing and leaning back to lock the door. It took thirty-five minutes more to crawl to our destination, and it was 11:35 as I got out of the taxi. I could have walked there faster.

The Moto building nestled right up against the bank. Like many buildings in Dar, it was a dirty gray. It sported a few tall windows with decrepit rusty balconies I wouldn't have dared step out on. I rushed up the stairs to the third floor, rather than trusting the elevator. Short power cuts occurred with alarming frequency and this building, unlike my hotel, didn't look like the type to have a generator. Mr. Oscar James was a solicitor, according to the plaque on the door. His office, with tasteful textiles on clean walls and a smart parquet floor, surprised me when I entered. An attractive young woman with a complicated woven hairdo looked up from a gleaming modern desk.

"*Habari za asubuhi*? she asked with a smile, to which I gave the only acceptable reply.

"*Nzuri. Habari yako.*" Once again I appreciated the ritual greeting. Somehow, answering "fine" helped maintain a reassuring sense of calm and didn't burden the inquirer with anyone's problems.

"Ana Lotner?" she asked. I nodded, and she ushered me through an inner door.

Oscar James, a tall European who looked about sixty, stood up behind his desk and extended his hand, glancing at his watch at the same time. I was relieved to be on time, as something made me think he wouldn't have waited a minute after noon for me.

"I'm glad to meet you," he said. "You won't mind if I call Giselle so she can verify your identity?" He was doing it as he asked. "Giselle, can you have a word with Ana, please?" He handed me the phone.

"Hi Giselle, it's me, and I'm here. Any problems?"

"No, Ana. Only that Oscar is very formal — and careful. I'll call you to be sure you're back in your hotel room before Mama Bakari brings the money at one. Goodbye for now, and please hand me back to Oscar."

He took the phone and listened for a few seconds before his eyes crinkled. "Regards to Luc."

He went to a wall safe behind one of the lovely tapestries I'd been admiring and took out an envelope. "Please count it."

I did so, as fast as I could. When I licked my finger, Mr. James made a soft *ahem* noise and handed me a rubber thimble. It helped. I finished and folded the neat stack of two-hundred-and-fifty bills into the money belt. He nodded — approvingly? — as I pulled my long tunic down over the belt. "You might consider an undershirt as well, tucked into your trousers under the outer shirt."

At noon, the traffic in front of the building was worse than ever, but I was not about to chance a walk back to the hotel with the money. Within a minute, I spied one of the high-end tourist taxis with a white license plate. I pulled open the car door and peered inside.

"Good morning, Mama," said the little man, sitting ramrod straight in the driver's seat. I hoped he could see out from underneath the large peaked cap he wore.

"I need to go to the Harbor View Suites."

"No problem, no problem," he said. I got in the middle of the back seat and locked both doors. He pulled into traffic, honking for no obvious reason. Without asking, he turned up the air conditioner full blast.

Five minutes later, we hadn't moved more than a few feet down Uhuru Road and, as far ahead as I could see, cars were stalled. No change after ten minutes. I shivered with cold. I looked at my watch: 12:20 p.m. By 12:30, we'd made it to the intersection with Bibi Titi Mohammed Street, where the driver made a sharp left instead of continuing on straight as I expected.

"Avoid the Clock Tower. Much better," he muttered from the front seat.

It wasn't much better, though. I shifted from one hip to the other, grinding my teeth as we inched along. The driver gave an impatient grunt and made a sudden right turn, forcing his way into the oncoming traffic. Horns erupted, but with the windows rolled up I was spared the oaths from the drivers we cut off. We increased our speed a bit, although I had no idea where we actually were. Several *boda bodas*, the ubiquitous motorbikes that ferried passengers all over the city, revved their engines as they wove in and out among the cars. Maybe I should have taken one myself. But I wasn't keen. Motorcycle riders were twenty times more likely to die from a crash than other motor vehicle users in Tanzania, according to a safety study I'd read a few months ago.

My phone rang as we turned left onto Samora, where my hotel was.

"Ana?" said Giselle.

"I'm still in the taxi, a few minutes away," I blurted, wiping my palm on my trousers.

"Will you be able to receive a package in the lobby at one o'clock?"

How should I know? A horn blared as a tiny Toyota truck narrowly missed sideswiping the left front fender. The driver mumbled something under his breath. We came to a complete stop as a huge delivery van pulled away from the curb, cutting us off. The hotel was one-hundred-fifty feet ahead and on the opposite side of the road. "Yes, I'll be there. Gotta go now," I said to Giselle, as I threw my phone into my bag. I leaned forward and tapped the driver's shoulder.

"Close enough," I said, waving a hand. I leaped out of

the taxi and dropped some bills over into the front seat. The snail's pace of traffic was in my favor now as I threaded around several stationary or creeping vehicles, across a river of autos, trucks, and busses. I hurried along the broken sidewalk to the hotel and dashed through the door.

The sudden quiet indoors calmed me, but the chilled air made me shiver again. The elevator panel showed it to be at the top of the building, so I made for the stairs. Huffing and puffing, I climbed to the fifth floor. In my room, I stripped off the sweaty money belt and crammed it into the safe. It was 12:57. I just remembered to grab my little pack before I sprinted back downstairs, where I slowed to catch my breath.

Across the lobby, a tall, dignified woman in a business suit and heels appeared to be searching for something in her purse. Her fancy braided hair shone, and gold earrings sparkled under the chandeliers. She looked over at me uncertainly. Sweaty and disheveled, I guess I didn't look like the person she expected to find. I met and held her eye, smiling hesitantly.

She approached me. "Hello," she said, evenly. "Are you...?"

"Yes. I'm Ana Lotner," I said, extending my hand. "Mama Bakari?"

Her face relaxed, and she took my hand in her own, which was cool and dry. "Pleased to meet you." She started to withdraw something from the inner pocket of her jacket, but hesitated, looking me up and down. "Is everything okay?"

"Yes, I was just stuck in traffic. Afraid I might be late." I said, offering an apologetic smile.

She smiled back, withdrew a slim packet, and handed it to me. "That explains a lot in Dar. Excuse me. I won't stay, as

I've got to cross town myself. Good luck."

"Thank you," I said, cramming the envelope into my pack. But I was talking to her back as her heels clicked across the lobby floor toward the door.

Bag clutched against my chest, I walked to the elevator, my pulse returning to normal. Back in my room, I took out the envelope and unstuck the flap. I counted two-hundred-fifty bills in the clean stack, thinking how good I was getting at this. I shoved the packet into the safe and debated between flopping on the bed or rinsing away sweat and tension in the shower. I headed for the cool water.

By 1:30, I was refreshed and stretched out on the bed to think. Giselle had said the last tranche of money would be delivered here to me at three. I ordered a sandwich from room service and tried to escape in Moscow.

At 2:30 Giselle called.

"Ana, I'm afraid there's a problem with the last delivery. Mr. Nelson can't make it to your hotel this afternoon. You're going to have to go to him to pick up the money."

Damn! That meant going back into the Dar traffic. I sagged at the thought. "Okay, where do I go?"

"He'll be at the Protea Hotel until three thirty. That's the Protea Courtyard. That only gives you an hour, but it's not more than three kilometers. Call me when you arrive there, and I'll let him know."

Three kilometers in Dar traffic at this time of day could take more than an hour. I didn't relish a repeat of the earlier stressful taxi ride. The best guarantee of getting there on time was either to walk or take one of the zig-zagging *boda bodas*. I strapped on an empty money belt under a tank top tucked into my trousers, as per Oscar's suggestion. I put on a long tunic and grabbed my little pack, wearing it in front and crossing my arms over it. At the last minute I threw an extra shirt on to hide the straps from someone who might want to cut them from my back and pull — I'd heard of it happening. I was going to roast out there.

I checked Google Maps for the fastest route on foot. I turned right as I exited the hotel, then trotted up Samora, keeping my eyes peeled for Zanaki, where I'd turn left. According to Google, the street changed names several times, and I had no sense of direction. The last thing I needed was to get turned around. I took care stepping across gaps in the sidewalk, some larger than the length of my foot and leading down into murky, wet depths. Warped boards overlaid a few of the openings, nothing I wanted to trust my weight to. I gagged when something furry jumped in one of the big gaps. The smell of motor oil and exhaust fumes permeated the dead still air. Large black thunderclouds were building out over the ocean. After ten minutes, at least two of my shirts were stuck to my back. A few beads of sweat oozed out of the soggy fabric and ran down to my waist. A different statistic from the Tanzania study popped into my head: three-quarters of accidents on the road involved *boda bodas*. Too bad.

"Hey!" I hailed one of the motorcycles, choosing one with a helmeted driver. If he wore it to create an impression of safety, it was effective.

"Protea Courtyard," I said, throwing a leg over the passenger seat. He peeled out before I was settled and I lurched backward. So much for safety.

I grabbed the luggage rack as my sunhat flew off my head. Still, the air rushing through my hair was sweet. Ten minutes of weaving and swerving, and we were there. There was time for a civil exchange with the grinning driver as I paid him, price unchallenged, and glanced at my watch. In fact, there was time for a cold Tangawizi before I called Giselle at three o'clock sharp.

"Ana? Good. Go ahead and call Paulus Nelson in room three-ten. He's expecting you."

A tiny weight rolled off my shoulders as Mr. Nelson, a balding, middle-aged European in a smooth linen suit, handed over the inch-thick stack of bills. This was the last tranche. He counted it in front of me, made me count it, and finally put it into a small manila envelope, which I zipped into my money belt.

"Good," he said. "I had a belt myself, in case you didn't have one. Never carry money in a backpack or purse."

I got that.

Outside the Protea, a uniformed doorman hailed a tourist taxi for me. I sank into the cool of the air-conditioned back seat, not caring how long it might take to return to my hotel. The clouds that threatened earlier burst and, for fifteen minutes, a wall of water cascaded from the sky. Slow traffic became slower still, as visibility dropped to a few meters. Cocooned in the back of the taxi, I sunk back and truly relaxed for the first time all day.

The downpour stopped as suddenly as it had started, and I emerged from the cab onto pavement steaming from the pounding rain. I blinked against the sun's glare.

Once I laid the last tranche in my room's safe, I called Giselle. "Thank you. I hadn't realized how complicated this would be for you, but the money is all secure in my room."

I opened the safe again and stared at the heaped envelopes. One-hundred-twenty-five-thousand dollars in cash. I took it out and aligned the bills into a stack five inches thick. I divided it between two money belts and fastened one over each hip under a large loose tunic top. I stood in front of the mirror, then walked back and forth. It wasn't obvious I had something around my waist and I gave my image a nod of satisfaction.

I ordered room service, because I didn't want to leave the room more than necessary. Besides, I relished eating in a bathrobe.

I was one step closer to getting Jared back.

22

FRIDAY, SEPTEMBER 8

H aamed called me at 10:30 the next morning, instructing me to go to a tiny café not far from my hotel. The sweltering day assaulted me as I stepped outside. I squinted at the sun and flagged a taxi. The driver narrowed his eyes at me when I gave the address. He gave a grunt and jerked the car into the oncoming traffic, making a right-hand turn. Horns blared and a man at the wheel of a truck shook his fist as we cut him off. In spite of that harrowing start, the taxi driver navigated competently through a maze of potholed backstreets. We wound into a warren where cracked sidewalks overflowed with bolts of fabric and tailors hunched over treadle machines. Heavy iron gas canisters littered the broken pavement, and a variety of electric goods — irons, hotplates, hairdryers, and radios — lay jumbled together on large shelves against storefronts. The driver stomped on the brakes, twisted to look behind, then backed up and delivered me in front of a row of narrow, wood-framed doorways, many with small signs in Arabic script.

"It's the one with the purple beads," he said, as I handed him the fare.

The beaded curtain clacked as I passed through the slim doorway. The relief from the clamor on the street was immediate. I stood still to let my eyes adjust to the dim light, and a tall man with an embroidered skull cap, a bushy black beard, and a flowing white jellabiya approached.

"How can I help you, Madam?" he asked with no warmth.

"I'm supposed to meet Haamed Hassan here," I said, glancing around at little tables overhung with the haze of cigarettes, where a few carbon copies of my greeter played chess and sipped tea. The man's face relaxed, and he smiled a little.

"Follow me," he said, striding toward a back exit. I hurried after him, out the door and into a sun-deprived alley. In a few meters, he turned sharply and ushered me through a narrow doorway into a dim room I figured to be another shop. There, amidst piles of carpets and two old, low, carved wooden tables, I was thankful to see Haamed reclining. He was speaking to two men. They looked at me, put their cups of tea down on a tray with a clatter, jumped up, and bolted out. My escort stayed, leaning on the door jamb.

"Haamed! What happened at the meeting with your friends?"

"Hello, Ana," he said, pulling himself into a more erect position. "The meeting with my friends," he started slowly. He blew air out one side of his mouth and gazed up at the ceiling. "I'm afraid they're no longer friends."

I couldn't tell if he was bitter or rueful.

"They believe, and possibly they're correct, that my actions led the police to them." He flinched as he took a deep breath and gestured at a stack of small rugs. "Sit down, Ana."

I sank to my knees onto the mound, alarm growing as I took in his appearance. Tan surgical tape around his ribs peeked through the gaps between his shirt buttons. He wore clean, neat, fresh clothes, but they didn't hide the derelict look created by the ugly purple swelling on his forehead and nose. His dark glasses didn't conceal much either. He'd been roughed up, and not just a little.

"I'm afraid the other guys may have been beaten as badly. I phoned one after we scattered, but got no answer. I last saw him fleeing down an alley, so I assume he got away."

I was staggered. "But *why*? And how'd they *know*?" And, I added belatedly, "Are you all right?"

Haamed took off his dark glasses, revealing a left eye nearly closed by swelling. But he managed to roll his right eye before he responded. "*Why*? Ana, I told you, these guys are part of a resistance group. Resistance against a government project — a *big* project." He shifted on the carpet pile and grimaced. "As for how they knew, they might have seen us together at the hotel and been suspicious that I was up to something." He shook his head. "I should have been more careful. I know I'm watched at times. A journalist talking to a foreigner?" His right eye bored into me. "And this government doesn't like people like me, as I think you know."

I slumped and let out a slow breath, humiliated once again by my naivete. I knew the current leadership in the country had an increasingly nasty policy of harassment of gay men, as did a number of eastern African governments. Covert lists of suspected homosexuals were published, and there'd been some brutal killings. Families had been targeted too. I hadn't considered how dangerous this might become for Haamed. "I'm so sorry," I said, and to my relief, he smiled.

"It's okay, Ana. This isn't your fault. I knew what I was getting into when I agreed to help. I need to be more careful."

"What happened?"

He shifted on the carpet pile and grimaced. "When I showed up, three guys I know from Mtwara were there, in the large back room of a more or less deserted shop." He reached for a small Turkish tea glass in an ornate silver holder, filled with steaming liquid, and sipped carefully around a swollen lower lip. "We'd barely started talking when the police crashed in, swinging their clubs. I didn't realize there was a back door, so I floundered around and took a couple of hits before I got away."

I shook my head. "I truly am sorry, Haamed."

He put down his tea cup and continued. "I had no chance to ask about resistance activities in Mtwara, or about possible abductions, before the police broke in, so I'm sorry too. This was all for nothing. I doubt those guys will talk to me again." He looked up at the ceiling. "I've been considering what we ought to do next. There's nothing more I can learn here in Dar. Are you ready to go south toward Mtwara?"

"I guess so," I said slowly. "But don't we agree that we shouldn't tell the mission hospital there about this?"

"I'm not thinking of going to the hospital. I want us to go to Lindi, on the coast, about an hour north of Mtwara. Where my mother lives. It gets us much closer to where Jared disappeared, and it's a safe place to make a base. I know the neighborhood and the villages around there."

I considered this and shrugged. "I guess we'll need to go down there soon anyway. I've always assumed the kidnappers would be in Mtwara and want the ransom delivered there."

Haamed signaled his agreement.

"I can be ready as soon as I pick up my bag from the hotel — and the money. I got it all yesterday."

Did I imagine he looked impressed?

"Good. Mustapha will take you to collect your belongings." He glanced at his watch. "We ought to be able to leave from here by half twelve and arrive just after dark. We shouldn't be on the road at night with so much money."

He inclined his head toward the man at the door, who'd been there the entire time. "Mustapha," he called, and they exchanged rapid Swahili.

I stood up. Mustapha beckoned me and, once again, I followed him into the alley. We walked the twisted cobblestoned passageway until we came to an old white Hyundai sedan, wedged into a recess. I wasn't sure how he'd enter the driver's seat on the right, but he was a skinny guy under the jellabiya, and, with a few contortions, he wriggled his way in. He backed out until the passenger door was clear, and I climbed in beside him.

I couldn't prevent a sharp intake of breath, once, as he maneuvered the car out of the tight alley. The rest of the time I just clenched my fists. Aside from an amused glance, he ignored me. We were at the hotel in fifteen minutes, without a scrape or a scratch.

Mustapha dropped me at the front, and I raced up to my room. I threw my clothes into my bag, then opened the safe. Lucky that I'd tried out the money belt arrangement the night before. I strapped on the belts, pulled a tank top and tunic over them, and sped down to check out.

The car was waiting outside when I emerged. The route back to the carpet shop struck me as long and circuitous, and I wondered if Mustapha was trying to confuse anyone who might be watching my movements. I went cold at the possibility, which didn't seem far-fetched after what had happened to Haamed.

We wove our way back through the alley. Haamed slipped out the doorway and got into the back seat, where he lay down. He grunted as he got comfortable among several large pillows. I stayed where I was, in the front seat, with the window rolled up and the door locked.

"It'll be hot with that window closed," said Mustapha.

"There's an air conditioner here," I said, fiddling with the dashboard.

He lowered his eyebrows at me. "Wastes petrol," I thought he said, but I turned it on anyway. I wasn't taking any chances. This might not be Nairobi, but car jackings happened in Dar sometimes too.

The air conditioner created a huge whooshing sound, accompanied by little more than a feathery breath of coolish air. We hugged the coast, ending up on the Nelson Mandela Road. Twenty minutes later, after we turned inland to intersect the B2 southward, Mustapha gave a sudden twist to the wheel, pulling the car into a small dirt alley. He stomped the brake, threw his left arm out toward me, and lunged across the seat.

Whap! I stiffened.

But he was merely arching back to face Haamed. "This is as far as I can go. I'm sorry," he said.

Haamed raised himself up a few inches on his elbow. "It's okay. I'm grateful for your help. I'm in a lot better shape now than I would've been without it." Mustapha rotated his shoulders further and offered an awkward shake with his right hand.

"Give my love to Fatima," called Haamed, as Mustapha left the car and slipped down the alley.

"I'll have to drive from here," Haamed said, starting to climb out of the back.

"Why don't I do it?" I pulled up the door handle. "At least for a few hours, to give you a chance to sleep a bit. Anyway, you've only got one eye open. Once we're going south on the B2, it's pretty straightforward. I won't have any problem."

Haamed sank back against a pillow. "You okay with the traffic?"

"I hate it. But I can still drive." Did he imagine I had limited experience with driving? Of course, I'd prefer to do it without him watching my every move.

He gave a weak smile. "Okay, Ana. A couple more hours of sleep would be most welcome." I clambered out and went around to the driver's side. Haamed watched with what I took to be faint amusement.

We were outside Dar, but there were still many houses, little shops, and occasional primary schools scattered beside the broken tarmac road. Traffic was dense and sometimes chaotic as I competed with large trucks hauling goods along the major route down the coast. Driving here was a full-time occupation, requiring my complete concentration. I hoped other drivers were giving it theirs. Sweat formed under the bulk at my waist. An hour crept by as we continued south.

Haamed stirred. "Ana, for the love of God, why don't you open a window?"

"I'm not taking any chances with this money. Traffic's too slow here. I'll do it once the vehicles thin out."

An hour or so later, I could drive for long stretches without seeing buildings on either side through the trees and bush. No houses were visible from the road, although the rare primary school and occasional speed bumps reminded me that people lived along this way. I cranked down the window, and the breeze, scented by the sea, was delicious.

We were moving down a gentle slope when the car lurched violently toward the middle of the road. I stomped on the brake as I tried to control the vehicle while pulling to the side of the broken-up blacktop. I tugged on the emergency brake. Haamed jerked awake in the back with a grunt and raised himself on an elbow.

"What's going on?" he said, alert in a split second.

"I think there's a problem with the tire."

Flat tires were the plague of all drivers on these roads. The stretch was empty, so I got out and walked around to the front of the car. Sure enough the right tire looked lopsided, a donut pressed too hard against the crumbling tarmac.

Haamed pulled himself upright, swung his legs around, and opened the rear door. "If we've got a puncture, I'll need to help you change it."

"You can't possibly help in the shape you're in. But you've got to climb out before I can jack up the car," I said, pleased to be in charge here. I knew how to change a tire.

I ducked into the front of the car and pulled the trunk release lever, gratified to hear the sound as it popped open. Haamed, leaning against a tree at the roadside, watched me remove our bags, expose the wheel well, and pull out a jack, a lug wrench, and the spare. The tools were black with oil and dirt but looked serviceable.

The battered sedan had no hubcaps, so I connected the wrench and loosened the first lug nut in a couple of seconds. A little bubble of empowerment swelled in my chest at this opportunity to demonstrate my skill, in spite of a slight difficulty in bending over, due to the bulk at my waist. When the lug nuts were too tight to yield, Haamed moved to help me, but I shooed him back.

I dug through the wheel well and ignored the pain when I rapped my knuckles on an enormous tire iron. The pipe I needed was at the bottom. I pulled it out, stifling a yelp as some heavy, unidentifiable, sharp iron tool took the skin off my bruised knuckles. Once I attached the pipe to the lug wrench, I had to jump on it, but I managed to loosen all the nuts.

"Men always tighten these too much," I muttered, just loud enough for Haamed to hear. I scowled at him.

His lip twitched, but he inclined his head with no other sign of humor.

I wedged a couple of large rocks in front of the tires, positioned the jack, and ratcheted the car up enough to yank off the damaged tire. I wrestled on the spare and replaced the nuts.

Was that admiration in Haamed's eyes? I slapped my hands together in a satisfied show of removing dirt and crammed the tools and the punctured tire into the trunk of the car. I threw in the bags. "Mustn't forget these," I said, flush with success.

Haamed continued to watch.

"Well, you can get back in," I said. "Let's go." I started to open the door and paused. "How're you feeling?"

"Not bad. A lot better. Would you like me to drive for a while now?"

"Nah. You should rest a bit longer." I got in the car, and Haamed went around to the passenger side.

"I'll ride up here, now. Good to be in a different position."

I smiled at him and started the car.

It wouldn't move forward so I gave it a little more gas. Then I remembered the rocks.

Haamed studied me. My cheeks grew hot. He assumed a deeply sorrowful face and, after a couple of seconds, the impish angle of his battered eyebrows made my lips twitch. A grin crept across my face, and a bubble of laughter rose up. It felt good and I laughed harder, letting my head fall back against the seat as days of tension flowed out of my body.

Haamed joined in. He reached over and patted my arm. "It's okay, Ana, you're doing fine."

I got out and kicked the rocks out of the way.

Traffic was sparse as I drove the last few hours. Haamed perked up, surprising me with a desire to chat.

"Ana, tell me more about your work — what you were doing here before Jared went missing."

I described the global health award and my hope to find projects to collaborate with.

"So you're looking for opportunities for American students?"

"No. It's not like that. We want to support projects that are mutually beneficial."

"Hmm."

"What does that mean? You don't think it's possible?"

"It may be. But some so-called 'aid' is just a new kind of colonialism. It's a sixty-billion-dollar per year business. As far as aid in the health sector, I've seen some situations that disturbed me."

"Like what?"

"These short-term gigs for medical students from

abroad don't impress me. Some seem to offer more to the American student than they do to the host hospital."

Visions of the "eye screening" in Rombo sprang to mind.

Haamed continued. "Let me tell you what happened to one of my uncles." He turned slightly to face me better. "He couldn't catch his breath one afternoon. Felt light-headed. So he went to the hospital. We watched as he sickened right before our eyes. The doctor was away so the nurses called a visiting American medical student, who thought he knew what was wrong. He said someone needed to stick a big needle in Uncle's chest — but he wouldn't do it. He said he'd never done it before, and he wasn't sure he'd do it right. So we stood there and watched my uncle die. Why'd they send a trainee without skills? For an exotic vacation?"

"I'm sorry. That's terrible, but the American program probably assumed the student would be supervised by a senior doctor."

"Senior doctors already have plenty to do. And do you think they were paying the supposed supervisor anything? Who benefited from the so-called exchange?"

"Look, I don't know. People have made mistakes. We've learned how to do things better. But does that mean it's all a waste? Should we forget about all foreign aid?"

"Oh, Ana, things are never so black and white as that. Foreign aid has saved lives. Vaccine programs have protected millions on this continent. And the increased availability of HIV medicines, paid by USAID, pulled some countries out of a nightmare. Measures to help control malaria have also made a huge difference."

Haamed smiled and held up a finger to make one more point. "And, outside the health sector, I have to mention that I had a great Peace Corps Volunteer as an English and writing teacher in secondary school. She's the reason I'm a journalist today."

"Okay. You admit some good things have come from aid programs. What did you mean by 'new colonialism?'"

He looked at me like I was an idiot. "You must know about the nightmarish situations where foreign aid's propped up dictators — provided them with political and economic powers. Somalia was torn apart by that."

"Well...yeah. But that was exceptional."

"Don't be so sure, Ana. Development's often about politics. Turf battles. It isn't easy to do it right. Sometimes it promotes top-down, short-term fixes, when what we need is messy political reforms." He gave a mirthless laugh. "And the politics in the donor country can shift every time there's an election."

He was getting worked up — talking faster and harder.

Part of me wanted to hear his ideas, but the uncomfortable realities he described and the ways they applied to the career I was struggling to build were too much to worry about. And anxiety over more immediate problems had drained me. My shoulders ached from hunching over the wheel, and my jaw was stiff.

Maybe Haamed sensed my exhaustion. "We're not too far now, Ana. I know where we're heading, and it'll be easier if I'm driving."

No argument from me. We pulled over to switch places. I retrieved a pillow from the back and relaxed in the passenger seat — or I tried to. Getting closer to the place where Jared disappeared revived every fear I'd had over the past week. Where was he? Was he hurt? Who'd done this and why? My mind played in an endless loop.

I sat forward. "Haamed, did you learn anything from your friend at the Dar hospital about Jared's work there?"

Haamed glanced at me and spoke with what seemed like reluctance. "Yes," he said. "Some of it may be rumors, and I don't understand all the details. Here's what I *think* happened. Two years ago, Jared contacted a Dr. Nganga, a senior doctor at the time, and asked him if he'd like to work together to expand training in the hospital."

"Yeah, that's the guy I met."

"Whether Jared knew it or not, Dr. Nganga was in rivalry with another doctor. Jared promised equipment and training opportunities that Dr. Nganga counted on. When Jared didn't come through, Dr. Nganga was left in a humiliated position. Didn't receive the promotion he'd expected — although something must have gone his way later, since he's now head of the department. Lots of animosity there, and it created a big rift in the unit. Some of the doctors claimed Jared had undermined their own practices by offering free surgery at a satellite clinic."

"So, politics?" I asked, pushing the thought of Jared's blunder out of my head.

"Yeah, I guess you could call it that. It's hard to drop in for a short stay to do good in a situation you don't know well — even more so if you're perceived as having money. And all Westerners are assumed to be rich."

"Okay, but would that make anyone angry enough to *kidnap* someone?"

"Maybe so, maybe not." He pursed his lips. "Might depend how much money was involved. People can hold grudges for a long time. And I learned Dr. Nganga comes from Mtwara."

Dusk was turning into dark as we reached the outskirts of Lindi. We wound our way through little hamlets on a maze of narrow dirt roads, with houses on either side. Most had at least a few plants growing in the hard-packed earth in front, including flowering bushes or what looked to me like coconut palms. Bougainvillea, color indeterminate in the fading light, twined over some of the wooden fence pickets. A gentle onshore breeze carried the smell of the ocean to us, but the air was still sticky and thick. Lights twinkled from a few houses and shone from an occasional front door or veranda.

"I hope you won't mind staying at our home," Haamed had said thirty minutes previously. "I want to keep a low profile, and I don't want people to connect us. Your presence in a guesthouse in town might make people start asking what you're doing here. This will be simpler. I told my mother you're coming, and she's expecting you."

We pulled off the narrow dirt road and entered the compound of a modest cement block house, distinguished by the profusion of plant life, mere silhouettes in the dim yard lights. "Mama loves her garden," said Haamed, smiling.

For the first time, I saw him as someone's son, with a life separate from his professional one. The impression was reinforced when his mother, a large, angular woman in a long cotton skirt, her head covered with a colorful hijab, ran out the door to greet us. Haamed climbed stiffly out of the car, flinching as he straightened out his limbs. "Mama," he said through swollen lips.

His mother spoke in rapid Swahili, and all I caught was *mwanangu* — my son — murmured several times as she enveloped him in her huge embrace. She stepped back and gently touched his puffy face. "*Pole. Pole sana.*" I'm so sorry.

She turned to me and smiled formally. "You're Ana. I am

Mama Amina. My son told me you'd be coming. *Karibu*."
Her *karibu* was as perfunctory as that word of welcome
could be delivered. She stepped toward the front door.
"Please, come in. We will make you as comfortable as possible. I'm sure you need to eat."

Haamed waved for me to go ahead. I followed his
mother up the two concrete steps onto a small porch and
into the house.

Inside, the single-story house was much larger than it
looked as we drove up. There was a big front living room
with a dining table and eight chairs. Thick, intricately
patterned wool rugs, such as those Haamed had been lying
on in the shop earlier that day, covered much of the shiny
red-painted concrete floor. An assortment of colorful shawls
and light blankets were laid across three couches and
several large armchairs. Wall fixtures held bare round bulbs.
A modern new refrigerator stood at one side near a door
that opened into what I presumed was a kitchen. A long hall
led out of the room and into the back of the house. The
table was set for three, so her comment about my need to
eat wasn't just speculation.

"Haamed, please show Ana to the guest room. I had
Falisha make it up for her."

Haamed smiled. He'd flinched as he picked up my bag
from the car, but he was steady enough as I followed him
down the long hallway. To my surprise, it exited into a little
lighted inner courtyard lined with large potted plants.
Several doors led off the enclosure. He opened a red one
and stood back for me to enter.

I found myself in a clean room about three by four
meters. Rich carpets covered the floor here too. The high,
heavy carved bed, with a two-step stool by its side, took up a
large portion of the room. It was enclosed in a canopy of

mosquito net, which draped gracefully to the ground. A small wardrobe completed the furnishings. Haamed placed my bag at the door and extended his arm to usher me in, but he didn't cross the threshold himself.

"Please refresh yourself and then join us for a light supper in the main room," he said, as he turned to go.

I turned, looking around the room. Through a narrow-arched doorway on one wall, covered by a curtain, I found a small room with a squat toilet and a water tap. A second doorway led into a larger room with a drain in the floor and a built-in bench. Water dripped slowly from a spigot into a plastic bucket, which held a dipper. Every surface here, including the bench, was tiled with beautiful patterned squares in a dizzying pattern of blue and red. Soap and a folded towel sat atop a small wrought-iron washstand.

I started to wash my hands and face, then gave in to the temptation to take off my clothes, plop down on the bench, and pour water over my tired body. The tepid stream refreshed me. I dried off, pulled on a clean blouse and loose trousers, and hurried out to the dining room.

Haamed waited there, lounging in a low-slung leather chair in the corner of the room, wearing a silky cream-colored jellabiya. His eyes were closed and legs were crossed at the knee. His feet were smooth and soft-looking in light leather sandals that exposed long slender toes ending in the same perfect oval nailbeds as his fingers. It was a different view of him than I'd had before, but it was all of a piece I was beginning to know. He opened his eyes slowly and smiled at me.

The supper, offered in a mishmash of pottery and painted tin plates, consisted of cold chicken, hummus with fresh warm flatbread, and slices of sweet pineapple and avocado. Amina waved me toward a straight-backed chair, fussed over dishes, and poured three glasses of water before she sat down.

"Now, tell me what's going on."

I was surprised by the detail Hammed gave her, but she took it all in, keeping her eyes on her son and making *hmming* noises at the right times. When he got to Mr. Ntabaye, though, she blanched and put down her fork.

"Oh, Haamed, you must be careful. He's a powerful man now in the TIC."

"That's the Tanzania Investment Company, Ana," said Haamed, before I could ask. "The organization I mentioned before." He looked back at his mother. "What have you heard about Ntabaye?"

"I know many people are afraid of him. He has power for getting required permits, visas, and authorizations — for those he likes. You can imagine the corruption." She grimaced. "I wish you'd be more careful."

Haamed gave her a patient smile. "Of course, Mama. Of course."

She excused herself as soon as she finished eating and left the room.

"She's not happy that I'm here," I said to Haamed.

"I expect you're right, Ana. But it isn't about you personally. My mother worries about me."

Haamed and I moved from the table into the living room area where we sat in the low chairs made of wooden frames with leather slings.

I was drowsy and relaxed after the long day, emboldened to ask Haamed some personal questions. "I liked the pieces I read from your reporting in West Africa. How'd you wind up there?"

He closed his eyes and smiled. "I got lucky I guess. I did an undergraduate degree at the University of Dar es Salaam in journalism. I also studied French, so when the French government advertised a scholarship for graduate studies there, I applied." He chuckled. "I think they liked the idea of getting East Africans involved in Francophone Africa. Their pride in language rivals the way Tanzanians feel about their 'pure' Swahili. The training was excellent."

He leaned forward, coming alive. "I felt freer in Paris in some ways than I ever had in my life. I loved the nightclubs, the music." His smile faded. "I loved aspects of the freedom — but it was also hard being an African there. You know the Tiken Jah Fakoly song, came out about ten years ago, 'Africain à Paris?'"

I shook my head.

"You'll recognize it," he said, scrolling on his phone, then sitting back.

Sting's "Englishman in New York," one of my favorites when I was in high school, rolled out, but with a soft reggae beat and French lyrics. It was irresistible, even through the tiny phone speaker, and I was transported to another era for a few minutes. Haamed and I sat in our respective chairs moving heads, shoulders, and feet rhythmically. It ended, and Haamed sighed. "Fakoly — from Côte d'Ivoire — had that aspect just about right. *Un peu en exile.*"

We exchanged smiles. He sat forward and the nostalgia dissipated. "Anyway, part of the program was to spend two years afterward in a Francophone country in Africa. I went to Senegal. When my time was finished, in 2004, I came back and covered the early days of the natural gas production in Mtwara."

A shadow crossed his face, and he looked down at the floor. "But I missed some things about the Francophone West African culture. They weren't stuck with the anti-gay laws the British left behind in East Africa. They had an unspoken tolerance that worked — until Western LGBT rights groups unwittingly stirred up a hornet's nest." He gave a half smile. "Another case of good intentions going wrong. I was caught up in a nasty situation in Cameroon in 2006. I moved around in different countries, keeping a low profile and reporting on non-controversial issues. I was still roaming the continent in 2013 when my uncle was killed in Mtwara and my mother had to flee."

He let his head fall. "I feel bad about that." He took a deep breath and let it out slowly. "And now I'm trying to figure out some kind of balance in my life, determine my priorities. I can't pretend to be someone I'm not, but being who I am has caused problems for other people."

Some things were too hard to talk about. We sat in the companionable silence that can follow a conversation turned unexpectedly personal.

The message notification from my phone jarred us both. I snatched up the device with a pounding heart. *Be in Mtwara with money Sunday morning. Instructions to follow.*

"Here it is, Haamed." I shoved the phone at him, and he studied the message for a long time. His face, irregular with swelling, was hard to read.

"Text back an okay."

I did. I also tried calling and got that damned voice mail message again, mocking me from cyberspace. I pictured Jared's phone, snug in the full-grain leather case I'd teased him about, now in some evil stranger's hand, left to ring unanswered. Was the guilty monster holding it, full of self-satisfaction? Or even laughing at my torment? A chill passed over me.

Haamed was practical. "Sounds like the penultimate message. We're in the right place, and now we wait. I'm going down to Mtwara tomorrow to check some things." He gave a half smile that looked more like a grimace on his battered face. "And no, you can't come with me."

It was time to call it a night, and we both stood up, breaking the intimate spell we'd shared.

In my room, I lay down but couldn't turn off my thoughts. A five-inch brick of one-hundred-twenty-five-thousand dollars, crammed into two money belts I'd gratefully taken off, rested under my duffle bag in the wardrobe near the bed. Haamed said there was no safe at the house, but also assured me that the chance of burglary was remote — no one expected to find that kind of money here. It was liberating not to have the bunchy wad around my waist, an awkward extra layer in the heat, reminding me of the reality I'd entered. But putting the cash out of sight didn't allow me to escape. Images of Jared lying somewhere bound and gagged — or worse — intermittently pierced my thoughts. The possibility of losing him, my remaining family, was like falling alone through the blackness of outer space. I didn't fall asleep until right before dawn.

23

SATURDAY, SEPTEMBER 9

Haamed was gone when I got up. It was nearly 9:00 a.m. when I emerged into the main room. I wandered into the kitchen, readying excuses for lying abed so late. The room was empty but, through a window, Amina and several young women were working in a small plot, laughing and calling out to each other as they pushed hoes and bent over to work the soil. I did a double take when I saw that a couple of the women were unmistakably pregnant.

"*Habari za asubuhi*?" asked a young woman, startling me as she came into the kitchen. She was also pregnant, heavily, looking like she might go into labor any time. She waited for my answer before she made a small curtsy with a bowed head. "*Jina langu ni Falisha*."

"*Jina langu ni Ana*," I replied. "*Lakini, najua kiswahili kidogo*." Best to admit right off the top how little Swahili I knew.

She laughed gently. "Oh? Well, you're most welcome. Mama Amina sent me to take care of your breakfast. Would you like tea or coffee?"

"Tea, thank you. But, may I help?"

Falisha answered by shooing me out the back door into a small flower garden with neat pebbled paths. Four white molded plastic chairs, some stained with orangish blotches, surrounded a table of the same substance in a circle of gravel. I wandered around, looking at the plants and enjoying the sun on my skin. I inhaled the strong floral smell and leaned over to enjoy the frangipani. Amina, visible in a plot farther away from the house and garden, but within shouting distance, continued to work with the women without looking up. Fifteen minutes later Falisha crunched her way to the table, carrying a tray crowded with a pot of tea, toast with orange marmalade, and a platter of papaya with lime.

Amina persisted with her labor, ignoring me as I ate in the garden. But she must have been aware of my presence, and as I swallowed the last bite, she finally put down her hoe and came toward me.

"Good morning, Ana." She spoke formally, with the same coolness I'd felt the previous night, so I was a bit surprised when she pulled up a chair to join me at the little round table. She drew a small paper fan from the *kanga* wrapped around her waist. "Hot in the garden already, so early." She waved the fan vigorously across her face and chest. "Haamed left hours ago, and he'll be away all day."

"Sure." I smiled in acknowledgment and finished off my tea. "Thank you for your hospitality. May I ask, who are all these young women?"

Amina swept her hand out toward the laboring women. "As you see, they're all expecting babies. There's no safety in the villages for girls like these without husbands." She grimaced. "Some die at the hands of relatives. I can't sit by and watch that. Some, like Falisha, have run away. Sometimes, a caring mother or sister or aunt smuggles them out to me. Here, they can live in security until they give birth."

Falisha appeared with a fresh pot of tea and a clean cup and saucer, which she placed in front of Amina with a slight curtsy. Amina nodded her thanks.

"And what happens to them after they have their babies?" I asked.

"That's hard," said Amina, pinching the bridge of her nose. "And it's different in each case. Some very lucky girls are able to go back to their people to live — maybe even with the baby, although that's rare. Sometimes relatives accept them back if the infant can be adopted out. We work with families to encourage them to take the girl back if we think it's safe."

She directed an unfocussed gaze across the field for several seconds. I wondered at the memories she must have stored.

Her face brightened. "We've managed to send a couple of the cleverest girls away for more education. We have a few volunteer tutors who come to us, so some girls are able to complete secondary schooling while they're here."

"Are you in danger by taking them in?"

Amina shrugged. "Maybe. Some of the most pious of their male relatives have made vague threats." Her voice hardened. "But I think they're grateful to have the girls out of their homes and out of sight. I've even had a few parents ask me to take their girls, since President Magufuli made it known that he'd enforce mandatory suspension laws for pregnant schoolgirls." She pushed a bit of light fuzzy gray at her temples back under her head scarf. "I'm limited in the number I can take. The girls work hard, and we're able to sell some of the produce from our fields. But it isn't a lot."

"How many girls do you have here?"

"Six expecting, at the moment. Two more have been here since they had their babies, and now they help run the place." She picked up the teapot and gestured to ask if I wanted more.

"Yes, please." I leaned forward to add milk after she poured.

She put the tea pot down and watched me in silence for a moment as I sipped. She looked away, sighed, and drew her arms up, crossing them over her chest. Finally, she looked directly at me. "Ana, I'm sorry about your brother, but why are you involving my son in this dangerous business?"

A thorn of defensiveness rose in my chest as I scowled and twisted my earring. I set my cup down and took a moment before speaking. Easy, Ana.

"Mama Amina, I'm sorry you're upset. I'd never heard of your son until three days ago. A friend recommended him and said he was a good journalist — someone trustworthy. I met him and explained my problem. He thought it over, and agreed to help. I didn't force him."

I didn't mention that he'd not been keen at the beginning. But he'd made his own decision. I had no power over Haamed.

"You can see now, though, can't you, how dangerous this is? You see what's happened to him already?"

"Yes. And I'm sorry. I was shocked at his injuries." My breathing quickened, and I reached out and turned my cup in its saucer. My head said I didn't need to defend myself, but the urge to do so was strong. "He never said he wanted to quit. He's been in charge of everything since this started. I'm not telling him what to do. He's a man who makes his own decisions."

I pushed the teacup away and looked at the ground,

imagining what Amina felt. I didn't know anything about her family. I wasn't going to ask if she had other children, as though their existence would somehow make Haamed less valuable. I knew nothing about his father.

As if reading my mind, Amina spoke. Her head sat straight on her stocky neck, and she crossed her arms on her chest. She'd make a fierce enemy. "Haamed is my lone living child. Or so I've come to believe. When he went to live in West Africa, I was afraid he'd never come back. He roamed for seven or eight years. My husband was Somali. He turned away from him years ago, when it became clear that Haamed was...different." She swallowed and shifted her gaze out across the field. "Imagine the pain of being abandoned by your father."

I knew exactly the pain she spoke of and I froze for a second. She brought her gaze back, and our eyes locked. I imagined the grieving of a mother for her son's rejection and she seemed less fierce than a few moments before.

"After Haamed's brother Mohammed disappeared in 2006, his father decided that he had no family, and we divorced. The two boys were like this," she said, holding up the index and middle fingers of her callused right hand. "Haamed blamed himself for his brother's disappearance, but it wasn't his fault. I don't want to see any more troubles put on the boy."

I TRIED all morning to work but couldn't concentrate. I picked up a novel, but lost track of the plot. The GHI was my best entry into the life I envisioned and I needed to make Andrew happy. Amina's concern for Haamed niggled at me. Over it all hung a big dark cloud of urgent reality. Jared was a hostage somewhere and I was waiting to hand over a ransom for his life.

Where was he? When would I get instructions to move this nightmare on to the next stage?

Amina didn't join me for lunch. I was resting in my room after the light meal when a knock sounded.

"Mama Ana?" said Falisha. "Excuse me. Mama Ana?"

I jumped off the bed and pulled on my clothes. I opened the door to find Falisha, shifting her weight from one foot to the other and twisting her hands. Her eyes darted into and around the room before coming back to me. "You need to come please. Police are here to see you. Mama Amina is with them." She pronounced the word *po*lice.

Jared. This had to be news about Jared. Silently, I slid on sandals and followed her down the hall and out to the back garden.

Mama Amina sat at the little table, along with two men in standard Tanzanian police uniforms — neat white shirts with insignia on the front and embroidered patches on the sleeves, tucked into blue trousers. They'd removed their peaked caps and set them down. As they stood up, one tall and one short, I noticed the billy clubs hanging from their belts and winced. How must it have felt when one of those connected with Haamed's cheek?

"*Habari za mchana*," I said, smiling and breathing slowly to calm myself. Waiting to let them tell me why they were here took every ounce of discipline I had.

They took my measure as they made the appropriate responses to my greeting with dead serious faces.

The tall one surprised me with a quick smile. It was perfunctory, but it reassured me a fraction. He gestured at the remaining chair and, when I moved to sit, he and his partner did the same.

"So, you are Mama Ana Lotner, is that correct?" asked the tall man. His smile disappeared, taking my confidence with it. He gave me a cold stare from under half closed lids.

I nodded, fear making me nauseated.

"And you are a visitor here from America?"

When I inclined my head again the short one leaned forward. "We'll need to see your passport."

"Okay," I said, attempting to sound light and agreeable. "It'll take just a minute to get it from the house. Do you want me to fetch it now?"

"Yes, please."

I walked at what I hoped was a dignified pace through the back door, then hurried down the hall to my room. I grabbed the passport and tried to think.

The money!

I didn't know why these guys were here, but whatever it was, I didn't want to be caught with wads of US cash I couldn't account for. I looked around frantically to see if there was a better place to hide it.

The room was simple, and the wardrobe was the only furniture, aside from the bed. Hiding it under the mattress seemed cartoonish. I separated the two money belts and laid each inside a different pair of trousers, which I folded with care and stacked among other clothes, leaving pieces of unwashed underwear on top of it all — as though this might stop them. I caught a look at myself in the mirror above the sink as I passed the door to the bathroom. It was almost a shock to see the same face from several days before. It made no sense at all that I was in the middle of an abduction and ransom crisis, hiding money while the police waited for me.

Out in the garden again, I handed the short policeman my passport. He thumbed through it in a desultory fashion, stopping now and again to point out something to his colleague. They studied the Tanzania visa at great length.

"What is your purpose here?" the tall one wanted to know.

I described my position at Honnelly and explained my mission to identify projects in Tanzania.

"Yes, but what exactly are you doing here in Lindi?"

I'd always been a lousy liar — definitely not one of those people in movies who invented credible excuses in a tight spot. This was much worse than making up stories for the doctor in the Dar hospital. I couldn't think of anything to say. I focused on the gravel under the table, noticing the little hills and valleys. I clamped my jaw, but thought of nothing to say. I hoped they couldn't see my chest thumping under my light summer shirt. The silence stretched.

"She's interested in my work with the girls." Amina's voice sounded to me like it came from miles away. I was surprised to look over and see her smiling at the policemen. "She'd like to find ways to help support these young women. Ana's family and mine have mutual friends in Moshi. That's why she's visiting."

I let out my breath. I wanted to embrace Amina for the lifeline. "Yes," I said, with a burst of enthusiasm. "Geoffrey and Fiona Walker have been in Tanzania for years. I think everyone knows them. They were kind enough to tell me about Mama Amina's work."

The two police conferred in low voices for a minute while Amina looked the other way, pretending not to listen. They pushed their chairs back and stood up. The short one handed me back my passport, and the tall one eyed me through his half closed lids.

"*Sawa*. You should take care. It's not safe for a woman to travel alone. Don't overstay your visa."

Falisha appeared at exactly the right moment to usher the men out. She must have been watching from behind the back door. Amina and I didn't move for a few moments, until we were sure they were gone.

"That scared me to death," I said, letting first my shoulders, then my entire body, droop over the little table. "Thank you for stepping in. I had no idea what to tell them."

Amina crossed her arms and looked at me. "It's the sort of harassment I feared with you here. It's aimed at my son."

"Amina, I am so sorry. I don't want anything to happen to Haamed. I don't want anything to happen to my brother."

She closed her eyes. "Do you know what those men were saying before they left?"

"No. I didn't understand it."

"They said these girls need to be punished."

My sense of relief vanished. I completely understood Amina's next words, spoken as she got up to go inside.

"I wish you success Ana. I hope your brother is released. But it will be good when you leave my house."

THE SUN WAS WELL PAST its zenith just after 4:00 p.m., when I snatched up my ringing phone with a shaky hand. I answered before I looked at the caller's name.

"Ana?"

It was Mark. I let out a long breath. Mark. Since I'd texted him from Paris, we'd exchanged one or two text messages each day, but we hadn't spoken — not unusual with the eight-hour time difference between East Africa and Eastern US time zones. The texts were brief — *How's it going? Fine. Miss you.* And mine were half-truths at best. Now he was on the other end of the line.

"Mark!" I grasped for equilibrium. "Mark, how are you?" The subsequent pause was overlong.

"Ana, why haven't you told me what's going on there?"

My mind raced, but my tongue was leaden. What did he know? And how did he learn it?

"I'm not going to play games. I ran into Beth last night. She thought I knew everything. She's a rotten liar — at least put on the spot like that. She couldn't come up with a tale to tell me, and the story came out. She felt terrible to be the one telling me — she was crying. Not over Jared, but over worry that she might've breached a confidence and let you down."

But she hadn't. That morning in Paris — was it only six days ago? — I didn't specifically ask her not to tell Mark. She'd probably assumed I'd told him, since that's what people did in relationships like Mark and I were supposed to have.

"Don't you think I'd want to know about this? Of course you have your own career, and it'll consume you sometimes. That's okay. But you gotta let me know when shocking things happen."

I tried to speak but my mouth was suddenly too dry.

He jumped into the silence. "Not so I can rescue you, Ana, but because I care what happens. Basic communication. Is there some good reason you haven't told me?"

I didn't have an answer. I was scalded — like I'd been slapped. My hands shook. "I'm...sorry." It was pathetic. I had to offer more. "The kidnappers told me not to tell anyone."

"And that includes me?" It was a genuine question, with no sarcasm, but his voice was rising, and my face got hot as he continued. "Ana, who counts in your life?"

"You do, Mark. But look at what's happening in my life! I'm confused, in the middle of a crisis."

"Yes, you are. And you're cutting me out. How do you think that feels? I don't want to compete with Jared for your loyalty. Where's the trust here?"

I spiraled into a vortex of internal rationalizations, but I felt mute.

"I'd like to keep the chance of a future together open, but you're going to have to let me know if you want the same."

"I do, but...I feel like I'm disintegrating. I'm scared to death about what's happened to Jared. Please. Just give me some time." I sat back and swallowed hard. My throat tightened, and I couldn't think of anything else to say.

I didn't have to. He was signing off.

"Good luck with your brother, Ana. I hope you'll call me soon."

I SPENT the afternoon in the back garden, drinking tea provided by the obliging Falisha, and sorting through careening feelings. I couldn't explain why I'd kept this secret from Mark. The deception *had* bothered me. But I hadn't lied to him except by omission — and I was only following orders not to tell anyone, wasn't I? My brother's life was at stake. Did I trust Mark to respect the bond I had with Jared? I was exhausted, bruised from the alternating waves of hope and despair tossing me up and down in the surf. It might be less tormenting to be stuck on the bottom.

Somewhere in the depths of my soul I knew I'd screwed up.

Gravel crunching in the drive around 6:00 p.m. alerted me to Haamed's return. He found me in the garden, before I could look for him in the house.

"Let me have a shower, Ana. Then I'll tell you what I learned. Meet me out here in half an hour."

He emerged from the house thirty minutes later, and Falisha appeared right after him.

"Can I bring something to drink?"

Haamed raised his eyebrows at me. I should take more fluids in the heat, but the thought of another pot of tea made my insides feel scrubbed.

"Thank you. Water will be fine." I turned to Haamed, leaned forward, and pulling my chair closer to his. "What did you learn about the resistance involvement?"

"It was difficult, frankly. Some old friends of mine from the movement were leery — but not like they wanted to hide something." He cocked his head. "More like they weren't sure they trusted me." He flipped his hands out, palms up, and shrugged. "I guess I expected that." He folded his hands back in his lap. "But a few were more forthcoming. I don't think they know anything about Jared's disappearance, although a couple had heard of the *mzungu* doctor doing eye surgery at the hospital. I can't be certain about them."

That told me nothing. "How about Mr. Ntabaye? Or that Dr. Nganga from the hospital in Dar? Any information about them?"

"Ntabaye, yes. There're interesting stories going around about him. He's got himself in trouble — finally — for some corruption that hurt the wrong people. The rumor is he needs money to flee Tanzania. A hundred-twenty-five-thousand would allow him to travel to another country and tide him over — and he's sure to have funds he can access stashed somewhere outside Tanzania."

Satisfaction at possibly closing in on a culprit battled

with alarm. Ntabaye was dangerous — and he'd had experience kidnapping. "That sounds suspicious, don't you think?"

"Maybe," he said in a flat tone. "Ana, I'm sorry, but
there's nothing we can do with suspicions. It'd be tricky
enough if we had hard evidence with a man like Ntabaye."

"Okay. What about Dr. Nganga?"

"I didn't have time to do much there. But he was angry
enough with Jared that his cousin here knew some of the
story. If we have time tomorrow I'd like to follow up on
that."

"And there's still al-Shabaab," I said.

"I suppose," Haamed said, with little conviction. "We
need to go down to Mtwara first thing in the morning to be
in place when instructions come for dropping the money."

24

SUNDAY MORNING, SEPTEMBER 10

I was awake before the *muezzin* started his call to prayer, glancing at my phone every few minutes, even though it hadn't made a sound. In my room, I pulled the money belts from the folds of clothing where I'd hidden them. Uncomfortable as it would be in the heat, I'd strap them on under the same long tunic I'd worn in Dar. I grabbed my brightly printed *kanga*, thinking it would come in handy for something, and strode down the hall to meet Haamed.

WE WERE in Mtwara by 7:00 a.m., reading book and newspaper at an outdoor table of a coffee shop, and exchanging occasional comments, never about the thing most on our minds. My phone, lying on the table between us, sounded at 10:45. We locked eyes as I reached for it, and Haamed's steady gaze gave me strength as I touched the screen with shaking hands.

Leave money in plastic bag at Catholic Church southeast of

*market. Rubbish bin near east entrance at 11:30 a.m. Then leave
immediately. Will release Jared at 3 p.m.*

"Why would they choose that particular place?" I
asked, handing the phone to Haamed. "Should I
respond?"

He read the message. "Text an okay." He pushed his
spectacles up, gazed at the cloudless sky, and narrowed his
eyes. "I wonder about the place," he said, punching
numbers into his own phone. He spoke in rapid Swahili, but
I caught a bit of English — "celebration of the birth of the
blessed Virgin Mary," he muttered, massaging the bridge of
his nose. "I see. Thanks."

He turned to me. "There's some kind of festival going on
there today, starting after services. Lots of people expected."
He looked at his watch. "That's forty-five minutes from now,
and it'll take us ten to reach there. I'll bet they're waiting,
watching, and they haven't given us time to set up
surveillance of our own. Let's go check it out anyway — if
you're okay to move ahead?"

I hadn't come this far to waver now. I nodded my agreement. "I'm going to tie a *kanga* over these trousers. I'll still
stick out but not quite so much."

He raised an eyebrow at me like I was crazy.

I was getting frazzled. "Wait. We need a plastic bag."

"There're several in the back of the car. Come on."

He drove fast to the church, in the middle of town. Even
from a distance I saw why the spot had been chosen. Dozens
of families were milling around outside the white cement
block building. In the front, heavy wooden doors were wide
open, and the dark interior looked cool and inviting. Little
kids raced around between tables laden with soft drinks,
snacks, and sweets, kicking up dust, while parents tried to
subdue them. Several folding tables were crowded together

near the east entrance. We'd have to move closer and look around to spot the rubbish bin.

I wouldn't stick out quite as much as I'd expected. "I'm surprised to see a few Europeans around," I said as we circled the area. We drove several blocks away to park behind some large flowering bushes.

"The church is known for its paintings, and the celebration's been well advertised," said Haamed as we got out of the car. "I'm going to watch what happens after you drop the money, so I don't want anyone who's there watching to see us together." He glanced at his wristwatch, "We've got twenty minutes. I want to look around the church grounds now. Are you okay staying here for another five or ten minutes?"

"Sure." Our eyes locked and gratitude filled me for just an instant before anxiety over the looming stakes rose again. "I'll make my way over in about ten minutes and make the drop." I touched the belts at my midriff. "Wait! I've got to get the money into the plastic bag."

"Put it in now, tie the *kanga* over it, and snug it up to your waist." He smiled. "That's where women all over rural Africa carry their money."

I managed a weak smile at the touch of levity. I took his advice and pulled the *kanga's* ends into a good firm knot over my new paunch.

"Where do I go after I drop it?"

"Come right back to the car. I'll be watching from nearby. If you notice me don't make any sign. They're not going to leave the money there long. I'll meet you at the car soon afterward." He pulled a multicolored knit cap down over his smart haircut. Between that, sunglasses, faded jeans, and an old t-shirt, I hardly recognized him.

"Haamed, no heroics, right?"

He took off the dark glasses, which still concealed nasty discoloration and abrasions. He rolled his eyes. "I like you, Ana, but I don't even know Jared. Don't worry. No heroics."

I wanted to hug him, but settled for a handshake. "We'll touch base by phone if necessary. Be careful."

"You too," he said striding away. My knees started to wobble the second he left.

TEN TORTURED MINUTES LATER, I did my best imitation of a stroll over to the church. In the wandering crowd, no one paid much attention to me, although I got a few smiles. I must have looked ill, with my arms crossed, cradling my abdomen. I forced my face into a pleasant expression and hoped not to look like a lurker around the laden tables near the east entrance. There it was, right up next to one of the tables — an old banged-up fifty-five-gallon drum, no lid, smashed in around the bottom. Once I got the rubbish bin in my sight, I avoided looking in that direction.

Two little kids approached with their hands out. Their mother smacked them away with harsh words, then smiled an apology at me. I pulled out my phone and pretended to be texting as I looked at the time: 11:27.

I homed in on the black rubbish bin. It would have served many purposes until, dented and leaking, it found its last use to collect waste. It was over three-quarters full, and it crossed my mind that that was no accident. Only in America, wedded to disposables, did people fill these oversize receptacles at one function. But someone had taken the trouble to fill it up this morning so it would be easy to reach into and retrieve a particular bag on top.

I'd imagined that I might notice something odd, but all I

saw was people meandering around the table, enjoying their samosas, biscuits, and Fantas in the warm humid air.

Sweat formed into beads and crept down my back. Large birds screeched overhead, and crows strutted around the ground, investigating the hard-packed dirt for edibles. Children ran everywhere, roughhousing and screaming. A little girl, dressed in a ruffled, pink organza dress, played hide and seek with her friend behind the drum, shrieking with delight.

At exactly 11:30, I shoved the phone into the folded waist of the *kanga* and edged up next to the rubbish bin, still fiddling with the knot. I pulled the plastic bag out, as casually as I could with trembling hands, and let it fall into the black container. It made no sound as it landed. I didn't look to see where it rested. Sweat dripped from my forehead. I pivoted and took a samosa from the table, smiling at a woman nearby. I walked away, willing myself to move quickly but calmly, so I wouldn't draw attention.

No one called out, "Mama, you dropped this!" or followed me. It took all the discipline I had not to look behind me. The walk back, past a few houses and a little shop, felt like it took hours. I got to the car and looked at my phone. It was 11:35. I exhaled.

I was dying to know what Haamed was seeing. I paced back and forth alongside the car, checking every minute or two to make sure I'd not missed a text. After ten long minutes, I recognized his lithe stride, coming toward me from the opposite direction I'd taken. I had to restrain myself from running to him.

"What happened?" I asked when he got close, my voice hoarse with dryness.

He blew out a big breath through closed lips, pulled off

his dark glasses, and shook his head from side to side. "I don't know."

My mouth fell open. "What do you mean? What did you see?"

"I watched you drop the bag. About fifteen seconds later, two boys came up to the table, near the rubbish bin. I couldn't see whether they spoke to the little girls who were playing there — you must have seen one in a pink dress?"

I nodded, frowning.

"The boys got into a scuffle. One of the legs of the table collapsed, and the whole slab came down. I lost sight of the bin for about a minute in the confusion, with a couple dozen people crowding around. By the time I elbowed my way forward there was no blue bag in the bin."

"But..."

"Wait. I glimpsed one of the kids running away and chased him. His family are regulars at the church. His main concern was avoiding trouble from his mother when she got hold of him. He claimed he didn't know the other boy, had never seen him before. Said he was some kid who started pushing, shoved him hard at the table leg, then disappeared.

"I found out who his parents were and managed to have a brief word with them." He produced a rueful smile. "The boy was right to be worried. He'll get a beating from his mother. But the family's completely legitimate. Members of the church and the community for years. He and his sisters are good kids." He took off his dark glasses and massaged his forehead.

"So the bag was gone?"

"Of course." He stuck out his lower lip. "It was well organized."

∾

I GLANCED AT THE TIME — almost noon. Three hours until I'd learn if we'd bought Jared's freedom and where we would find him. There was nothing to do but wait.

"Let's get a coffee back at the café. I need to decompress," I said, taking the first deep breath I'd managed all day.

But we didn't make it into the café. As we pulled up to the front, my phone signaled me. I didn't recognize the number.

I read the screen and my jaw dropped. "Haamed! Jared's free!"

He slammed on the brakes, and I lurched forward against the seat belt as the tires skidded on gravel. "What? Already? How?" Our eyes met. I handed him my phone. *Ana, I got out. Where are you? Waiting at Ng'onye Inn Mtwara.*

I grabbed the phone back with a trembling hand. "I'm calling the number," I said, my voice cracking.

I don't know what I expected, but Jared answered the phone. "Ana? Ana!"

"Jared?" I had to force the word out of my constricted throat. "Jared! Are you okay? What's going on?"

I heard the smile in his voice, calm and smooth in contrast to mine. "I'm fine. I'm waiting at the Ng'onye Inn in Mtwara. Where are you?"

"I'm in Mtwara too."

"You're in Mtwara? Oh my God! What are you doing here?"

But the connection was breaking up his words. "Gotta...phone back...explain...Inn."

Haamed drove the four kilometers to the Ng'onye Inn faster than I'd have believed the old Hyundai would go. It was as close as I ever saw him come to recklessness, but I had no criticism. We blasted down the potholed Zambia

Road, and I bounced up and down, hanging on to a plastic strap over the passenger seat window with my left hand and gnawing the knuckles on my right. I forced myself to stop chewing my hand only to find I was chewing my lip — and trying to talk at the same time.

"Escaped? But how'd he get to this Inn? We just dropped the money."

Haamed glanced away from the windscreen long enough to give me a calculated stare. "Easy, Ana. We'll find out shortly."

The sign for the Ng'onye Inn was faded almost beyond reading, but Haamed knew the place.

"That's him!" I pointed at my brother as we pulled into the little brick-paved parking area. "That's Jared."

25

SUNDAY AFTERNOON, SEPTEMBER 10

I was out of the car before Haamed shut off the engine. Jared stood three meters away. He threw his arms open as I leaped from the car and I flew into his embrace. His unshaven face scratched my forehead as he bent to envelop me. He wiped tears from my face and stroked my hair.

"Ahh, Ana," he said, his voice catching. He pulled back and looked around. "Where's Sean?"

Of course. He didn't know what I'd been doing the past few days. "Don't worry. Sean's safe. He's back in the US with Beth."

"What? In the US? I've been looking forward to seeing him." He slumped a little.

I understood his disappointment. He'd probably have trouble thinking straight for a while. "You didn't think I'd risk someone grabbing him too, did you? His safety was one of my first worries."

"Yeah. Of course." He tightened his embrace. "Thank you, Ana."

I pulled back to take a good look at him. "You're really

okay." I studied him in detail. He was dirty, his hair matted, his pants sagging, and his shirt stained and torn. His face was scraped, his arms and hands dotted with rough red patches.

He turned as Haamed unfolded from the driver's side of the car, slammed the door, and walked toward us.

"Did you pay your driver?" asked Jared. "I'm afraid I have no wallet. No phone. Nothing."

"Oh." I smiled. "Jared, this is Haamed Hassan. He's a friend of the Walkers who comes from this area. He's been helping me the past few days."

Haamed extended his hand. "Welcome," he said gravely. After a moment's hesitation, Jared took his hand and nodded. For a moment it was like two bull elephants sizing each other up. He and Jared shook hands, but Jared didn't smile, and he turned back to me.

"I thought no one knew about this. I mean, the man said he told you not to contact anyone."

"We can trust Haamed. Let's go inside for a drink," I said, starting for the door of the Inn. "This is no place to hear everything."

He still hesitated. The poor guy was overwhelmed. I grabbed his arm and pulled him toward the door of the yellow concrete-block guesthouse. Haamed walked right behind us.

Inside the cool dimness of the Inn, we passed a modest reception desk with an artificial floral arrangement in a shiny gold plastic vase. The entry led into a small lounge with several plastic-covered tables and dining chairs. The smooth, dark red concrete floor was slick with polish.

We took chairs in the empty lounge. Jared and I leaned across the table toward each other and started to speak at the same time. I stopped, hand to my throat. "Okay. You start. Tell us what happened."

Jared stretched back, tilting his chair onto the rear legs. He glanced from me to Haamed, who watched him with slightly narrowed eyes. He let the chair fall forward with a thud and leaned over the table on his forearms, hands folded together. He looked straight at me. "I've been held for nine days. I escaped last night."

Haamed raised his brows.

I threw my hand out. "But we just paid the ransom. We got a message where to drop it this morning. That's why I'm in Mtwara."

Jared's mouth fell slack. "What? No!" He shook his head and massaged his forehead. "You mean you gave them the cash? All of it?"

"Yes, I got it from the Loubets, as you suggested."

"What time did you get the message?"

"Right before 11:00 — at 10:45."

"I don't think they'd have sent the message if they knew I'd escaped. That old guy must have been tied up in the room all night. I bet they've found him now." He groaned and frowned, deep lines emerging between his eyebrows. "But they must have also got the money."

I reached across and pulled his hand from his forehead and I held it in both of mine. "Jared," I breathed out in a whisper. "I'm just so grateful that you're safe. I need a chance to get used to this." I took a deep breath and let it out in a long sigh. "Start at the beginning. What old guy? Tell us what happened."

"Okay." He patted my hand, extracting his own. "But let's have that drink." He rocked back on the chair again. "Haamed, can you see if there's someone in the reception to bring us drinks?"

Haamed studied him for a second, shrugged, and went out to the front desk to have a word. He was back in less than a minute. "Help yourself to the beverages in the cooler." He took out a bottle of water. "Ana? Tangawizi?"

"And I'll have a beer," said Jared before Haamed closed the door. "Safari."

The three of us moved to the back of the room, where a pink overstuffed couch and matching loveseat sat on opposite sides of a coffee table. I shifted a centerpiece of plastic flowers so we could see each other.

"So," Jared said, "to start at the beginning — we had a great surgical session in Mtwara. People were thrilled. The nuns asked us to return." He let that sink in, smiling. "I headed out on Friday morning as planned, after checking the last group of patients. It's always so satisfying to take off the bandages.

"I'd received a text message from a local businessman — at least that's what he claimed to be — on Thursday. He wanted to meet before I left town to discuss the chance of me returning to do a free surgical camp to honor his mother, who passed away last year." He rolled the bottle of beer between his palms before taking a swallow. "I think the guy said he worked for the Tanzania Development Corporation — or maybe it was some other big organization around here."

Jared shifted on his end of the couch. "Anyway, it was a possibility to support my non-profit, so I agreed to meet him at the Himo 2 café on the way to the airport on Friday. My flight was supposed to leave at eleven thirty that morning. The sisters insisted on driving me to the café and we left the hospital early. I said goodbye to them around nine fifteen and went in to wait for the guy." He shook his head. "He never showed up. I texted him and called his number, but no answer."

Haamed leaned in and listened without moving a muscle as Jared continued.

"By ten fifteen, I had to leave to make my flight, so I went outside to find a lift. An old blue Toyota sedan pulled up, and a young guy in the passenger seat asked if I needed a taxi. He spoke to the driver, then said they'd take me to the airstrip. I threw my duffel in the rear and got in next to it."

Jared raked his hand through his hair and frowned. "Should have been a straight shot down the A19 to the airport, but, at some point, the driver took a left as the young guy turned to me and said, 'I'll stop here.' The driver braked in an alleyway and the young guy jumped out. He whirled around, opened the door, and was in the rear seat next to me before I knew what'd happened. I'm sure I could have over-powered him if I'd been expecting it — but I wasn't. He had me down in the seat, bound, and blindfolded before I could resist. I yelled, but he gagged me fast. The car was moving again. I admit I was scared, but I figured they wanted my wallet. I got really worried when we kept going. I struggled, but the guy was strong, and I was tied up. We drove for an hour, maybe hour and a half, with a number of turns. I have no idea where we went."

I was riveted — hadn't taken a single sip of my Tangaw-izi. Haamed was watching Jared with the intensity of a stalking predator. Jared tipped his bottle up again, and I watched the muscles in his throat ripple as the beer went down.

Haamed waited till Jared finished his long guzzle, then spoke. "Was the road tarmac or dirt?"

"Some of both," said Jared. "Both pretty rough."

"Did they have a gun?"

"I don't know. Remember, I was blindfolded, and they had me down behind the front seats. I could hardly move. When we finally stopped, they pulled me out, took my phone and wallet, and shoved me into a small room. They untied my hands before they pushed me through the door. I took off the blindfold and untied my own legs.

"The room was cement block with a foam mattress on the floor, a plastic bucket for a toilet, and an unopened two-liter bottle of water. The door was one of those solid iron ones with a little sliding panel cut in it, but it wouldn't budge from the inside. Light filtered into the room through a high window on one wall, but I couldn't see out."

Haamed nodded. "Did they speak to you?"

"Not a word. They talked to each other, but it didn't sound like Swahili."

"All right. No more interruptions. Please go on."

"Okay. No one came to me all afternoon. I yelled until I was exhausted. The window was way too high to reach. Around dusk, someone slid the panel open to look in, then opened the door a crack and pushed through a small plastic bucket with a lid — you know the type." He held his hands in horizontal planes to demonstrate. "About this tall. Full of *ugali* and beans.

"I had a terrible night lying on that mattress — don't think I ever closed my eyes. The next morning, maybe an hour after dawn, the young guy slid open the little panel to talk to me." Jared narrowed his eyes. "He hadn't said much the day before, but he spoke English pretty well. He told me he'd used my phone to send a text message to you, Ana. To say they had me." He shook his head and pursed his mouth. "He wouldn't let me see the text. I asked how he knew about you, and he just laughed."

Goosebumps rose on my arms. They knew who I was.

Maybe *where* I was, and what I'd been doing. Creepy.

"They probably knew about Sean too," I said, letting out the deep breath I'd been holding. "Good thing we got him back to Beth. Who knows what they might have planned?"

"Yeah. That morning, the guy wanted to talk about getting a ransom. He said I had to prepare a message for you, how to get one-hundred-twenty-five-thousand dollars. I thought about it all day and decided the Loubets were our best hope. That evening, I had to record it twice. They thought something was funny the first time — that "doable" wasn't a word and I was trying to pull something off. After I recorded that message, I didn't see much of anyone for the next week. Just got food and water at irregular times."

Haamed hadn't taken his eyes off my brother.

Jared leaned forward, arms on his thighs, lower jaw protruding. "From the first day I was locked in that room, I was looking for a way to escape — but I needed to understand the routine — if there was gonna be one. They were careful to open the door only enough to slip things in, so I couldn't see outside. I sometimes heard voices midday, but nothing at night except insects and a few dogs barking far away. I was isolated. Besides giving me food twice a day and emptying the slop bucket, they left me alone."

He rubbed the back of his neck with a shudder. "When they came, they always rattled the little window. I was supposed to put the buckets next to the door and put on a blindfold. Then I had to lie on the floor in the far corner, facing the wall. Once all was positioned, they opened the door and swapped the buckets in a couple of seconds." He leaned back and held out his hands, palms up. "So I never got a look at anyone. One time, I kept the slop bucket in the far corner of the room, to see if they'd come in to retrieve it. They didn't."

Haamed was so still that his breathing was imperceptible. Only his eyes looked alive.

Jared let his gaze drop to the floor before he took a breath and continued. "I counted the seconds it took for the bucket swaps — the time when the door would be open. On Thursday morning, something changed. It took longer for the exchange, and whoever did it had a hell of a wheeze. Labored breathing, wet cough. Hawking phlegm. Sounded sick and unfit. The door was open longer, and that meant I had an opportunity. I practiced and timed myself by counting seconds. I could get to my feet and over to the door from the corner in a little over half the time the door was open. Of course, I had no idea if the person was armed, how big, or what. But I figured I had to take a chance the next time the wheezy one came at night.

"Last night I did it. I lay in the corner as always, with my back to the door and the blindfold on loosely. I heard the wet breathing and the second the bucket scraped across the floor I jumped up, moving fast. I dragged the guy through the door into the room with my hand over his mouth and had him bound in a couple of seconds." He looked down and waved his hand at his tattered clothes. "I'd torn fabric from inside my waistband and from the bottom of my shirt to make ties for his hands. Plus I had the rope I'd taken off my own feet. I was right about him being old and weak. No fight, and no chance to make more than a feeble cry before I gagged him, using the blindfold.

"I ran outside. It was too dark to see detail, and I wasn't going to stick around. A small house sat about fifty meters away, with a dim light inside. I went the opposite direction, toward an area that looked wooded. I sprinted in what I hoped was a straight line for maybe two hours. I had to slow when the undergrowth got heavy. When I convinced myself no one was following me, I lay down for the night.

"In the morning I started walking again. After a while, the brush thinned and I came to a dirt road. A truck driver picked me up there this morning and dropped me off here at this place. He let me use his phone to text you."

I hadn't said a word as Jared spilled out his story. When he stopped talking, Haamed scribbled hard for a minute. The only sound was his pen and the soft *thwap-thwap* of the revolving ceiling fan.

I moved closer to Jared on the couch and threw my arms around him. I leaned limp against him, as pent-up tension poured out of me.

"Jared, I might have lost you." I sobbed against his chest. "I can't believe what you've been through — that this happened."

"I know, Ana, I know." Jared's muscular body relaxed beneath me. He seemed thinner.

Haamed watched us with a faint smile. He leaned forward and cocked his head. "Strange situation. I know the area well. Mind if I ask a few questions?"

"Sure. Go ahead," said Jared, extricating himself and settling back on the couch.

"Do you know which way the window in the room faced? Say, by the sun?"

Jared beetled his eyebrows and frowned. "The sun didn't come directly through the window. It was diffuse, but maybe it faced more or less north."

"Did you say your captors spoke to you in English?"

"Not really. Except when we talked the second day about money and the voice message. Otherwise, they didn't talk at all."

"Who gave you the instructions for lying in the corner

blindfolded when they brought food?"

"Oh, right. That routine was established the first day by the young guy — the one who made the voice message with me. But nothing after that."

"Did you hear anything outside the room? Animals? Voices?"

"Roosters, of course. And the dogs. Once, some children shouting. Adults once or twice. I didn't recognize the language."

"Sound of the ocean?

"No."

"How high was the window in the room?"

Jared closed his eyes and stuck his top teeth over his lower lip for a second. "The roof of the building was slanted at a steep angle. Say, thirty degrees? So the wall at one end was higher than the one opposite. The window was high in the wall — maybe three-and-a-half to four meters up?"

"Was it a thatch roof?"

"No. Corrugated metal."

"And what did you say was the name of the local businessman you were supposed to meet?"

"Mujit Dhamji."

Haamed closed his notebook and slipped it back into his pocket.

"What about the money?" asked Jared. "What happened with that?"

I related an abbreviated version of my visit to the Loubets. I pulled out my phone and showed him all the messages I'd received. "So, we hoped to see you later this afternoon — that is, if the kidnappers followed through and released you."

"I'm glad I got out when I did. I'm not sure they'd have let me go."

"I agree, Jared. I'm just relieved you're here now. The Loubets will be thrilled, and I ought to let them know. And the Walkers and Grace. They've all been waiting for news."

Haamed stood up. "I'd like to suggest that you wait on that, Ana. You didn't give them precise details of when we expected the release. How about if you and Jared go to Lindi and spend the night? I'll find someone to take you. I'd like to ask a few questions around here, and I'll drive up there later."

Jared shifted and used his arms to push himself up straighter on the couch. He nodded several times and narrowed his eyes almost imperceptibly at Haamed. "Why are you going to do that?" He ran his tongue over his lips. "I mean, is it a good idea? Won't you be stirring things up? The guys who did this are serious — and they might still be around."

"True. They might be. Or they might be long gone with the money."

"Sure," said Jared. "But they're dangerous. I don't want you to do anything that might put us — or you — at risk." He shook his head and expelled a big breath. "I'd like to set this behind me."

"I understand," said Haamed. "I plan to be careful. But I grew up here. It's still my home and I like to keep up on happenings. Let me find a taxi to take you to Lindi."

"No blue Toyotas," said Jared, with a weak smile.

"Of course not," said Haamed. His face was dead solemn.

JARED SLEPT most of the way to Lindi, in the back seat of our taxi — no surprise. After what he'd been through, I was impressed by his composure. But that was my brother. My heart brimmed with gratitude, relief, and love. I had to rouse him when we got to Lindi.

Amina, warned by a call from Haamed, expected us. She was hardly effusive, but warmer than she'd been previously. Or maybe it was me. I was a different person than she'd met two days before. The heaviest weight I'd ever shouldered had fallen away in the past few hours and I was ready to fly. Sure, the gratitude buoying me up at that moment would ebb. With time, I'd go back to taking Jared for granted — but it wasn't time yet.

He wanted a shower. He'd lost his bag, of course, along with everything else. Amina was prepared with old, but clean, jeans and a t-shirt. "Or if you'd rather, I can give you one of Haamed's jellabiyas. One-size-fits-all."

Jared, a bit shorter and broader than Haamed, studied the denims. "I'll wear the jellabiya, thanks."

"And would you like a light refreshment now or prefer to wait for dinner later?" asked Amina as she handed over the jellabiya.

"I'd love a snack and a bee...soft drink," he said, awareness dawning on his face as he looked at the jellabiya. "Thank you." He gave Amina one of his beautiful grins, and she smiled back. "But may I have some time to recover, please? Say, an hour? Hour and a half?"

Jared disappeared into the house.

"I'll fill you in now if you'd like," I said to Amina.

We walked together to the back garden chairs and I explained what we'd done that morning.

"So, Haamed is still down there talking to people about this?" she asked, scowling. "He didn't tell it quite like that. What difference does it make now? Your brother is back and safe."

"Yes. And I'm beyond grateful to Haamed for that. As far as I'm concerned this thing is over. I have what I wanted — my brother safe."

"I hope I'll be able to say the same about my son," Amina said, rising.

I understood, but couldn't do more than smile at her, and she walked away.

A minute later my phone vibrated. I glanced at the screen and answered. "Haamed, what's going on? Your mother isn't happy with me."

I heard the smile in his voice. "Nor with me, I suspect. How's Jared?"

"Showering before donning your jellabiya."

"Ask my mother to give him some *malapas*. It'll look ridiculous with his trainers and athletic socks."

I smiled. "He can go to town for some clothes tomorrow. He'll want to go home as soon as possible, and we need to plan that."

"Okay. I'm at the hospital with the religious sisters now. You can imagine their shock. They blame themselves for leaving him."

I grunted my understanding.

"I've learned a few things about people he met and spent time with here. I'm going to stay around so I can meet a man later tonight or tomorrow morning. No problems. I only want to follow up a couple of things."

"Okay. Haamed, please be careful. Don't take any chances. I'm fine if this ordeal ends right now. You've gone beyond the call of duty. I think I can speak for Jared in saying that we're satisfied to leave it. The money is gone. It was intended to ensure his return, and we've got him, however it happened. I don't think the Loubets will regret this outcome at all."

But Haamed was a journalist.

JARED STROLLED out to the garden in the late afternoon. Haamed was right — the footwear wasn't right.

"Nice look, bro," I said, staring at his feet.

He grinned and tousled my hair. "So, Ana, you know what I'd like? I want to talk to Sean. God, I've missed that boy. What time is it anyway?"

I glanced at my mobile. "Just before five."

"Hmm. Five p.m. here means...nine in the morning at home."

"Remember that Sean doesn't know about the kidnapping," I said. "I spoke to Beth two days ago, and she hadn't told him. He thinks you had to stay a bit longer to take care of some patients. She's trying to protect him."

Jared raised his chin. "Well, I'm his father, so I've got some say in what he hears too. And now it's a happy story."

I frowned. "It may have a happy ending but it's never going to be a happy story. I think Beth's right to protect Sean from some things." But I shrugged and handed him my phone.

He scrolled down the screen and leaned back in the chair, rubbing his freshly shaved jaw. His right ankle rested on his left knee, and the late afternoon sun glinted off the golden hairs of his calf, exposed as the jellabiya slid up. "Beth?" he said louder than was necessary. "Beth, I'm free."

Silence for several seconds.

"Yeah, I escaped. That's right." His ear-to-ear grin showed off the excellent teeth I'd always admired.

He deserved privacy so I walked out into the *shamba*. But I heard his booming bonhomie turn short and clipped in a few minutes. The announcement had turned into an argument.

I wandered the *shamba* thinking about the conflict between them. When I was sure he'd finished the call I ambled back and raised my eyebrows in a question.

"Damn it, Ana! She doesn't want me to talk to him on the phone about it." He glanced down impatiently. "Of course, he's in school now anyway. I'll call later but she doesn't want me to tell him until we can talk face-to-face. Says it's too traumatic for a phone conversation."

"Sorry. But you can at least hear his voice later, can't you?" I sat down. "Beth may be right. What's a day or two matter?"

His angry face softened. "Okay. I guess it can wait. I only want what's best for Sean. But I've been thinking. People'll be interested in this and we need to figure out how to tell them." He scratched his jaw. "Maybe a press release from my NGO?"

I frowned. "I'm not sure, Jared. We don't need to do anything yet. We should tell the Loubets first. They shouldn't find out about this from the news. Ditto for the Walkers. Let's see what Haamed thinks."

Jared bit one side of his lower lip and narrowed his eyes. "Now don't be annoyed, Ana. I know he's been a help to you — moral support, I guess — but I don't see what he's got to do with this now. Who is he anyway, besides a friend of the Walkers?"

"He's a journalist, Jared, but he doesn't introduce himself that way unless it's necessary. He's been in political trouble and needs to be careful."

"A journalist!" Jared lowered his brows, then pursed his lips and cocked his head. "Why didn't you say so? He might be useful. I've been wondering whether I ought to talk to someone in Dar before I put out word about my escape back home — Haamed could facilitate that for sure."

"And all the more reason to wait to speak to him before telling everyone about this."

We had dinner with Amina, much like the night Haamed and I arrived, but Jared sat in Haamed's place. He wanted to talk about Sean. I pulled out my phone to show a few pictures, and Amina indulged us, although perhaps she didn't think he was quite as magnificent a nine-year-old as we did. Amina excused herself after the meal and left the two of us.

Jared and I stayed on at the table. He wanted all the details of my time with Sean, and he smiled every time he spoke of him.

"We need to make a decision about going back," I said. "I guess you want to go as soon as possible."

"Yep. Can't wait to see Sean. We were supposed to do another game drive after I finished at the hospital." He rubbed his brow. "Let's see, our tickets were for Wednesday, the sixth." He shook his head. "Wow, I'm confused. It's Sunday now — the tenth, right? I lost a week." He scratched his head. "Hey, did you contact my office? They expect me to be back at work tomorrow. The days just slid together."

He sounded drowsy and, for the first time, I considered that he might not have come out of this trauma unscathed. It had to have taken a toll on him.

"Your office doesn't know anything. We need to tell them now that you're delayed. The best you're going to do at this point is to leave Tanzania tomorrow night on the KLM flight out of Dar — if there's a seat. And we've got to let the embassy know you've lost your passport. Better to try for Tuesday. I'll arrange it, as well as call your office. I can tell them you need a day or two more to recover from sinusitis or something."

His lids drooped.

"Jared, you're exhausted. The only thing holding you up the last few hours is sheer tension. Let it go. We'll talk when Haamed gets back in the morning. We'll work out a plan to get to Dar and on a plane back to the US."

"Okay, Ana. You're right." He pushed back from the table, looking drained.

I stepped over and hugged him with all the strength I had. "I am *so* glad to have you back."

He staggered off to bed.

If Jared had been damaged by the past ten days, he wasn't alone. Adrenaline had kept me going and now I was a rag doll. I was scheduled to return to the US on Tuesday, the same date I'd advised Jared to go. I should have spent the previous week investigating projects. Now I could either go back with Jared or pull myself together, extend my stay and hope to wrench some useful work out of this trip. Since the threat to Jared was over, maybe I could level with Andrew and suggest a week's extension. He'd have to understand when he learned what I'd been through. The prospect was exhausting, but it was better than returning empty handed.

An hour later my phone alert sounded. It was a text from Haamed. *Got some answers. I'll be in Lindi tomorrow morning.*

In spite of the fact that I was dying to know what he'd learned, I slept well that night. I should have enjoyed it more — it was the most peaceful night I'd have for a long time.

26

MONDAY, SEPTEMBER 11

The crunch of gravel alerted me to Haamed's arrival around 8:30 the next morning. I'd been up for a couple of hours, drinking tea in the back garden, and basking in the morning sun.

"Where's Jared?" he asked.

"Still asleep," I said with a smile. "I'll go wake him up."

I started to rise but Haamed stopped me. "No. Wait, Ana. I'd like to talk to you first." He looked back toward the house. "In fact, let's walk over to the far side of the *shamba*. There's a little bench we can use where we won't be disturbed."

I forced myself up. "Okay. But I'm dying to know what you learned. Can't you tell me as we walk?"

Haamed hesitated and squinted across the field for several seconds. "No. Let's sit down."

Unease ruffled my mind as we made our way along a hard packed path. Under a big mango tree, we sat on an old wooden bench, worn smooth by sun, wind, and rain, and intended to give women a rest in the shade.

"Ana, how well do you know your brother?"

Huh? I frowned. What was I supposed to say? "He's my *brother*. I've known him forever." I threw my hands out at the impossibility of describing the lifelong relationship. "He looks out for me, and he's one of my best friends. He's a good person who works to help people. What are you looking for?"

Haamed watched me without a word, and I was once again reminded of the graceful big cat who'd approached me in the hotel lobby five days before. This time, I recognized the deep sympathy in his eyes, but something inside me was crumpling. I wanted to touch Haamed's warm brown face from some sense that I'd draw strength there.

He took a long chest-expanding inhalation and let it out. "Ana, Jared was not abducted. It didn't happen the way he told it."

The earth dipped and spun, and I put both palms on the bench to steady myself. A lump in my throat turned into a boulder, and the hoarse whisper hurt coming around it. "What are you talking about? He...wasn't abducted?"

Haamed locked eyes with me. Across this bridge into his soul lay a deep well of strength and I drew from it.

"It's been a hoax, Ana. A hoax. Breathe slowly and listen. I need to tell you what I've learned."

I heard my harsh dry breath. Haamed looked hazy through air that seemed to shimmer.

He began his story.

"Jared's work at the hospital was fine. He left behind grateful patients who can see again, thanks to his efforts. The nurses and religious sisters liked him, once they sorted out an issue about patient fees. They said he insisted they drop him alone at that café. They never heard of Mujit Dhamji, the guy Jared was supposed to meet. In fact, *no one's* heard of him."

Haamed laid a warm hand on my arm. Something inside me was crumpling and dying.

"One of Jared's first patients was an old man from Msimbati — you know, the place I told you about, where there was trouble when government forces tried to quell unrest over the pipeline? Anyway, the old man, Jared's patient, had a wife, and she was killed that night. I know this because I learned it from the man's son, Amal. It was his mother who was killed."

He glanced away and I studied the intricate pattern in the worn wood of the bench. After a few silent seconds, I felt his gaze, and our eyes met again.

"Turns out Jared heard Amal's story too. The sisters said the two of them spent a bit of time together, even shared a meal on Wednesday, connecting first over the old man's surgery." He shrugged. "Amal speaks pretty good English, and he was grateful to Jared for the fact that his father can see again. I guess they started talking, and Jared was especially interested and sympathetic toward Amal's bitterness over the pipeline project.

"On Thursday, Jared sent a message to Amal to say he wanted to meet again. He had a plan he wanted help with. He told Amal all he had to do was provide a place for him to stay out of sight for a few days and to help retrieve some cash."

I tried to breathe slowly. Clammy sweat seeped under my arms.

"Jared told Amal that part of the money would compensate him and his family for the wrongs they've suffered. It would also go toward building an eye clinic in the area. Amal was uneasy, but he's not a sophisticated guy. Jared convinced him that no one would be harmed and that the payment would be coming from some of the 'bad guys'

responsible for the injustices associated with the natural gas
project."

I slumped against the warm wood bench. Only
Haamed's gaze kept me from dissolving around my racing
heart.

"But Jared had never been to Mtwara before. How could
he have planned this?"

Haamed nodded slowly. "I think it was a scheme he
contrived on impulse — a sort of crime of opportunity."

I couldn't accept what I was hearing. "So, did you talk to
Amal?"

"I did, Ana. The sisters told me about him and, once I
had his name, it wasn't hard to find his house. It was a bit
harder to find Amal, who'd been lying low. He's the man I
stayed down there to speak with last night."

"And you believe this Amal? You take his word over
Jared's?"

"I do, Ana." He looked down.

"But maybe Amal's the kidnapper."

His smile was pitying. "That's exactly what he's afraid
the police will think now, if Jared's story gets out, but it can't
be true. I've spoken to a number of people around there.
He's not part of any group that might be behind this, like the
resistance, and he doesn't have the wherewithal to do it on
his own. Most kidnappers want credit for their work —
they're promoting a cause. Once I found Amal's house, there
were other things that didn't make sense. The building
where Jared says he was held actually exists — pretty much
as he described it — but I doubt the door could be secured
well enough to hold someone as fit as Jared."

I was limp with dread. "Why did you suspect Jared of
lying?"

He shifted. "I didn't assume he was. I wanted to find out

what happened. It's my job to question, and several things didn't make sense. The sound of the ocean. I was sure I heard it in the voice message. Anyone confined alone in that building for days on end wouldn't forget the steady pounding of the nearby surf. And, another thing: if you kidnapped someone, wouldn't you take his shoes? Then, once I started asking I learned that Mujit Dhamji doesn't seem to exist."

I had one last protest. "But, if he made this up, why come out right after the money was dropped? Why not emerge at three o'clock, like the message promised?"

Haamed's face was soft with pity. "That timing was important. If Jared waited till three, he wouldn't be able to claim he escaped his captors."

Sickeningly, that resonated. Jared wanted to be a hero.

Haamed continued. "Amal wasn't at his home, but I tracked him to a neighbor's place. Once I mentioned abduction, the poor guy fell apart and told me everything. I think he was glad to have it off his chest."

"Why the hell would Amal go along with this scheme?"

"Ana, you see Jared as your brother. Put yourself in Amal's position. What do you think he sees? A powerful, wealthy man he has no reason to distrust. Jared's a white doctor with status."

Haamed let me process this for several seconds.

"And then, there's the money. Amal said Jared promised him ten thousand dollars." He frowned. "Amal got involved on Thursday, the day after he and Jared had dinner together."

"And the day after Beth's revelations in a phone conversation," I said, seeing the whole sorry story coming into focus.

We sat in silence for a while, me trembling like the

leaves blowing in the mango above us. My life lay in pieces, like after I learned about my father's death, except I didn't have Jared to help me through this. Tears rolled down my face.

Haamed was still for several minutes, head bowed. "Before you fetch Jared, I want to tell you something." He swallowed and looked out across the *shamba*. "In 2006, when I was still living in Cameroon, my brother Mohammed came to live with me, looking for work. It was a great time, although I worried a bit about some of his activities. I was right to worry. He got involved in a land deal he couldn't afford. It was stupid and he was in over his head. Of course, people knew who I was and who I loved. That's the way it was in Cameroon, and no one cared — until my brother got in trouble. When a list of gay men was published, my name was there. It was an attempt to take revenge on Mohammed. He felt responsible, and he was devastated. To make the story short, he had to run from some nasty men. He disappeared completely. I spent years searching for him. At first, I was driven by anger, but, eventually, it was love. I wish every day I had him back to forgive. No one is irredeemable as long as he is loved."

He stood up. "I think we should talk to Jared now."

JARED WAS up when I knocked on his door. I couldn't face him, so I called out for him to meet me in the garden and went back outside. Haamed asked Falisha to bring coffee, tea, and toast, and we sat at the table with the scent of frangipani to wait for my brother. I was shaky and nauseated — like when I waited to hear the result of my mother's exploratory surgery, whether she might live or die.

"Haamed, will you do the talking — at least start it off? I'm not sure I'll find the words. I want to watch Jared."

Haamed nodded and smiled at me with a kindness that soothed my whole being. His calmness seeped over to me, and I quit wringing my hands. We sat in silence as he drank his tea and mine went cold.

Jared bounded out into the garden with a smile a few minutes later. I followed Haamed's gaze and caught his grimace when he saw Jared in his jellabiya.

"Coffee! Great. You read my mind. Haven't started a morning with this elixir for many days."

I winced at the falseness I imagined in his voice.

Jared flopped into one of the plastic chairs and poured himself a cup of coffee. He swirled milk in it and gave us a smile. He looked like a family dog expecting to be scratched.

Haamed maintained a solemn face. "Jared, Ana and I need to talk to you."

My pulse raced.

Haamed cleared his throat and leaned forward with his arms crossed on the table. He kept his eyes on Jared, who was scrutinizing the far reaches of the *shamba*, as though searching for something. Haamed waited to continue until Jared looked at him.

"Jared, I know where you've been the past week."

Jared, coffee cup poised above the table, raised an eyebrow. Not another of his muscles moved. "You do? You mean you found the place they kept me? And you caught them?"

Something curdled in my heart.

Haamed kept his eyes on Jared's. "I met and spoke with Amal."

I watched, struggling to accept, as Jared pretended not to understand. We let him speak.

"Amal?" Jared set his cup down, lowered his eyelids a fraction, and massaged the back of his neck. "Is that the name of the guy who kidnapped me?" He shifted his attention to me, before he looked back at Haamed. "Is he part of al-Shabaab? I figured they might be behind this."

How far would Jared carry this lie?

I watched Haamed, and an image of a leopard stalking its prey slinked into my mind. I was a voyeur at a slaughter.

But Haamed wasn't cruel. He didn't torture Jared. He ended it as cleanly as possible.

"Jared, I know you weren't abducted. Amal is in the house right now. He has a bag with a load of US dollars in it. I didn't count, but I'm guessing it's one-hundred-twenty-five-thousand."

Jared's face melted. His jaw dropped open and hung there for at least five long seconds.

The curdling in my heart spread through my body.

He tried to justify his actions that morning.

"Ana, that money would allow me to do a lot of good. Imagine an eye clinic here. And you've gotta agree that Amal and his community deserve some compensation. Look what they've gone through! What's wrong with using the money for a good purpose?"

I had no answer for his entreaties — or maybe articulating it would require digging back so far into basic moral precepts that I hadn't the strength to start. I stared at Jared, brokenhearted and speechless. Maybe my silence encouraged him to think he had a chance.

"And anyway, are you telling me that you believe this man," he jerked a hand at Haamed, "who you've only known for a few days? Believe him over me? What would Dad think of that disloyalty to family?"

That unleashed me. Sadness gave way to fury. "I don't remember Dad speaking of loyalty to family. It was loyalty to the truth he cared about." My voice started to rise. "Do you plan to tell the Loubets what you've done? About your plans for their money?" I wanted to shake Jared and hear his teeth rattle. My voice escaped, and I was screaming. "And what about what you've put me through? And the other people that've been drawn into your lie? What about the work I was here to do?"

Jared was ashen and silent. Haamed had slipped inside and now he reappeared with a plastic sack I recognized all too well. "I gave one thousand dollars to Amal and sent him away."

THE HONORABLE HAAMED left it up to me to decide what to do that morning.

I was wandering the garden, alone, when he approached. "I've thought a lot since yesterday. I'm not going to write this story."

"What?" This was one hell of an exposé, a real scoop for a journalist.

"As you said, Ana, not everything's about money. Islam also teaches us to make the world a better place. Sometimes compassion toward one individual sends out ripples of goodness. Sensationalist stories aren't what I want to write." He produced a sad smile. "Remember, I had a brother I loved, too. I've probably lost him for good."

I've thought about it often since and I think I made the right decisions. I told Jared he had to return the money to the Loubets and tell the truth. Beth and the Walkers had to know the facts too. I shrank inside, thinking how my parents' kind friends would feel, but I wouldn't carry this lie any further. I wouldn't invent or support stories for him.

I wondered if I could have stood strong if we had to tell Sean, destroy a nine-year-old boy's belief in his father. Thank God Jared hadn't yet bragged about his escape to his son. Truthfulness could include omission when it came to Sean, at least for the time being.

I didn't tell Jared that Haamed wouldn't write the story. I wouldn't give him that satisfaction.

Jared left Lindi just before noon. I saw Haamed send him away in a taxi.

I CALLED MARK THAT NIGHT. "Better sit down. I've got a lot to tell you."

"Are you all right?" was his first response, with none of the coolness with which we'd ended our last call.

That made it easier to tell him everything.

"Oh my God, Ana! I'm so sorry. It's shocking. Can I help you?" He was furious with Jared but he never said he was surprised. He didn't make me feel like I'd been a fool either. He only showed that he cared about me.

I didn't talk to Grace until the next day. She was sympathetic and angry, but, like Mark, she never expressed disbelief that Jared would do it.

Before we hung up she said something odd. "Remember talking about *Three Cups of Tea*?"

"Yes."

"I don't think I got around to telling you that you should read *Three Cups of Deceit*."

EPILOGUE

I stayed an additional week in Tanzania. Beth and I met at her apartment two days after I flew home. She'd seen Jared the previous week, on his return.

"Oh, Ana!" She embraced me. "I can't imagine how painful this must be for you."

"Yeah. But anger's still holding me up." I leaned back and studied her face. "How's Sean? And what did you tell him?"

Beth released me and grimaced. "On this, at least, Jared and I agree — although for different reasons. We're not telling him at this stage. No mention of abduction." She kneaded her forehead. "Thank God I stopped him from talking to Sean when he called from Tanzania."

I nodded. And felt a surge of gratitude to Haamed for stopping Jared from bruiting around his heroic escape the day he emerged.

"He told me he reimbursed the Loubets. Other than that, besides discussing what we'd tell Sean, we spoke very little." She looked down then back up, squarely at me. "I think he was deeply humiliated."

I knew about the Loubets, since I'd received an extraordinarily kind message from them. *So very sorry, Ana. Our deepest sympathy to you. You are not to blame for this.* They must have been reeling with shock and pain, but they'd tried to make me feel better.

I'd gone back to Moshi the day I left Lindi and stopped to see the Walkers. Jared had called them. My shame was deep but my anger was deeper.

"Oh, Ana. I am *so* sorry," said a teary, white-faced Fiona, hugging me hard.

What else could they say? Little, really, and Geoffrey must have agreed — he stood stiffly and said almost nothing. I guessed they were relieved my parents weren't alive to see this. I was grateful they didn't say so.

THREE WEEKS after my return to the US, Brad, Andrew and I sat down to debrief. It was the same bar where we'd gathered back in April but the six-month interval felt like six years.

In the extra week I'd stayed in Tanzania I'd made up for time lost to Jared's betrayal. Bolstered by Grace and fueled by fury I pulled myself together and did ten days of work in a week. I rescheduled appointments I'd missed while "saving" my brother, including the KI training. I talked to local health NGOs — several recommended by Grace. Most ran small projects aimed at improving the lives of women or children's health. I met an entrepreneur in Moshi who built small stoves vented to the outdoors to decrease respiratory problems from charcoal cooking fires. I saw a big university program focused on children's nutrition and a large USAID-funded project promoting safe childbirth practices.

Community education programs for the exploding numbers of diabetics were popping up and I visited two.

Some projects were genuinely improving Tanzanian lives, and some were providing more for the donor agencies than for the recipients. I found myself viewing them through the eyes of Haamed and I picked Grace's brain about several.

Over bar snacks, I described the best of the options. Andrew liked the diabetic education ideas but grumbled about the small size of the KI project.

"What about that nurse training?" asked Brad. "Wasn't that a good opportunity for building up local health workers?"

"It looked good on paper but whoever designed it didn't realize the nurses would have no place to work after training. Probably didn't invest enough time on the ground to get it right. I don't think we're in a position to make too much of their mistakes, but I'll use it as a case study for teaching our students."

Brad presented programs he'd investigated in Mali.

"I like the clean water project, Brad, but it sounds like it's mainly an opportunity for French graduate students. Can't we offer more opportunities for the Malians in the collaborating NGO? And how do we make sure Honnelly students who visit aren't a burden?"

"Yeah, I'm worried about that too," said Brad. "Needs more thought."

We agreed that Brad and I would move ahead with four proposals.

"And one other thing," I said, shuddering at the memory of the school eye screening. "We need to start a pre-req course for students who go overseas to any of our projects."

Andrew raised his eyebrows and nodded. "How about if

you two sketch out curriculum ideas and we make it the subject of another meeting." He glanced at his watch.

"You have time to stay for another drink?" asked Brad, after Andrew left.

"I'm wondering if I'm really gonna be able to do what I want in this position," he confessed, half way into his beer. "Development aid's been so corporatized. And Andrew's the quintessential academic. Pressure to bring in funding will never end."

"I know. But it's no different in the NGO world. It all requires money. I think Andrew's learning, too. The academic pathway offers the chance to work with students, both American and foreign. I like that." My head was starting to buzz with curriculum ideas. "Plus, we get to be part of interesting research."

"Yeah. And be pressured to publish papers."

We laughed, because it was all true. I was looking forward to working with Brad. Maybe there would be room for both of us in the GHI or maybe there wouldn't. Either way, I'd enjoy his friendship.

I left the bar and skidded across the icy sidewalk to my car, found the scraper and cleared the windscreen. Winter was starting early.

My phone rang as I was about to pull into the traffic. My father's former lawyer was on the other end.

"Ana, I wanted to let you know as soon as I could. Your father's remains have been recovered and identified from dental records. An instructor in an ice-diving training program found him. His leg was trapped in a chunk of old anchor chain so that he couldn't free himself. His death is now officially ruled an accident. I haven't reached Jared yet. I presume you'd like to tell him yourself?"

For a second, I felt the old wound, thick and rough as

Jared's sweater that night. Then it dissolved, to be replaced by a lightness. Dad hadn't meant to leave us. Why had Jared tried to make me believe our father didn't want to swim to shore? Did I want to call Jared to tell him? I'd not spoken to my brother since my return from Tanzania.

"I'd appreciate it if you'd call him," I told the lawyer.

FOUR MONTHS after I returned to the US I still hadn't spoken to Jared. I thought about it often and, as anger ebbed, pain flowed in. Our mother's adage, "Least said, soonest mended," was utterly false. It wasn't going to get me through this. I couldn't bring myself to call him. Haamed's story of his own brother frequently played in my head. I believe he wanted to impress on me the importance of forgiveness. I wanted to reach that stage but it wasn't just a matter of will.

"He's never even said he was sorry, or shown that he learned a lesson. I don't trust him anymore," I said to Grace, in one of our many phone calls.

"I'd feel exactly the way you do. You can't take a shortcut to forgiveness. People talk as though it's just a decision but I don't believe it. Forgiveness follows healing — not the other way around. If you try to suppress the anger you'll never heal. And how can healing even start if Jared doesn't admit his wrongdoing?"

"What if he never does?"

"Then the best you'll manage is accepting Jared as he is."

I guess acceptance was what Beth had achieved. I saw Beth and Sean frequently, usually with Paul, but she rarely mentioned Jared.

"He's dissolved his non-profit," she told me one time.

"He said he wants to stop traveling so much and have more time for Sean. I didn't fight a joint custody agreement."

Was this Jared's effort at admitting wrongdoing? It wasn't good enough.

I hated the raw wound that sat in the space where affection and admiration for Jared used to dwell. But it was out of my hands.

AS FOR HEALING, trust, and forgiveness, Mark and I had a lot to sort out. Rage and pain at Jared's betrayal turned out to be powerful forces for breaking open the protective walls around my heart, and Mark's love cascaded in. I see things from my childhood through a slightly different lens now. The lines sketching Jared and me aren't as black and white, but they seem truer. I'm freer than I've ever been. Since I admitted, first to myself and then to Mark, how much I want him in my life, he's been here, every bit the good man Beth suggested he was. He never tries to fix the hurt or banish the rage. He doesn't push me to talk about it, but he's always ready to listen. He simply bears witness and his empathy soothes and warms me.

As for development aid, we discuss it endlessly — when it works, when it doesn't, how it ties in with academic initiatives, aid programs, or the social entrepreneurial approaches he favors. And we talk about life's possibilities: how we might carve out careers that would be compatible and allow us to live somewhere in the great region of eastern Africa. It's exciting stuff.

We're also talking about marriage and kids.

We hope to go to Tanzania in the spring. I'm looking forward to introducing him to Haamed and Grace.

GLOSSARY OF SWAHILI

- *boda boda* motorcycle taxi
- *baraka* happiness
- *boma* compound
- *dalla dalla* minivan that provides local transportation
- *habari* the news
- *habari yako?* What's your news? How are you?
- *habari za asubuhi?* How are you this morning?
- *habari za jioni?* How are you this evening?
- *habari za mchana?* How are you this afternoon?
- *haina* does not
- *haraka* haste
- *jina langu ni...* my name is...
- *kanga* patterned cotton wrap 1.5 meters x 1meter, worn by women (like sarong or pareo)
- *karibu* welcome
- *kazi* work
- *kidogo* a little
- *kuku na chips* chicken and chips

- *kuku na wali* chicken and rice
- *lakini* but
- *malapas* flip flops
- *mambo* slang greeting
- *marahaba* polite response when a young person greets an elder with *shikamoo*
- *muezzin* a man who calls Muslims to prayer from the mosque
- *mwanangu* my son
- *mzungu* a white person from abroad
- *najua* I know
- *ndiyo* yes
- *ndovu* elephant
- *ng'ombe* cow
- *pole sana* very sorry, condolences
- *safari njema* good journey
- *sawa* okay
- *shamba* small farm or field
- *shikamoo* respectful greeting for an elder
- *shuka* plaid blanket/cloth worn by Maasai
- *nzuri* fine, good
- *nzuri sana* very fine, very good
- *ugali* maize staple

QUESTIONS FOR DISCUSSION

1. Have you participated in or read about development aid to low-income countries? What is your opinion about the effectiveness of aid and how did this story change your ideas?

2. Ana says her mother was the chief offender in the family's propensity for letting sleeping dogs lie and not discussing difficult emotional issues. In what ways did Ana manifest that same trait?

3. What price did Jared pay for his perfidy? Would you like to see him pay more and, if so, how?

4. What is Ana's motivation for working in the global health field? What is Jared's motivation for his work in Africa? Are these motivations what you expect of people in this field? Is there a moral issue here?

5. At the end, Ana says she sees her childhood through a different lens. What aspects of her family life do you think she might have reconsidered?

6. Grace says that forgiveness follows healing, and not the other way around. Is she right? Is this your experience?

7. What general principles for effective development aid can you suggest?

8. Who was your favorite character in the story and why?

9. Do you think Ana and Mark have the foundations for a good life together? Defend your answer.

10. Were you familiar with the concept of "third culture kids" before reading this book? What do you imagine are the advantages and disadvantages of such an upbringing?

11. How does Ana's affection for Sean influence her relationship with Jared?

12. Dr. Nganga is skeptical about the possibility for "reciprocity" in health partnerships between north and south. What are the issues that get in the way of reciprocity?

13. Do you think that Jared was as close to his father as Ana was? What is your impression of Jared's relationship with his father and where is this demonstrated?

14. In what ways do you think that Haamed's time working with Ana changed him?

ACKNOWLEDGMENTS

Many people pitched in to help me with this book. James Courtright, with his impressive knowledge of current events in Africa, suggested the natural gas fields around Mtwara with the surrounding political unrest as a likely spot for the plot I was hatching. He also steered me towards information on journalism in West Africa and I stole a few lines from him for Haamed. Tom Courtright read several early drafts and challenged a number of scenarios he found unlikely — he was mostly right.

Jan Lewallen read the very first draft and, without her comments, Mark would have been a paper-thin shadow of an afterthought. Haamed's story was also much improved from her comments. Lilita Hardes provided important feedback, reading at least two versions. Nancy Smith read patiently and carefully and caught some awful misuses of words. Shannon Cave helped make Ana's goals clearer and ratcheted up tension at critical points. Greg Engle, former Ambassador to Togo, talked to me about US policies on missing Americans. Ron Pickett's writing group provided encouragement throughout the pandemic. Judy Levine put her own writing aside in order to go through the manuscript line by line; she saved me from several blunders. Maryn Lewallen made important suggestions. I am so grateful for all this help.

Several publications were useful as background for creating this story. In particular I relied on qualitative research done by V.R. Kamat about the development of the natural gas fields around Mtwara, and on Robbie Courey-Boulet's excellent book, *Love Falls On Us. A Story of American Ideas and African LGBT Lives.* Any errors in portraying related historical events are solely mine.

Finally, as always, Paul was there throughout to bounce ideas around and he had many good ones that found their way into this book. I hope to convince him to join in the next one.

ABOUT THE AUTHOR

During twenty years of living and working in health development in eastern Africa, Susan Lewallen co-founded an NGO in Tanzania, published over a hundred academic papers, and garnered a number of international awards. She knows the complexity of foreign aid from the West, and especially how it plays out on the ground. Her first novel, *Crossing Paths*, demonstrated that well-informed fiction is a great vehicle for enlightening westerners about complex issues in a part of the world she loves. She lives now in San Diego with her husband. Her two sons, raised in Tanzania, are carving out careers in Africa.

THANK YOU FOR READING THIS BOOK

Thank you for reading this book. To follow the author and progress on future books, please subscribe to blog updates on her website: www.susanlewallen.com and like her facebook page: Susan Lewallen Author. If you enjoyed the book please leave an honest review with your favorite retailer or on Goodreads and encourage your local bookstore to stock it.

Made in the USA
Middletown, DE
19 April 2022

63916605R00189